Yellow Me

CW01645589

First published by Bleak House Books in 2008

This edition published in 2025 by Fahrenheit Pocket Noir, an imprint of Fahrenheit Press.

ISBN: 978-1-914475-88-7

10 9 8 7 6 5 4 3 2 1

www.Fahrenheit-Press.com

Copyright © Anthony Neil Smith 2025

The right of Anthony Neil Smith to be identified as the author of this work has been asserted by him in accordance with the Copyright, Designs and Patents Act 1988.

All rights reserved. No part of this publication may be reproduced, stored in a retrieval system, or transmitted in any form, or by any means, electronic, mechanical, photocopying, recording or otherwise, without permission in writing from the publisher.

F 4 E

Yellow Medicine

By

Anothony Neil Smith

Fahrenheit Pocket Noir

An Imprint of Fahrenheit Press

<u>*By the same author.*</u>

- *Slow Bear*
- *Slower Bear*
- *Slowest Bear*
- *The Butcher's Prayer*

"On my list of the most original voices in crime fiction today, Anthony Neil Smith easily makes it into the top five. YELLOW MEDICINE is a terrific read, a crime noir bullet-train ride on unsafe tracks."—Scott Wolven, author of Controlled Burn.

"YELLOW MEDICINE gets its hooks into you from its first turbulent pages. It is the novel's complicated, captivating hero, Deputy Billy Lafitte, who holds you from beginning to end. He's a liar, a cheat and a pretty bad guy, but so richly rendered that, before you know it, you find yourself following him through the darkest of terrains, and eagerly."—Megan Abbott, author of the Edgar-nominated Queenpin

"YELLOW MEDICINE starts with one of the most memorable and engaging anti-heroes in recent memory. Mix in bent cops, a psychobilly band called Elvis Antichrist, meth cookers in the Minnesota sticks, and a truly nasty pack of wannabe jihadists. Add a liberal helping of guns, knives and explosives. You're gonna love it."—J.D. Rhoades, author of A Good Day in Hell and Safe and Sound.

"Anthony Neil Smith has taken the stark, freezing landscape of rural Minnesota and brought it to life with an injection of Louisiana Hot Sauce in the form of Deputy Billy Lafitte. A violent, bawdy, thrilling, edgy, gut-churning masterpiece."—Victor Gischler, author of Go Go Girls of the Apocalypse, Pistol Poets, and the Edgar-nominated Gun Monkeys.

"Smith deserves credit for taking a risk by creating a character like Lafitte, whose private code of honor-if any-is far more obscure than an antihero like Mickey Spillane's Mike Hammer."—Publishers Weekly

"Smith has a powerful voice and delivers quite a romp, offering along the way a sort of Tony Hillerman glimpse into a part of the country that is not often the subject of crime fiction."—Steve Glassman, Booklist

To Brandy, the best thing I found in Minnesota.

ONE

Today

After two weeks of being shuffled around to similar bland cells, bland interrogation rooms, and bland Federal types asking dull-as-dishwater questions about my "contacts in the criminal underworld," Agent Rome finally walked into the room. I'd wondered when that would happen. I was worried about Drew, hoping she had made it back to safety. I wondered how the murder of Graham, my ex-brother-in-law and boss, would be received at home—both in Yellow Medicine County and with his family down South. I wondered how many people would blame me. Maybe Rome had the answers.

I'd been given a loose blue outfit, some rubber slippers. Real prisoner gear. No one had told me what I'd done wrong. They just asked question after question after question of which I could only answer a few. They were unhappy with the answers but kept asking the same questions anyway.

They had fucked with my sleep, so I only figured out the date when a lazy agent brought in a folded USA Today and I scanned the headline: "Congress Stall On" and the rest was out of sight. Could be that our little adventure with terrorism was being hidden from the public. Fine with me. That had been the point of the trip to begin with—make the lunatics go away.

Then, Rome.

All Federal in his suit and tie, ID badge hanging around his neck, carrying a laptop computer, a legal pad, and some pens. He was alone, although he stopped at the door a few seconds, delivering a lunch order to one of his peons. Lunchtime. Could've fooled me. I thought it was more like two in the morning.

He closed the door, grinned at me from across the room. "Deputy Lafitte, you're not holding up too well, are you?"

He was the first familiar face I'd seen in a long time. Tall, thin, black, with military hair. "Please tell me you're here to get me out. It's just a big mix-up, right? You only now heard I was being held against my will, right?"

He made a pathetic little grunt before stepping over to the table, pulling back the chair slowly, maximum scrape across the floor. He sat, opened the laptop with his bony fingers. I scoped out the rest of his haul—the legal pad was blank. I imagined he'd try to get me to write a statement of some sort. Not a confession. He wouldn't call it that. No, a "statement" by a material witness to help reel in the bigger fish. I stole a look at his wristwatch. 11:30. Put that together with the lunch order and I had my bearings. Or maybe not. Could've been a ruse again.

"It's not that easy," Rome said. He took on the posture I'd seen from other administrators when they wanted something—leaning forward, fingers laced together, middle of the table. *Tell me your secrets, and I'll give you a hug.* "I've been fighting to get in for a while. It was only when I convinced them that I was sure you'd talk to me if given a chance. We can clear this up, then we can get you out."

Lies. All lies. I slouched low in my chair. "I've told them everything I know. You *know* me, man. You were there when those dealers almost killed me."

His eyes flicked to the side. Camera in the corner, someone on the other side of the glass. Maybe he hadn't told them about that night.

"You remember? The girl with the gun? How you nearly let them kill me instead of stepping—"

"That's enough. They tell me all you've given us is bullshit, night after night. You should come clean."

"That's what I've been trying to do."

"Really, Billy?"

I shrugged. "You think I like it here? There aren't seventy virgins waiting for *me* in the afterlife, so you think I'm lying for the sheer fun of it?"

Rome looked at his screen. The blue reflection off his eyes made them seem holographic.

He said, "Where's Paul Asimov?"

No one had asked that yet. They'd all gone straight for the stuff about the terror cell in Detroit. I'd wondered if they had realized my former partner was even missing.

He waited a moment. Pushed his hands closer to my side of the table. "Hm?"

"I haven't seen Paul in a long time. He came

to my house, told me what was going on. I haven't seen him since."

Rome's leg was bouncing under the table. His teeth tugged his bottom lip. The guy needed to ease up.

"And that's that?"

I shrugged. If they had found pieces of him along the road, his stuff at my house, I could say I didn't do it. The terrorists did. "Paul fucked up. He made a big mistake. If I could bring him to the table right now, he'd try to make things right, tell you everything he knew. The problem is that I have no clue where he is."

Rome nodded. This was a game of *"Gotcha!"* if I'd ever seen one.

He spun the laptop around so I could see. On the screen was a jpeg of a face. Looked like it was made of clay or wax, and it resembled Asimov just a bit.

Rome said, "That's him, right?"

"Close."

"You know what this is a picture of?"

I almost had it, something I'd seen on TV, something they'd done with old skulls.

Rome's grin crept higher. "Yeah, that's right. Facial reconstruction. Got a skull but no ID? We let some of our people do the math, throw some clay on there, see who turns up. This time it was your buddy Paul."

I cleared my throat. I had to act surprised. "He's…dead?"

"Exactly. All chopped to pieces. We've only recovered half of him."

I couldn't look at the screen. Seeing his fake face was more gruesome than remembering what we'd done to the body. At least that was an act of kindness. "Jesus."

Another minute or two slid by in silence. Rome broke it with, "You didn't ask where we found him. You want to know?"

"I don't care."

"Come on, throw me a bone."

I shook my head, closed my eyes.

"I'll tell you anyway. A wild dog in Wisconsin was chewing on charred scalp."

I gagged and tried to hold back, couldn't. Rome grabbed the laptop away just in time. There wasn't much in me, but I couldn't stop. Sad pools of pink-tinged saliva. Maybe I had a bleeding ulcer. Then just dry heaves.

Rome was quiet in the back of the room. He finally knocked on the door, told the agent standing outside to hand him a box of tissues and a Sprite. A couple of minutes later, he brought them back to the table, pushed them across.

"Take a few minutes, clean yourself off," he said to me. "Man, I was giving you the benefit of the doubt. Heard nothing but praise from the Sheriff about you. Fooled me one hundred percent."

I wiped my lips, layered a few tissues across the wet spots on the table. The smell of the stomach acids was still heavy in my nostrils. I took the Sprite, sipped, felt the burn push through my esophagus.

"But now we've got all this evidence that says you're just as dirty as I first suspected. Don't you want to tell me all about it? Make you feel better." He smiled. Why'd he have to smile?

I coughed, felt a sting at the back of my throat, then said, "I don't know what else you expect. I did my job. I wasn't involved with terrorists. I didn't make any deals with them. I just wanted to protect those kids."

"Yeah, good job you did."

"How was I supposed to know?"

He rested his elbow on the table, leaned his chin against his fingers. Looked bored. "It's only a matter of time before your story will get wobbly. Facts will contradict you. Until then,

I'm just a dentist. One tooth at a time."

"And when it doesn't wobble?"

He shrugged, slow-blinked. "I said a matter of time. Didn't say how much time. We've got the whole calendar cleared for you."

I was confused. If Rome had the proof, the rest was gravy. No need for his tough guy bullshit. That told me half of this act depended on my response. But I couldn't shake the feeling he was hiding something big.

"Why don't you ask me something?" I said.

"No need. I've already told you, I'm your last shot. Those guys in there—" he nodded towards the glass. "They want to scare you. Want you to do the hardest time there is. Traitor time. Even the baby-rapers will spit on you. Seriously, talking as friends here, I don't want to see that."

"Good buddies, right? This how you treat your friends?"

He laid his hand on his chest, mock-hurt. "I don't chop them up and scatter them across three states. Yeah, after finding parts of your old partner, I started thinking maybe you weren't so innocent after all. And even if it wasn't you, I don't see you giving me what I need to put his killers away."

I didn't answer. I couldn't. Losing two friends in one week, knowing I was the only one connecting both of them, if I had spoken then, it would be to damn myself to hell. But maybe I'd do that on my own time, not as a "guest" of my own government.

Rome waited me out a few minutes, then said, "But hey, Billy, after what we've been through? You can still come out okay. All that corruption is like rust. You can sandpaper it off. There's a boy scout underneath."

"I appreciate that. Really sweet coming from an undercover man. Takes a real good liar to pull off that sort of work, doesn't it?"

He nodded, eyes on the table. He pulled the cap off a pen, laid it on the legal pad. Slid it over to me. "Your involvement with this group, from the first time Paul Asimov brought it to your attention until you were found in the backyard of the house where the cell operated, possibly a witness or participant to a double homicide."

"I want a lawyer." A phrase I never expected to say.

And a response I never expected to get.

He laughed. "You didn't just say that. And I mean, literally, you didn't just say that."

"I want a lawyer."

"Hell, shout it out loud. Write it on the walls in blood. I'll still say it never happened." He leaned closer, dropped his voice. "Is this real enough for you yet? Do we have an understanding?"

I looked at my reflection in the mirror, imagined emotionless black-suited automatons with FBI stamped on their foreheads.

"What happens to me after I write the statement?"

Rome gave it some thought, tried to think of a way that wouldn't sound like a lie, I supposed, since there was no way I would be set free.

So he said, "Tell us the truth, and maybe it won't be so bad for you."

How bad could "not so bad" be? A few privileges—maybe a TV in my cell? More exercise time? Slightly better food? Protection from rapes and beatings?

Nothing I could say would get me out of their web. Exiled from the real world.

I shoved the pad across the table. "Not good enough."

He turned angry, lines wrinkling his face.

"We don't make deals."

"I'm not asking for anything. It's just that I

won't make up lies to get myself a nicer pillow in prison. Waste more of my taxes on me if you want, but it won't change the story, wobbles and all."

Veins on the backs of his hands swelled as he balled his fists. "We are *all* on the same team, my friend."

"I used to think so."

Another staredown. This time Rome didn't keep up the charade very long. He said, "You know where you are right now?"

I looked around the cramped beige walls and said, "Your rec room?"

Flicker of a grin. "Outside, I mean. In the open air."

I had no idea. I hadn't even known the time for at least a week until I saw Rome's watch. I'd been blindfolded when I was moved, carted around in silence for hours on end. I was in a small jet once without the blindfold but with the shades drawn. Must've been at least an hour or two in the air. Not given much sleep. Not given newspapers. Soundproof cells so I couldn't eavesdrop on the guards' conversations. And this motherfucker wants me to *guess* where I am?

"Disney World?"

"Exactly. Of course. You're in line for Space Mountain as we speak. Try again."

I didn't take the bait. The games were tiring, working my brain to find an answer only gave me more possibilities to trip up.

He finally said, "You're not far from home, actually."

Where exactly was that? I was born and raised in Mississippi, and only moved to Minnesota after Hurricane Katrina. "Can we go to the beach, then?"

Rome straightened in his chair, his face long with surprise. "Hey, good one. I'd forgotten about that. No, I meant not far from Pale Falls. We're in Minneapolis."

The thought of being back made my heart beat a little faster, made me think about Drew, Graham, Layla, Ian, Heather. I missed the place, the people. The emotion was a surprise. I'd only come to think of Yellow Medicine as home when it looked like I might lose it. What I'd hated about Minnesota wasn't the people or the scenery, not when I really thought about it. What I had hated was *me* in Minnesota, the bitter and disgraced me that could take any sunset in any big sky and turn it into something ugly. Bringing me back after all this, though, he might as well have castrated me. I'm sure the natives would've wanted to. Yet I couldn't think of anywhere else I wanted to be.

"So?" I said. "My cell in Minneapolis looks like my cell in Detroit or Chicago or wherever the hell else you've shuffled me."

He sighed. A good performance. "Just thought you'd like to know how close you are to the people you betrayed."

"I never betrayed□□"

"Hey, you can be noble in your own head, but I've *talked* to Spaceman's mom. I told her the truth, how you probably had something to do with his disappearance and left her hanging. How those guys she described that met you in the diner were working out financial details for your part in their scheme. You want to deny it?"

Pissing me off. He saw me as his one-way ticket to Washington D.C., a cozy office, and the power to change lives—or ruin them. I didn't blame him. He was doing his job, doing it well. Wasn't I trying to achieve the same thing, just under the table? Rome was the good guy. I was Samson brought low by my own arrogance.

"Keep it up," I said, just trying to rile him up. "You'll get promoted right out of this backwater. They always need another token black guy to help fight the evildoers."

He reached across the table and slapped me hard. Felt like a brick. The look in his eyes, I was surprised they weren't on fire.

Call it a reflex. I was instantly on my feet lunging for him, but the shackles on my ankles fucked me up. Arm muscles tightened as I reached for his neck with my fingers.

He was safely away, hands on his hips while he waited me out. But I raged on. Screamed myself hoarse. Fought through nausea and fear, even though I couldn't make it past the table. I'd rather die of a stroke than let these bastards manipulate my strings.

Rome let me pulse and yell and swipe and pound my fists on the table until it wasn't funny to him anymore. "You just flushed your *whole life* down the drain, you understand?"

"That the way it is? I hurt your feelings and I pay forever?"

He pounded on the door, said something to another agent I couldn't hear because I was shouting, "*I will rip your fucking heart out! I will eat your fucking heart!*"

The agent handed him something. A gun. No. Not a real gun. Goddamn stun gun. As he lifted it and aimed at me, I thought, *Oh, that's not good.*

You don't plug fifty thousand volts into a guy whose wrists and ankles are bound by steel and shackled to a steel ring on the floor. You just don't do it. Unless you're a goddamned sadist.

And it was all my fault.

Lightning strike. But it wouldn't end. Stiff, unable to move or breathe. The prongs felt like rattlesnake teeth pumping fire inside me. If I'd ever been afraid of death before, the stun gun changed my mind. I wanted to die. I looked forward to being dead. Anything to stop the pain.

When it finally stopped, I was hoping that the room was just an afterthought. What I was seeing was only an echo of my life. Any second the pain would flitter away and my soul would give up looking for heaven and hell and just fall asleep and that's all she wrote. My story would be over.

But I kept breathing and jittering and burning—smoke rose from my wrists, circled with charred skin. I don't remember falling to the floor, one ankle twisted badly in the snarl of short chains. I was alive, and I hated it.

Rome knelt beside me. Maybe he looked sorry for me, I don't know. He said, "Bait me all you want. It won't stop what's next. Tomorrow I'm taking you back to Yellow Medicine County, let you to see firsthand the damage you've done. We'll need you to take us to the bodies, show us where the Malaysians were hiding out. See how much of a badass you are then, *boy*."

I let him have the moment. I pictured the streets of Pale Falls in my mind, terrified of what Rome had waiting for me there. I'd come full circle. Home sweet home.

TWO

Three Weeks Ago

Drew joined me at the bar after her band finished its set. She played bass for a psychobilly group called Elvis Antichrist. They were too good for empty bars during snowstorms here in rural Minnesota. I told her they should take that act to the Twin Cities. She told me they tried, got turned away with, "Psychobilly is deader than Elvis."

It was mid-March, the melt still weeks away. She sidled up to me, asked the bartender for a glass of Chardonnay, then, "Billy, I need help."

Must've been hard for her to say that. She knew the cost of asking. I was the one who taught her how to fuck on prom night last sping after arresting her drunk date. Now they say, *Don't let Deputy Lafitte get you, boys, or he'll steal your girls.* A few have tried to catch my eye, encouraged their guys to drink *more.*

Drew was a special case. As long as she understood my price.

Better than chasing divorcees my own age. I had enough baggage from when I was married with kids.

Drew repeated that she needed my help.

"What kind of help?"

"Big help."

Probably meant someone needed to be punished. I looked her over—the too-dark mascara and thick stage make-up, the black hair with canary yellow streaks, her ample figure in a black goth dress and knee-high boots. Hot damn sexy freak of nature. On prom night she had worn a maroon gown that bared most of her back. Her hair had been a boring brunette and you wouldn't think she'd ever *heard* of psychobilly. She even won the state spelling bee once.

I spun off the volume on my radio, not expecting a call in this weather. I often lazed through most of my shift at this bar, fully uniformed, drinking beer and listening to half-assed local bands. Took a swig and turned on my stool to face her. "Go ahead."

"It's Ian."

Shit. Her boyfriend since July. He was into dealing meth, but who wasn't? I'd arrested him for possession several times and finally decided it was easier to take a "fine" from him than carry his skinny ass to jail for the night, since his father would just guilt the sheriff—my ex-brother-in-law Graham—into setting the boy free anyway. What a washout. Twenty, acted fifteen, thought he was going to make a fortune organizing "raves" on the prairies. Dropped out of the university in Marshall. He couldn't better himself and didn't have enough sense to take over his old man's farm one day, so drugs suited him just fine.

Why oh why did bright and sparkly little Drew go nuts over that loser?

I said, "I've already helped that asshole more than I ever intended. You're not winning me over, sweetie."

"It's not a *legal* problem exactly. It's that some guys he was, um, considering working with. He lost something of theirs. It wasn't Ian's fault. Could've happened to anyone, eh?"

"Not anyone."

"Look, I know he's into some bad stuff, and I'm trying to straighten him out. He's got a good heart and all. Thing is, these guys, they already gave him a warning."

She got my attention. It didn't matter that Ian was a pain in everyone's ass. He was *my* problem—I was the enforcer around here. Nobody pushed my people around.

"What type of warning?"

She frowned, her cheeks droopy, eyes on the bar. A sad sight. "They burned him. They put a brand on his ass."

I didn't know whether to be pissed or to laugh. I spewed beer and tried to look concerned. The bartender shouted at me. I flung a coaster at him.

"With a real brand?"

"Oh, yeah. I don't know where they got it. It's an "F" and a quarter moon. He's lucky it didn't get infected."

"And I take it he had a great nursing student with a good bedside manner helping out, right?"

Drew blushed. Once she outgrew the crazy costumes and cult-music, she was going to be a lifesaver. The yellow dye would always wash out, the goth look her nighttime mask only. It suited her, but then so did the shyer aspect of her personality. She truly lived two lives. I planned to be Drew's guardian angel until the day I died, and even then for long after.

She said, "Can you get these guys off his back? Yes, I *know* that drugs and all are wrong—"

"This was drugs he lost?"

After a quiet moment, she scrunched her eyebrows and said, "I don't really know. He won't tell me more. I assumed."

"Either drugs or money, right?"

"Guess so."

I snapped my fingers at the bartender. "Hey, put Drew's next drink on my tab."

He shrugged like I missed the joke. Drew had barely touched her wine anyway.

I told her, "I'll talk to Ian tomorrow, all right? We'll get this taken care of."

That brightened her whole face, more babydoll than vampire, and she hugged me awkwardly. "I knew you would. Thanks so much."

"Why didn't he ask me himself?"

"You know. You and him, right? Don't let him know I said anything."

The kid probably put her up to this anyway. With that in mind, I felt bad about the next part, the thing she knew was coming. That's why she was hanging around, pretending to study the bottles behind the bar, waiting for me to ask:

"Busy after the gig?"

She shook her head. "Might need a ride home in this storm."

You're thinking I'm a bastard. A real nasty piece of work. All I can say is that I don't force anyone to do anything they don't want. I'm willing to risk my neck night in and night out to protect my citizens, so if I go above and beyond to help a young lady in need, how she shows her gratitude is entirely her decision.

Still, something about Drew, about this night, this favor, made me cautious. I was willing to check into Ian's situation without getting anything in return. That branding shit wasn't right, some upstart hicks trying to bite a piece of my pie. The other thing was the way Drew made it seem like a direct tit-for-tat. Goddamn it, I'm not supposed to feel bad about taking home a girl who's telling me she's willing.

I did this time.

So when the phone behind the bar rang and the bartender brought it to me, saying, "Dispatcher," I breathed a little easier.

I took the handset. "Yeah?"

"Jesus, did you turn off your radio again?

What did I tell you about that?" The dispatcher was Ms. Layla, who reminded me of my dad's sisters. They acted like traditional aunts, full of advice and cookies, but they chain-smoked and gambled a lot.

"Sorry. I had to take shelter. It's loud in here—"

"All I asked is for you to keep the damn radio up in case...forget it. Get over to the casino. They've got a problem with Doctor Hulk."

"I'm on it. See you soon, Ms. Layla. And I do apologize—"

"You can bring me a roast beef sandwich if you really want to be forgiven."

I handed the phone back to the bartender. Drew had gotten the gist of the conversation and was standing. I jerked a thumb towards the door.

"We'll talk later, and don't worry about anything. I'll handle it tomorrow."

She wrapped the fingers of both hands around her wine glass, as if she were about to offer it to me. "Really? Don't worry?"

"You guys be careful. Call me if you need me."

After she headed back towards her bandmates to help dismantle the stage gear, I said to the bartender, "You laughing at me earlier?"

He crossed his arms. "You wanted to pay for her drink. The band drinks free. Especially her."

Son of a bitch was getting territorial. I said, "Oh yeah, Clark. Like you've really got a shot. Whatever fantasy keeps you warm at night, go with it."

Clark shrugged, turned away, wiped down the far end of the bar. I'd taken the fight out of him, which made me feel pretty good. Being feared had its perks. I lifted my hat from the bar and snugged it on, ready to face the snow.

THREE

I had time to think about Drew and Ian's problem on the way to the casino, which was on the Upper Sioux reservation at the edge of the prairie across the street from an endless field of corn. They called the joint Jackpot Harvest, slightly better than a bingo hall or slot room, but not up to big-time resort standards. Dr. Hulk was a gynecologist from Cottonwood who worked in Marshall, a larger town to the south. His real name was Hulka, but when he drank, he turned green—envy, jealousy, vomit stains, all of them.

The snow was wet and slushy, making the drive slippery. The cruiser had good tires, a good engine, handled well, but I wished I had my Ram 4X4 instead. In a few weeks this would all start to melt, flooding the river I lived on and filling the lakes all over the state, leaving us thick with muck.

My guess: Ian was trying to open a franchise for some larger players. Too bad. He was the last person even drug dealers should trust. For a minute or two, something to take my mind off the snow, I thought about lending him a hand, doing all the talking to these guys and making sure we got a fair cut. Plus, with the law involved, I could guarantee safety for drops and meetings, provide an abandoned farmhouse for a lab.

I laughed, thinking like I did in the old days, the sort of shit that got me fired in Gulfport, Mississippi after the big hurricane. Lost my job, my wife and kids, and a lot of money. The whole point of taking the job in Minnesota was to make a clean break, start all over. Sure, I still took the handouts, worked the angles when it didn't seem too out-of-bounds, but I'd say my hands were mostly clean these days.

Nothing that would hold up in court, I mean.

The head of security at the casino was waiting for me at the entrance. Name was Rome, and he was tall and black, skinny as hell. Classy in a suit while he held his bulky radio. Part Sioux, of course, but the truth is they hired him to avoid a lawsuit. He had friends in The Cities that helped out, made a few threats. I don't know why he wanted to work at a dump like this. There was something deeper, but since it hadn't elbowed into my space yet I wasn't digging.

He held Dr. Hulka by the collar. White shirt covered with a patch of vomited taco and whiskey. Some blood, probably his own from the scratch on his cheek. I climbed out of the cruiser at the covered entryway, empty of guests. Everything was too bright, our little pocket of light you couldn't see ten feet outside of. The wind was a steady screech.

"The usual?" I said to Rome.

"He's friskier. Drank more than he typically does. It started with some blackjack dealer he was hitting on, just a kid. Maybe twenty-three."

"Yeah?"

"I put a stop to it because she was getting nervous, forgetting her routine. She's new here."

Hulka tried to grin. It wasn't good. The way he bobbed, you'd think he was on a boat.

I said, "What else?"

"Then he moved over to slots, shouted at a cocktail waitress that we were dirty Indian thieves, and grabbed the server's buttocks." Rome was all business like that, and probably religious. The rumor was that he sometimes witnessed to the big losers, trying to get them to accept Jesus. "That was the ball game."

I pointed to the blood on the doctor's pants and shirt. Hulka's forehead was half-covered with a bandage. "Eh?"

"He didn't want to listen to reason. As I tried to accompany him to the office, he walked into a column."

What I wouldn't give for the videotapes. Rome's stories about his battered patrons always involved walking into a column. None of the bruised troublemakers disputed him once they were sober.

Hulka swung towards me. Rome tightened the grip on the collar until the doctor gagged. He rasped at me. "I wan' press sharges."

"Excuse me?" Either the alcohol or the fat lip. Couldn't tell.

"Guy here, abuse, tha's what it is. Nigger thin's he can take me on."

Rome's lips curled. He was enjoying this. Hulka would sleep it off, get back to work, then after a week or two cooling off, he'd be back. That's when Rome would request a little chat, remind him who'd got the upper hand—maybe show him edited portions of the tape, especially this part. Tuck a favor away in your pocket, that sort of thing. Maybe a nice contribution to Rome's Baptist church.

Hulka gagged on another threat and let loose on the concrete, more alcohol and bile, the hot sick smell like a slap in the face, splashing onto my shoes. I stepped back, took a look down there. The drops had nearly frozen on impact, an abstract pattern. I'd seen worse.

When he was done, I cuffed him and asked Rome, "What do you want me to do?"

We'd been through this before. "Keep him away for the rest of the night. Keep him safe."

"You got his keys?"

Rome spread his hand on his chest. *You think I would take the man's Lexus?* "I heard them in his pocket."

"Have a good one."

"Same to you."

Hulka puked in the cruiser. I watched in the rearview as he tried to aim some at the back of my head, but wasn't strong enough to lift his neck that high. In small towns and rural counties like ours, it's a blessing and a curse to be as addicted as the doctor. Everyone knew, but they were too polite or repressed or embarrassed to say it to his face. Because of that, he lived a daytime life and a nighttime life, neither having much to do with the other. I'd heard he was married, but to a wife who was never home. Also heard he had a couple kids, one in college and one in high school. People said his son was just like Hulka, and that didn't make either of them very happy.

I didn't plan on taking him to the station or leaning too hard. Easier to drop him off at home, help him inside, and let him forget it ever happened. That was before he started talking.

"Thin' you're pretty powerful, don't you? Got the whole county wired."

I didn't respond.

"Too goo' t' talks to me now?"

Glanced in the rearview. Caught his eyes. "Let's just get you home, doc. Don't want to make your headache worse."

"Fuck it. Jus'…treating me li' a child, put me in cuffs. Get you fired for that shit."

"Nobody's getting anybody fired. Five more minutes." It was getting harder to see, the snow blowing and spattering into slush on the windshield, gathering on the sides where the wipers missed. Mostly two lane roads out here, had to be careful, especially making a turn, and the turn to Cottonwood wasn't too far away.

"Everybod' feel sorry for me. All feeling sorry, the poor drun' doctor. They got sticks up their asses. Here's wha' they don't know. Wanna hear a sec..rrrr…secret?"

Of course I did. If it weren't for all the secrets I knew, I wouldn't have been the deputy I was. "Lay it on me."

He leaned forward, lost balance and scraped his face against the divider screen. Heaved a few breaths. I thought he might puke again. Then he said, "I fuck all their wives."

Well, goddamn, that wasn't much of a secret. I just assumed. "While you're examining them?"

"Wha'? No, no. Ew, tha's tha's th…tha's just gross, man. Not like that. I mean, like, we'll get to talking an' these women just want a man to talk to, y'know? They star' telling me when to come over, the husban' out town. They wan' be treated like sluts."

"Remind me which road it is after we turn." I clicked the turn signal. Disappointed, actually. I didn't believe him. A drunk rich guy boasting, nothing more. Maybe he'd slept with one or two waning socialites, but Hulka wasn't the monster gigolo he imagined himself to be. "I can't remember the street name."

"Don't change the subjec'. Ask me for names. You wanna know." He slumped back on the bench, tumbled to the side. The vinyl stuttered. "I fucked your wife, too."

That was his mistake. I gripped the wheel tighter, cleared my throat. "You did? Tell me about it."

"Said her cop husban' only had one big gun, an' not in his pants."

"She did?"

"Oh, geez, I rode her int' the ground. Broke the bed." Lowered his voice, tossed some attitude into it. "I fucked her in th' ass, yeah. I came all o'er her face."

Drunk boasting, all lies. My ex-wife was originally from South Dakota, but she lived in Mobile, Alabama. She moved back home with her folks after the hurricane. After what I had done. She filed papers, didn't even want my explanation. That's what I deserved, though, for marrying a strict evangelical Christian. Thought she could change me. I let her think she had, until the storm ripped my mask clean off.

Dr. Hulk hadn't screwed my wife. He hardly ever screwed his own. But all his bullshit had flicked a switch in me.

"So, my wife? And all these others? You proud of that?"

"Prou'? Who needs prou' when you've got grateful pussy?"

I clucked my tongue, caught his eyes in the rearview. They widened some.

"Naughty boy," I said. "Stupid, too. You don't tell a man with a gun that you fucked his wife. I don't think we can let this be."

The turnoff to Cottonwood was in the headlights, but I slid off onto the shoulder, the anti-locks clacking against my foot as the tires glided on the iced-over pavement. The Hulk looked green indeed. Sickly, even. And suddenly goddamned sober.

He said, "No, the turn's up there."

"Get out."

"You can't do that. I can't walk home in this condition."

"Who said you're walking home?" I opened the door and stepped into the wind and snow, my feet sliding on the glassy ice, snow that had melted during the day and frozen again after sunset. Even in my departmental jacket, the wind bit like snakes. Hulka's jacket was probably hanging in Rome's office. That's why this was so much fun.

He leaned away from me when I opened his door, but was still too loopy to resist, especially with the cuffs on. I pulled him out while he yelled at me, "What the hell do you think…Outrage! I'm going to sue….no, press charges! Jesus, Billy, c'mon, stop fucking around!"

I hauled him behind the car, then pressed my knee against the back of his. He turned to spaghetti. I eased him down until he was kneeling. I wanted him to see the cruiser. Exhaust poured out of the tailpipe. I stepped around him and leaned against the trunk. That's when his breath went short.

Pulled my pistol lazily, let it hang at my side. I didn't slide my finger over the trigger, played fair. I said, "Anything else you want to tell me about my wife before I do this?"

"What are you talking about?"

I let out a long sigh, watched it turn to vapor, and stared across the cornfield. "After you, I'll need to confront my wife, too. Then there's your wife."

"Listen, I swear I never touched your wife.

That was the booze talking. I promise. Please, just take me home now. I won't even file a complaint."

"Sounded to me like you were serious. I want to know what else you two did. It'll be easier to take care of her if I've got a clear mental picture."

"Billy, for God's sakes, look at me. Look at me!"

I looked at him.

His face was chaotic. "I never touched your wife. I don't even know who she is. I was very wrong to say that, and I apologize. I'm an asshole. I'm so sorry."

"Really." I nodded. "You sure about that? How would you know which one was mine? After all, if you're fucking everyone else's wives, how would you know?"

Hulka inched toward me on his knees, hit a slick patch that sent his knees flailing wide like a gymnast. He fell onto his stomach, craned his neck. "There's been a few, not all of them. Jesus, forgive me. Oh God. You can't be in my business without making a few mistakes. I'll never do it again. I swear."

I lifted my gun, squinted, centered my aim on his forehead. "I don't believe you."

He started to cry. Barely able to understand him, but I figured out: "I don't want to die I don't want to die please don't I'll change I'll change I never expected it to be like this."

"How many wives? Currently, I mean."

"Two."

I slipped my finger over the trigger.

"No! Shit! Two, two! I mean it! Only two!"

That was the part I'd been waiting for. None of the bluster. I wanted the real deal. Crouched before the crying, freezing doctor, I said, "So tell me, Doctor Hulka, who are the two married women you are currently committing adultery with, and who are their husbands?"

He told me as if I were his best friend. I was surprised. One was the wife of a very wealthy man whose family owned half of Marshall—made his money in frozen foods. The other was the wife of a college professor. I didn't know the women, but imagined they must be very different from one another. Interesting choices. He babbled on a bit more and I let him have as much rope as he wanted. This type of info was what helped build my rep so quickly here, so far away from home, barely any friends or allies.

In the distance were headlights coming fast. Should've paid more attention to the road. I hoped I could get Hulka off the pavement before the driver saw us. I tucked away the gun and stepped behind the doctor, helped him up.

"Sorry about all that, Doc. Sometimes I just lose my temper, you know? Especially when I feel my chain's been jerked. You were jerking my chain, right?"

He nodded, or maybe he was just shivering. I didn't care. He was on shaky ground those four steps back to the cruiser, nearly falling into the backseat. The headlights were right on us now, and the electric company truck swept by, creating a vortex of snow and wind that stung my eyes. I closed the back door, got into the driver's seat, cranked the engine.

I rolled up to the Cottonwood turn, got up to speed. Silence from the backseat except for Hulka's wheezing.

"Remember to let me know which street it is. Hard to see in this snow." I caught a whiff of something sharp, sniffed the air to make sure. "Doctor, did you piss your pants?"

He said, in the most pathetic voice I'd ever heard, "I'm sorry sir."

Like I said, being feared was a wonderful thing.

FOUR

Well past two in the morning, I couldn't sleep. I sat in the den of my river valley home, which reminded me of a hunting lodge, and drank an Australian Cabernet, my third glass since getting home just after midnight. Pretty soon I was on the phone to Mobile, my ex-in-laws house, convincing myself I was calling to talk to my son Ham. If I hadn't been drinking I would've known better. Problem was that I drank so I wouldn't have to know better.

Three rings. Then a woman's voice, Ginny's mom. "Billy."

Must've glanced at the caller ID. Or she knew I'd be the only asshole calling this late. "Sorry it's late. I truly am. Re…really."

"What do you want?"

"Wanna talk to Ham. Maybe Savannah, too."

"They're asleep, Billy. You don't want me to

wake them up."

"Yeah, you're right. I am sorry. I wish…I wish it wasn't like this." It just kept coming, my brain unable to roadblock my mouth.

Her husband's voice rose in the background. "Is that him again? Let me talk."

Ginny's mom whispered a brush-off , then said to me, "You can't keep doing this. You know when they're awake. You know the rules. And you can't talk to them when you're drinking." Always so level and calm when she spoke to me. She never showed emotion, and that pissed me off even more. I don't know what I wanted, though. Maybe I was ashamed. Maybe I just liked fucking around with their grandparents' "rules".

Don't take the bait. "Yeah? They're my kids. I should be able to talk…you know…whenever, and however."

She didn't even let me finish the rant. "Goodnight, Billy."

She hung up. But as I started to pull the phone away from my ear, I heard some background noise. Someone had picked up another extension down there.

"Ginny?" I said.

A short exhalation, and then she clicked off.

I knew it was her. One day she would talk to me like we used to, like normal people do. After all, I would probably be in worse shape if it hadn't been for Ginny's help after the divorce. Maybe it was all a test, a temporary thing. I needed to show her I could change, could be a good dad. This job was my one shot towards earning her trust again. And goddamn it if I wasn't blowing it a little more each day.

The TV news scrolled info across the bottom of the screen and weather to the side, but I had muted it while on the phone. Closed captioning added to the mess. The wood stove was stoked and burning, one of the little extras I liked about the place. The house was pretty run down, had flooded twice, and was always damp. It needed work. I bought the four acres for a pretty good price, thinking I would turn it into something special. Nearly a year and half later I still lived out of boxes and suitcases, unable to feel comfortable although I didn't have much choice. I was lucky to get the job, and grateful, but I hated Minnesotans and hated the goddamn wind.

The howling started on one end of the house and caught every crack and hole on its way across, a real zombie chorus that made it hard to sleep. Not that I was sleeping. Most nights I drank wine and stared out the windows into my frozen front yard, the twisty dirt driveway cutting through to the tree-lined county highway, until I passed out, trying to pinpoint the moment my life turned to shit.

When Katrina hit, she washed away half our home. We'd been somewhat prepared, stowing our important papers and treasures in a storage shed or the attic, but no one knew just how devastating the storm would be for Gulfport. We found out the storage shed flooded, too. All I had left was a damaged police cruiser, a .45, a 12-gauge shotgun, my wife Ginny, and my kids Ham and Savannah. It took twelve hours to drive them over to her parents' house, only eighty miles east. After that, it was back to work helping my fellow citizens. We needed power and gas, clean water and ice, clean-up crews with chainsaws and backhoes, roofers and building contractors.

Imagine this: thousands homeless, left with nothing, in the late August Mississippi sun. You had to know the right people or pay the right price to get higher on the list. It didn't seem fair.

I took matters into my own hands. I directed power trucks to places most needed. I stopped incoming supply trucks and took a portion to deliver on my own to those who couldn't make it to the pick-up points. Knocked open a door at a department store so people could get new shoes, clothes, diapers.

Being the Good Samaritan had a price, costing me time and effort, some out-of-pocket expenses. I didn't think it was unethical to ask for reimbursement from those I helped. Or upfront payments if the need was dire enough. After all, they thought of me as a savior for the moment, their personal hand of justice.

What got me in trouble was the other side of things—when you play Robin Hood, one side always gets shafted, a little less gold in the saddlebags and an arrow in the thigh, and that's the side with muscle. In my case, it wasn't so much the federal government or the old money families. In order to get what we needed I had to cross the upper-middle class, not rich enough to get a jump start but certainly spoiled on their creature comforts.

Well, fuck 'em.

Cops got paid jack-shit and we put our lives on the line every night. An embarrassment. If I hadn't played the angles and taken some moonlighting gigs as "security", my family would've probably dipped into food stamp range. Not on my watch.

After the storm, they were on their cell phones bitching at their insurance companies: "Look, we know there are people out there with greater needs, but the sooner we're taken care of, the sooner we can get back to work and help them." So said the bankers, general practitioners, pizza franchise owners, beauty shops owners, pawn shop owners, car lot general managers, on and on…

The people I was helping? Hourly wage-earning blackjack dealers and cocktail waitresses out of work since the casinos—huge floating barges because our lawmakers thought gambling on land was morally reprehensible, but had no problem taking the tax revenues if the goddamn things were on the gulf had broken from their moorings, washed across the highway, crushed buildings and cars along the way, while flooding out slot machines and gaming tables. Mighty lucky debris, we'd call it.

Again: fuck 'em. They say that to us and we say it to them and the liberals and the media tell the republicans they shouldn't say it to those poor folks in New Orleans (but by ignoring the Mississippi Coast the liberals and the media are saying it to we of the gambling-addicted Redneck Rivera anyway) who've been fucked for years and ignored by the same liberals and media-types who were now complaining that everyone else was saying Fuck 'em.

In other words, I messed with the wrong people. I got pulled in on an IAD complaint. In the wake of the storm surge, plenty of officers were glad to rat me out in order to help out their own shitty living conditions. I was strung up as an example of corruption, an example of the "good" police filtering their own ranks to protect and serve. Third page news (the hurricane would dominate the first two for months). A scapegoat, a whipping boy, a martyr. Yeah, a martyr to those cops I *didn't* squeal on, the ones who knew they owed me their livelihoods even though most couldn't spill my name fast enough.

My options sucked. Roll over on my fellow cops? Not on your life. Private security? True, there were plenty of jobs since so many people had disappeared—they didn't even want to salvage their belongings. Easier to start over, be new people. Yeah, I could see standing in front of the same store I'd helped loot only weeks earlier, this time hired to shoot anyone who tried to do it again.

With Ginny sticking to the divorce plans, I knew my life on the Coast would never be the same. I was born and raised there, knew too many people who knew Ginny and me, who knew what I did. I'm sure her parents pushed a little, too. I remember sitting in their living room while Ginny lashed at me. She paced while they sat on the edge of the couch cushions, staring me down, all holy roller condescension. They didn't even own a TV, real hard-liners.

"Tell me the truth. This is what you did? Took advantage? Stole? That's what you did?"

If the Old Testament Prophets hadn't been watching I would've felt stronger, able to twist it my way. Shade the truth. I wasn't like those cops in New Orleans who fled, taking their squad cars and abandoning their duties. Not like I was preying on citizens—they *wanted* my help.

I said to Ginny, "You've got to believe me..."

"'Thou art snared with the words of thy mouth.' Proverbs," her father said.

"—that everything I did was for good of those people."

She said, "You took their money. You were like some mafia."

"No, please, they gave me gifts. I couldn't turn that down. It was for *you*, for us."

Ginny's father butted in again, still as a statue but loud as a walrus. " 'For the good that I would I do not, but the evil which I would not, that I do.' Romans."

I lifted my head. "Got anything in there about forgiveness? About sacred vows between man and wife?"

The man's face was a storm. He wanted to lose his temper. I knew he had trouble with that before his first heart attack, even slapped Ginny's mother around a bit. I would never do that to my wife, so the holier-than-thou shit got to me.

Waited him out. He looked at his daughter and said, "'If the unbeliever departs, let him depart. The wife is not under bondage in such cases.' First Corinthians." Then to me, "God's patient but he ain't stupid, boy."

I stood. "Well I'm not leaving. This is between Ginny and me. We'll work it out."

"No," Ginny said. "Not this time."

I couldn't see my kids—they were supposed to be playing in the back bedroom—but I sensed my son listening at the door, opening it a crack. He'd make a fine detective one day, join the police same as me. Make his father proud. At that moment, though, he was probably confused, and if I had stuck around for visitation weekends, he'd grow resentful after being filled with his mom's anger towards me and his grandparents' pious lies.

And yet, even with the pain of the divorce, the anger between Ginny and myself, it was she who presented me with my second chance. Her family had moved south from Sioux Falls, South Dakota because of her father's transfer when Ginny was fifteen. Her brother was five years older than her and already a junior at Iowa State in Criminal Justice, so he stayed behind. I came along another ten years after that, met Ginny and whirled her up in romance, asked her to marry me. I'd only met the brother, Graham, a few times. Seemed like a decent guy—quiet, nice Christian leanings. Married with kids, loving it. He also seemed a bit of a stiff board. But, hey, he was just my brother-in-law and I only had to see him every couple of years. I didn't mind watching the game with him or shooting the shit on the phone before Ginny picked up.

After a respectable run of years as a deputy in Yellow Medicine County, he got himself elected sheriff. Not all that grand of a job—babysit the citizens of a rural farming county, occasionally deal with stray shots and rumored meth labs. Cozy, except for the snow and wind. A boring job for a boring man who didn't mind the boredom.

The ink hadn't even dried on the papers before Ginny called him, pled my case, and got me hired. I didn't hear it from her. There I was, sitting in a hotel room without power, staring at the gun in my lap, when Graham rang and offered me a job.

"I believe in second chances, and believe it or not, my sister still believes in you." he said.

"That's the dumbest thing I've ever heard. If she still believed in me, I'd be home with her and the kids right now."

"You know it's not that easy. Listen, this is a one time offer. Lots of people in your position don't get this handed to them on a silver plate."

I took a deep breath, did all my thinking in as long as it took to exhale. "Okay, all right. Yeah, I think I want to."

Minnesota. A new start out on the frozen plains. My purgatory.

The bottle of wine nearly drained, I was drifting in and out of dreams, one about my wife and kids in a plane crash. They walked away unharmed. Maybe I was dreaming it because the TV news was droning on about a crash in Russia. The internal blending with the external, none of it making sense. I slapped my cheeks and shook the sleep away, ready to go climb in bed under heavy quilts to make up for the drafty bedroom and lousy heating system.

That's when two beams of light sliced across the yard and front window. I blinked and switched off the lamp for a better look. A pair of headlights at the end of my driveway. They weren't coming towards the house. Sitting there, burning, waiting.

I lifted my pistol off the coffee table. The gun was always within reach. I lived next door to a boat launch and a decaying house that probably housed a meth lab. People would get lost or overshoot the meth house and use my driveway to reverse course. But the car out there at three in the morning, snow still blowing enough to obscure the make and a glimpse of how many people were inside, stayed put. I was drunk enough that even with clear skies and a telescope, I'd still have trouble telling who it was.

I wondered if they could see me inside. I stumbled into the kitchen, flicked that light off. Back to the living room, killed the TV. I eased closer to the front windows and tried to focus. Somewhere in my head, a little voice said, *You know you're an easy target.*

I wasn't thinking about bullets. The way I felt, they'd bounce right off my chest.

Those headlights just sat there. I thought I saw movement, like the back passenger's door opening. I ducked, eye-level with the sill. Checked the pistol to make sure the safety was off. I never put it on anyway.

How long did I crouch like that? Forgot to check the clock later. All attention on those headlights. The cramps, the fear, the anger. I'd made some enemies, sure, but I never bothered them at their homes this late at night. Have the same fucking courtesy for me.

Then the lights moved, retreated to the road and headed away.

Plenty of explanations: teens looking for a place to make out, got a little freaked (it seemed too long for that and not long enough for fucking), or some guy got himself lost and needed to check his map (then why didn't I see the interior lights?), or some drunk needed a few minutes to rest his eyes, get himself five minutes more sober for the trip home.

That didn't stop me from obsessing about all the other reasons. Like someone in the bar overhearing my conversation with Drew, pointing those outsiders my way before I found them first. Or the worst possibility—the friends of the gangbanger I shot in Gulfport after the storm finally tracked me down. I was pretty sure no one knew except Paul Asimov, my shift partner, but could be he sold me out for a piece of the profits. I'd rather he did that than let them torture it out of him. I dropped the big bad *gangsta* with a gut-shot, then we dumped the guy out in the woods north of Biloxi, an area hard to get to with all the downed trees, and let the animals have a buffet.

It was a stupid thought. All that happened a thousand miles away. I was careful when I left, made sure the trail only led so far, very few of the people in my life knowing exactly where I had landed. Not even Ginny.

Still, instead of going to bed, I sat up in my

thrift-store recliner, gun in my lap, listening hard for footsteps on crispy snow, or fallen limbs snapping, or whispers. There were a few noises—crunching snow, probably rabbits or deer, and tricks of the wind. No one tried coming inside. I sat dead still at the ready until gray sunlight showed me the world outside again. Only then did I fall asleep.

FIVE

After waking up late in the afternoon and cleaning out the cruiser, I shot down to Marshall while listening to the HorrorPops on my MP3 player. They were a European psychobilly band. I'd been listening to more of the stuff since meeting Drew. We were both punch-drunk after fucking that first night and she lay sprawled on my bed smoking menthols and telling me all about this music she loved—a mix of punk, rockabilly, and horror flicks. Kinda like the soundtrack of my life. The HorrorPops had this chick singer, so I thought of Drew every time I let it blast.

Flying down Highway 23 at about ninety, the trip takes fifteen minutes on the two-lane road, me taking chances by tailgating, passing the law abiders even with oncoming traffic. It wasn't like the badges would dare pull me over, the only reason I was in the cruiser anyway. My first time through, driving my pick-up and hauling a small U-haul, a trooper lit me up.

Guy was so mad he stuttered at first, wanting to lecture me. "Do you have *any* idea how dangerous it is pulling a trailer that fast? Got some sort of death wish?"

I handed him my Mississippi license. "I think you'd better look me up before you say another word, pops. Chill out."

If a perp had ever talked to me that way, he'd be on the pavement while I searched his vehicle and called in the drug dogs. Pops didn't do that. Seeing how his girth strained the buttons on his shirt, I understood. He was much less red after he called in and was told who I was and why I was in his state. He handed back my license and said, "How about keeping it down just a bit? Lot of semis through here can nearly blow you off the road. At last until you unhitch."

"That would've been fine, sir. But because of this stop, I'm running late. Gotta drive like the wind." I pulled away. He didn't chase me down. Since then I've never been stopped.

I was on my way to see Drew's boyfriend. Drew had told me Ian's hangouts, whose dorm he'd been crashing, hiding out from whoever had branded him. He might try to hide from me, too, even though I was trying to help this time. Something squirrelly about that kid. Same with the whole story. I cleared my head and kept the churning music up loud while battling the winds that so desperately wanted to sling me off the road into the snow-patched soybean fields. In mid-winter the snow made the whole place look majestic, peaceful. In mid-summer the tall corn and the beans reminded you of the importance of our midwestern farms. But in early spring they just looked like shit.

Past the university campus, squat-red brick buildings. Hung a right and circled the campus until I found the visitor's parking lot, got out and followed my scribbled directions to the residence hall. Drew said Ian was staying with an art student in his dorm room. Pretty risky, could get the guy expelled if the university figured it out. I passed farm girls dressed in sweatpants and ski jackets, some viable candidates and some porkers, and some drastically plain. Mouthbreather guys, others with those haircuts kids get in their twenties and regret almost immediately. Found the right building, hung around the front until someone came out. I didn't care that I didn't blend in, thirty-three and hard like steel, a full mustache and ‘burns, something about the seventies’ look of my dad appealing in these days of shaves and waxes. I climbed the stairs two at a time to the third floor. Room 305. Pounded hard.

No answer. Pounded again. This time I heard rustling, groans. I tapped my fingers on the door, a peppy rockabilly rhythm, until the kid inside got pissed off enough to fling the door open, muscles flexed, ready to wail. He was in boxers, hair sticking in eight directions. Sleeping all afternoon. Goddamn lazy kids. Not that I’d been any different, or even was now.

“You Josh?”

He nodded. “Who the fuck are you?”

“Looking for Ian.”

“Who?”

“Skinny pale kid, probably the guy you buy weed from.”

“Hey, man, that shit ain’t cool.”

“Is he here? I need to talk to him.” I wasn’t dressed like a cop—jeans, black CAT steel-toes, and flannel.

He knew, though. Didn’t want to rat his source out. He pasted this lazy smile on and started to shut the door. “No idea, man.”

The hall was clear. I stopped the door with my foot and palm, pushed him back by willpower alone. Inside, I closed the door and looked around. Mounds of clothes, smelling sour. Plus the weed. Plus the incense he burned to cover the weed.

The guy balled his fists and wanted to bump chests, a hip-hop stand-off. I slapped him hard across the face. That put an end to the posturing.

"I need to speak to Ian. He's in trouble. I'm the answer to his prayers. You dig?"

The guy was stunned, stoned, cheek flaring red. "Yeah, I dig."

He was protecting Ian's dirty secret, one Drew must have been blind to. I sneaked around the girls' res hall until I found the propped-open back door. They had to have some way to let the boys get in at all hours. Second floor this time. I found the door and knocked politely.

A chick's sing-songy, "It's o-pen!"

Stepped inside just as the girl kept on, "What, did you forget your key again?"

She looked at me, stopped smiling. "You're not my roommate."

Her long hair cascaded over her shoulders as she sat Indian style on the bed, topless. Ian's head was in her lap. The other bed was empty.

When Ian saw me he began to jitter and say, "No no no, shit shit shit."

"Hey! Get out of my room!" The girl tried to cover her breasts with her hair. Almost worked.

"Soon as Ian gets his pants on."

He was struggling into them, since I'd caught him in tighty-whiteys. Cheating on Drew. Didn't surprise me. Ian thought he should act like a rock star but without playing music or having money. Would I tell her? If I thought it meant she'd get with me instead, then of course. But even the hint of obligation would spoil it for me—I wanted her to want me with no conditions. Besides, she had a bright future and I didn't want to stand in her way. She needed to get out of the backwoods while I needed to hide in them.

Ian mumbled and moaned while zipping his torn-to-hell khakis. I took in the room—cleaner than the guy's, of course, but not by much. The smoke detector was covered with a sub sandwich bag and duct tape. The window was open and the heat was blasting to compensate.

The girl managed to pick her T-shirt off the floor with her toes without showing me any more nip. A tattoo of a vine ringed her ankle.

Still indignant. "You can't do this. I'm going to tell the RA right now. It's illegal."

I made a show of sniffing the air. "Are you really so immune to the smell that you think potpourri works? While you're off complaining, bring the RA down here so we can discuss what you guys are smoking."

She crossed her arms, wadding the shirt against her chest. Then a smile, slight, and a lift of the chin. "I have rights."

"You can have rights, sure. Just have to defend them in court, see if those rights will keep them from kicking you out of school. Looks to me like you've got a pretty sweet situation. Parents paying for classes and books and pot and condoms. Pretty sweet. But if you want to throw that away over *rights*—"

"Fine, I get it. I'll shut up."

I grabbed Ian's shoulder and pulled him towards the door. "You'll do more than shut up. What's your name?"

She didn't want to tell me, but worked out that I'd learn it eventually. "Heather."

"Well, Heather dear, I'll be back to see you later and we'll try to work something out."

She swallowed hard, kept quiet. That was okay. After another couple of hits she'd realize how much she liked the dope and how much she'd like to keep things exactly as they were. At least she'd learn something this semester.

I dragged Ian's scrawny ass outside and found a concrete ledge to sit on, one that lined a central area outside the administration building, near the flagpole. Ian shook a cigarette loose and offered me one. I shook my head.

He looked at the ground, shrugged. "Whatever, man. Look, you can't tell Drew about this. It wasn't what it looked like."

"It looked like you were getting some strange. That hippie chick strange with the hairy armpits. Like you're being led by your pecker and will fuck anything that makes a move on you first."

"Man, it's just...look. I *love* Drew—"

I took his cigarette. That shut him up. I turned it around, placed the lit end an inch away from his bottom lip. He pulled back. I grabbed the back of his head and held it, a shaky mistake waiting to happen.

I said, "You don't know what love is. It's a goddamned verb, remember? It's something you do. And you do it by not fucking around on the side. I would usually admire fucking around, but you seem so weak-willed that I can't believe you think about it all that much."

"Billy, please." Like a five-year-old.

"You don't love. You do what feels good at the moment. If it weren't for Drew having a soft spot for you, I wouldn't be here trying to help."

"Jesus!"

The wind slapped us around and ripped the ash off, staining my fingers gray. I flicked the cigarette onto the pavement and let go of his head. "Goddamn telling me it's love. You just like how different they are. Drew, nicely trimmed, sweet and innocent, a nice tight fit."

The look on his face told me he didn't know I'd been with her. He shook his head, paled. "Can't believe this."

"It was before you, and after that she gave me up quick."

"I'm going to be sick."

"Shut up." I stood up and paced in front of him. Wanted him off-balance. "I won't tell her about hippy chick, but you'd better come clean right now. These two guys leaning on you, what's the deal?"

"I don't need you. I'll manage."

"Sure, great. One more time, what's the

deal?"

He shoegazed more, shoulders bobbing. For these kids, *I don't know* was a goddamned way of life.

I pinched his chin between my thumb and middle finger, forced eye contact. "This ain't about you. This is about visiting players coming into my county wanting to change the rules. Where I come from that's cheating. Nobody wins by cheating."

He jerked his head. I gave him space. Thinking it over, working it out. Weak kid, all it took was a little nudge.

He huffed and finally said, "I didn't know they were so hardcore at first. This guy I knew asked if I—"

"Who?"

"Hey, I don't want to get him trouble."

I held out my fingers, waved them towards me like *Give it.*

"Fine. But don't say, you know. Guy's name is Vis. That's all I know, his last name."

I nodded, knew him. Tracy Vis. Hated "Tracy", never answered to it. Getting to be about thirty-eight, not a successful criminal. He ran a lottery scam sometimes when he couldn't get anyone to make meth for him. Fucker was too dumb to figure out what fifteen-year-old drop outs learned in twenty minutes off a website.

"What did he want from you?"

Ian said, "He wanted me to check out some places in Yellow Medicine County, guys working labs that might be interested in a bigger operation. Hook up with these two guys—they were both Asian, I think."

"You think?"

Another shrug. "I dunno. Not, like, Japanese or Chinese, but not Nepalese like the foreign students around here. You could tell. They were all business. One spoke great English, barely an accent. None, really."

"Definitely meth, then? Not heroin?"

"Yeah, like a franchise. They organize the labs, get the distribution in line, and take a big cut. But since there's more stuff coming in than before, everybody wins."

Shit, and I hadn't gotten one hint of it. That meant people thought it was a good enough deal to keep it secret, even though I paid them to keep me in the loop.

I said, "Drew says you lost some of their product."

He grunted. "It wasn't anything like that. I

could've understood if I'd lost product."

"Then what was it?"

Ian shifted his weight, probably thinking about the brand on his ass, itching now that he was watching that mental movie all over again. "I lost their trust. After talking to some guys near Wood Lake, they laughed at me. No need for a mob. The labs out here, like moonshine stills, they said. Thing is, they followed me after. Barged in on the next meeting with the Asians."

"Son of a bitch."

"Yeah. I didn't expect what happened next, though. Soon as the guys said that this was their territory and that they didn't appreciate being hustled out of business, well…"

More wind. Biting me. I shoved my hands into my pockets. Ian bared his teeth.

Then, "These Asians killed Trigger and Spaceman. You knew them, right?"

Sure did. Both ran a red phosphorus lab upriver. Spaceman was in my pocket. I helped those guys out if he kept me informed. They should have come to me instead of getting all macho. Macho came easier for me because I meant it.

"I knew them."

"They're…dead, you know, on the floor and

all. Guys shot them in the head. Then they blame me. I tell them I didn't have anything to do with it. Doesn't matter. I wasn't careful. I needed to be reminded. Drew told you what they did."

"They had the brand with them? How did this go down?"

Ian's lips curled, staring off into space, students passing around us now between classes. "They put a bag over my head, put me in the backseat of their car and we drove. I don't know how long. They left the bag on. I couldn't see anything. I only heard, like, wind. Their jabbering. Then they bend me over…what was I supposed to think?"

"Shit."

"Man, when that fire hit my ass, I almost did. I screamed. They didn't mind me screaming, so we must've been, like, pretty far out somewhere. I screamed a long damn time. They didn't hit me or anything. Just held me up by the arms. After, when I had calmed down, they told me it was a reminder to be smart. I've been hiding ever since."

More students, coming too close, smelled the cop on me. Girls in flannel pajama bottoms and fleece slippers going to class unwashed.

Goddamn wind made it hard to think. Definitely sounded organized, all this honor-system bullshit. I wondered if laying low was really working, or if the Asians knew exactly where Ian was and would now end him for talking to me. Maybe they were watching us at that exact moment.

Once the crowd thinned, I said, "Let's see it."

The kid shrunk more. I thought he would fold in on himself. "See what?"

"I have to see it to track it down. Don't get all shy. I won't even touch it."

"Not here."

"I don't have time for a private peek show." I probably did, but I just wanted to see if he'd drop his pants in public with icy winds swirling. Between me and the drug lords, I was hoping we would provide enough mental scars to set him on the right track. Sometimes being feared is an educational thing as well.

The kid did his James Dean shrug again, said, "Fuck you, I don't wanna."

I pulled my hands out of my pockets, cracked my knuckles. Innocent enough, but Ian freaked.

"Why can't you leave me alone? Don't track

them down, let me handle things. You'll just get me killed."

"Dude, I've kept you from getting killed once or twice already. I'm your de facto bodyguard. Better to be under my wing than a worm I'm aiming for."

He squirmed, looking around and over his shoulder and I wondered what this would look like if a security guard happened to round the corner at just the right moment. I'd have to tell him I suspected the kid was keestering drugs.

Eventually he stood, sighing and jerking his body, like that would make me call it off. He turned around, unbuckled, and thumbed his waistband down far enough to let me see the bandage. Pants were so baggy I wondered how he kept them on at all.

"I need to see the mark. It'll be like a fingerprint, you know."

He said, "*Gaaawd*" and peeled the adhesive off. The skin was charred, leaking yellow, and the area surrounding it was red and puffy. What Drew took to be an "F" looked more like a Chinese symbol, and it was resting in a waning quarter moon. I didn't get it—not a ranch symbol. I had a hunch, though. Made my stomach drop. Needed to do a little research.

"Zip up. Listen, I'll need to take a photo later."

"Do you really—"

"Sorry." Quiet. "Really, I'm sorry."

Shrug. "'S okay."

We let the gusts shove us around. I felt bad for him once I saw it, but not enough to ease up. He was still a petty troublemaker who was lying to a woman I'd die for, getting mixed up with outsiders who knew how to outflank me, and who caused the death of a good informant. If I hadn't promised Drew, I'd have thrown the kid in jail for a couple weeks. Maybe she would have preferred that, too. At least then we'd have known where he was sleeping.

"All right. Stay put. I'll be back tonight at eight. Be here."

"Out here?" He looked around.

"Just, *here*, on campus. One of those two dorms. Okay? Drew will let you know when I'm coming."

Ian cringed at her name. "Promise you won't tell her, man. It's one little mistake, you know. I'm under a lot of pressure."

I wiped the frost off my mustache. So whiny, the young folks these days. Nothing's ever their fault. "Men don't rat out other men. You break her heart, though, I come after you."

He slumped, pulled the sweater's hoodie over his crown, and started towards the girls' dorm.

"Where are you going?"

He spun. "Back to Heather's."

I shook my head, pointed towards the first res hall I tried. "Back to your own kind. No coed hideout for you."

"Give me a break. Why not?" Then he figured it out. "Shit, man, you weren't serious."

My finger still outstretched towards the men's dorm. A statue. Tried not to grin.

He finally got the message and stormed off. "Unbelievable. No fair. No fair at all."

However pissed Ian was at me, at least he understood that I was in charge. I expected no fight from him later on. It would keep him safe, I hoped.

The difference between my love for Drew and Ian's was that she didn't feel the same way about me. Somehow he'd risen to the top of her affections in spite of all the obvious warning signs. Coming to me to protect him, that's a big act of love. Agreeing to a night with me she didn't want as payment—I couldn't accept that.

Drew needed to want me freely, her whole heart in it, in order for me take her again. I'd kill for her, but I wouldn't fuck her. Well, not unless she asked me to.

I didn't knock on Heather's door this time. I tried the handle. Still unlocked. I stepped inside. She was lying on the bed, same clothes, her bare feet crossed at the ankles. Staring at the ceiling. I went to her and sat down, ran my longest finger along her leg, traced the tattoo on her ankle.

"Have you considered your options?"

She turned her face to me. "I can't believe you. Is this how you get your kicks?"

I swirled my fingertips on her T-shirt. She flinched. I made a move to the bottom of her shirt, slipped under. Her skin was warm.

"I don't think the punishment for this sort of thing fits the crime. Why ruin your college career over something that should be legal anyway?"

She propped on her elbows. "Exactly. See?"

"I couldn't do that to you. I'd be a hypocrite."

Her expression brightened like spring sun on her face. "A little pot never hurt anyone. Mild stuff."

Aw, yeah. There it was. Hope. She saw light at the end of the tunnel.

Too bad the train was coming.

"Wish I could overlook it. But the law is the law."

The bright face went sour. "Please, I'm sorry and all. Can't you forget about it?

I grinned. "Sorry, it's part of the deal."

"I don't mean to be like this. I'm just having fun. God, I'm only, like, nineteen, you know? I promise I won't do it again."

Her voice rattled like ice cubes in a glass. Fear all over her. Jesus, I'd read all the signs wrong, thought she would be into it. What the hell was I doing?

I scooted down to the end of the bed, my hand trailing down her leg. I could have done it if I wanted. Really. She would have liked it, too. I remembered Drew on her prom night, the way everything seemed natural between us, the way she played with the radio in the cruiser while her boyfriend stewed in the backseat. I never felt one moment of resistance or fear from her. I'd fooled myself into thinking it was about the badge, the gun. Chicks dug that shit.

Not this one. And I didn't want to be that guy after all.

I stood, said, "Give me the pot."

Heather's face relaxed some, and she reached for a stuffed yellow and green dragon on her bedside table, shoved two fingers inside its mouth, and brought back a sandwich baggie with hardly enough marijuana for two or three more joints. I took it from her, started to close my hand around it, then changed my mind.

"I'm not going to take it. I almost did. I'm just saying be careful, okay?"

She nodded, her head hunched against her shoulders. "What…what about…you know?"

I grinned, took a step back. "As long as you don't tell Ian, I suppose we can let it slide. As far as anyone else is concerned, I just fucked you fiercely, darlin'."

I left the room in a hurry. I didn't want to think about what I was missing under Heather's skirt. Instead, I pictured Drew on stage, the lights on her face, bass slung low. My punk rock baby. Took the steps two a time until the wind bit into me as good as any cold shower. The only time I'd ever been grateful for that bitter fucking wind.

SIX

Yellow Medicine County was named after the root of the moon seed plant, something the Indians used for, you guessed it, medicine. With so much Indian heritage and history out here, obvious in the names of towns, counties, rivers, and lakes, you'd think things would be pretty cozy between Native Americans and the descendants of Norse Vikings. But my first few weeks in Minnesota, it was a little shocking to find so much racism towards the Sioux. Down South, it's an honor to say you have Indian blood in you. Here, there's tension over land, money, entitlements, education, heritage, dating, you name it. Not as subtle as the white/black line in Mississippi, where everyone has to live and work with each other every day, much more so than the Scandinavians and the Sioux.

I wasn't trying to make the world a better place, except for myself and my children—you better know I sent those checks every month—and once I knew about the racial pressure cooker, it made sense to exploit it. I learned which band leaders could use a little cooperation or appreciate a blind eye. I was able to get the inside scoop on all the players on both sides, a good ref enforcing the ground rules but willing to let things slide since it's a rough game and all. But one flagrant violation gained the offender a severe penalty.

Even after a year and a half, it felt as if I was missing something. Somehow being blocked from seeing the real game. I couldn't quite understand it at first until it hit me that I was still thinking like a Southerner, all casual and charming. The Minnesotans were layered, masterminds of playing politics, dual-operators. All that chit-chat about the weather? The way you answer helps them figure you out. Cold repressed sons of bitches. Whoever coined the term "Minnesota Nice" must have never been around truly nice people, raised by a family of killers or something. Friendly on the surface, but it was forced. The only "nice" I'd seen was from the women I fucked, and even then it was obvious they were hiding something.

At the same time, the whole state was pretty

goofy. These people held the world record for "Most People Doing a Cartwheel". They sculpted a beauty pageant winner's head from a big block of butter. They really liked food on a stick. They deified Garrison Keillor, for Christ's sake.

Said all that to say this: I still had a lot to learn, I had to be very careful, and sometimes I tripped over my ego.

The sheriff asked to see me before I started my shift. Graham had been Chief Deputy for three years before the good citizens voted him into office. And pretty young for the job at thirty-seven considering the two previous sheriffs had each held the post over twenty years—started in their fifties. One guy had been stone deaf the last year of his term but faked hearing, none the wiser until he didn't turn around when his son tossed a chunk of firewood at him, put him in a coma. So my brother-in-law was a soft-hearted evangelical peace officer who thought I was a reckless liability.

I thought he was a pussy.

He brought me a coffee with too much cream in it—he liked to fix his own instead of asking Layla—and then took his chair. The desk was arranged to soften you up, with his wife and two children smiling from framed photos. My niece looked like an angel in the family photo, but outside of the house I'd caught her dressing way too sexy for fifteen, meeting up with college boys. My nephew, seventeen, was in a Christian rock band. Jesus, what a horror show.

"How's it going? Done any more work on the house?"

I shook my head. "Maybe I'm not the DIY type after all. Still like to try, though."

"You ever need a hand for painting, carpentry, let me know. George and I could help out. Maybe even get Layla and Kirk, make a day of it."

Aw, how about that? He wanted to be my brother for real. Yeah, sure. He just wanted me close, wanted me to trust him. Like I had a new family or something—George was his second-in-charge, a nice enough guy, liked to dress well but still a hard-bitten country guy. Layla's husband Kirk was also worth bringing along for a fishing trip, although I preferred my way of doing things to theirs. Our one and only ice fishing trip together was the least "fishing" I'd ever seen.

I could enjoy their company for a few hours, sure, but I didn't see how I'd ever really fit in. Not that I had to with Minnesotans. We drank beer, we watched a game, we complained about politics, especially when they found out I wasn't voting for their team.

I said, "Sure, I'll let you know."

He hovered over the desk, finally resting on his elbows, one hand covering the other. His Mac laptop was closed, pushed off to the side. No papers on his desktop at all.

"Billy, I heard that you had a suspect on his knees off the shoulder of the highway last night. Had your sidearm out, too. I checked this morning for your report but it doesn't appear to have been filed yet. Plus, there's no record of you logging someone in to the holding area."

He waited, expecting me to jump in and defend myself. Half the fun was having him do all the work. The choir boy hated confrontation. He liked spontaneous confession so much better. Cleansing souls and all. I told him, "So?"

"Was my witness correct? Did you threaten a suspect last night and then not bring him in?" Lines of concern around his eyes.

Time to let him off the hook. "It was a

courtesy for Terrell Rome at the casino. He had a drunk who needed a ride home, and I wasn't busy."

"That's not really our jurisdiction."

I let out a long breath. "You should have seen the guy, though. Puking on himself, bumping into walls. I just wanted to get him home safely. We stopped on the way because he was feeling ill, vomiting in the car. Did Layla mention that? She told me to clean it out myself."

Graham had pulled a small notebook from his desk drawer and a goddamn fancy pen, took notes. He was thinking I would be more apt to tell the truth if I thought he might check up on me. But Layla would lie for me. We hit it off nicely. She liked the way I saw the world. Plus, her husband and I could talk cars and war movies all day long.

"Keep going," he said.

"Not much more to it. I brought him outside, let him finish, and then took him home."

"Was he handcuffed?"

It was that truck driver from the electric company. I'd have to look him up, see if he had any secrets. "No sir. He was just a drunk man needing a ride. I felt some pity. You might even know him. A doctor who works down in Marshall."

Something in Graham wanted to ask. He would love to hear the gossip, would love to question the man and see if our stories were the same. To do that, though, would stain his dignity. Even if he could check my story with Hulka, he knew the good doctor would keep his mouth shut. Not worth the embarrassment, not in small towns like ours.

Graham tapped his pen on the pad. A flat sound. Chinese water torture. Other men might be willing to confess just to fill the air with *any* other sound. He finally sighed and said, "We're not a taxi service. Next time tell the fine folks at the casino to arrange other modes of transportation unless it's an emergency, will you?"

"Got it."

"And file reports, even for favors."

I nodded, waited. This wasn't the only reason he called me in, right? I expected him to tell me they'd found Trigger and Spaceman's bodies. He knew I kept track of the meth activity around here. My references all agreed that my specialty was being able to think like a dealer, like a businessman. Like a gangsta.

"Something else, Billy?"

Or maybe I should be the one to tell him. Redeem myself before the whole world came crashing down in some sort of turf war where I try to be a one-man army. Better to get all the county's law enforcement involved. Protect our citizens from the scum of the earth, the demons looking to damn the souls of our children.

Too bad I'd lost my soul in a hurricane.

"No. Nothing. Just thinking we should get lunch one day this week."

"I'd like that. Let's try for Thursday."

I rose from the chair and gave him a thumbs-up. "You got it."

He wrote it on his pad. "Heard from Ham and Savannah lately?"

So word had gotten back about my latest late night drunk call. I'm sure he meant well, but it stung. He thought it part of his duty to keep me in line if Ginny complained. Son of a bitch.

I answered on my way out the door. "Wouldn't want to disturb their sleep."

On my way out I sat on the edge of Layla's desk while she talked to her husband on the phone and flipped through a *Motor Trend*. She and her husband collected old sports cars, restored and sold some of them. I think she only had the job because she liked the guns.

I said, "You remember me calling in about my passenger last night, right?"

She gave me The Look over the top of her glasses, then said to Kirk, "Just Billy. He's up to no good."

I held my hand to my chest, tried to look wounded.

She said, "The sheriff knows who it was?"

I shook my head. "Don't think that's any of his business."

"Okay, I can agree with that." She winked at me.

"Thanks doll. Tell that husband of yours he'll have to fight me for you one day."

"Fuck off, prick."

On the way to my car, I heard someone else in the parking lot call my name. I looked over, saw Nathan Eberle coming my way. We started here about the same time, but he was a lot younger, fresh out of college. A scrappy little go-getter. His greenness got on my nerves, but I'd ridden with him a few times, tried to instill a bit of my policing philosophy in him. He didn't seem to approve. More like Graham than me. Still, good to have along when I didn't feel like fishing alone.

"Afternoon, Nate. Just getting off shift?"

"Couple more hours." Skinny kid. A meth dealer could probably break him in half. I hoped he would at least take my advice on shooting his perp in the leg if it looked like things might get frisky. He said, "Almost time to hit the river, right? Reel a few in?"

I let out a sigh. "You'd better not be talking about ice fishing, for Christ's sake."

Nate and everyone else had heard my bitching and moaning about that trip. He laughed. "What, this still too cold for you? Another two or three weeks, I'd say the ice will be gone. I've got a canoe."

"We'll see. You guys still have thicker blood than mine."

"You can wear a coat or two." Kid was fucking with me, I swear.

Shook my head as I opened the door to my cruiser. "At least I can get laid, young man."

I went to see Spaceman's mom, but I wasn't sure if I wanted to let her know he was dead yet. I wanted to see the bodies myself, but I imagined the Asians had already gotten rid of the evidence. At least no one had found them so far. It was probably guilt that led me to see her, thinking of how I'd let these guys keep up their business for selfish reasons. They were stupid enough to think my invulnerability had rubbed off on them. Soon as Ian told me they were dead, my stomach ached.

His mom was named Sheryl and she worked at the local diner in Pale Falls. Most mornings you'd find the old men in town at the horseshoe breakfast counter betting dimes on the roll of a die. They didn't say much. When they did it was so thickly accented that I couldn't make it out. The breakfasts were tasteless, the sausage like cardboard, and hash browns never a convincing substitute for buttery grits. The coffee, well, I started bringing my own. The other half of the joint was a sit-down restaurant that hadn't been changed since it opened—tables, chairs, overhead lights, all stuck on "1963". The salad bar was suspicious. I swear I've never seen anyone touch it, but it was always only half-full.

Sheryl must have been in her early forties, and she slept with guys sixty and older most of the time. Not unattractive, but certainly worn down to the frayed edges. The thing you couldn't help notice about her was her breasts.

Pretty much your average C cup, except that her left was three times larger than her right because of a benign growth the size of a cantaloupe. She tried to have it removed once but nearly died from bleeding before they even got started. She had to learn to live with it.

How'd I know all this? Yeah, I fucked her my first week in town. Had to. Just no way to see those breasts and not wonder. She had to hold the left one up when she was on top. And be careful not to let it hit you in the face—bruised my nose.

I also knew that Spaceman had been stashing away some money so he could send her to a better doctor, maybe even one in Europe. He was tired of all her men treating her like an amusement park ride and then disappearing. So he had planned to surprise her on her birthday. He dealt drugs so his mom might be happy one day.

This time of the afternoon, the diner was mostly empty. Sheryl was perched on a stool, hand holding up her chin, listening to the swap shop on AM radio. She grinned at me, the tired type that highlighted the lines around her mouth.

"We're not serving breakfast, baby."

"Slept late. The night shift, you know."

"I thought you usually came in before you went to bed."

I set my hat on the counter and took a stool. Our faces were close. She smelled like a deep fryer and vanilla. "Last night I needed something stronger than chocolate milk and waffles."

"Anything right now?"

"A root beer."

She grabbed a hard plastic cup, scooped a tiny amount of ice from below the drink machine.

"More ice, please. Remember."

"Fine, fine. I don't know how you can stand it."

I'd found that Minnesotans didn't like a lot of ice in their "pop" and tea. Say it waters down the taste. They're right, but we Southerners want it right to the rim anyway. She double-scooped and then ran me a root beer, handed it over. It gave me time to think how I should tell her about her son. Probably some sort of reverse psychology.

I thanked her, took a teeth-freezing sip. Then, "Heard from your boy lately?"

She rolled her eyes. "They get that age, they

don't want to call their mothers as much. It's been a couple of days."

"I thought he lived with you."

"I guess he always will. Not like I'm going to give his room away or anything. Mostly he stays with his friend, you know. I know what they're into, but I've been talking to him and I think he might be convinced to try looking for work in The Cities. Or maybe try college again."

She sounded a little excited talking about it, but her spirit was broken, heavier than the weight of her huge tit. The way those words cracked at the end. She cleared her throat. I needed another sip to give us both a moment. A caller on the swap shop said, "It's practically new. My husband liked to shovel the sidewalks himself, you know. He died in December while cleaning the driveway. Anyway, I'd bought him the snowblower and he barely used it, so…"

I said, "Out where I am, there's no reason to shovel anything."

"Well, if you ever want to get snowed in, let me know and I'll come keep you company."

I raised my eyebrows, pretended that was a nice offer, but my one time with her had been enough. The flirting since was just flirting, at least on my end.

I couldn't tell her. Let her find out without me. "Sheryl, next time you talk to him, maybe mention he should call me?"

"That's why you're here?" She crossed her arms. "I'm a pigeon all the sudden?"

Another sip. Watered down indeed. "How many times I come in here and not ask for anything but breakfast?"

"Why don't *you* call him? Seems to me you're in touch more often than I am."

"I don't have time to hunt him down. Probably hiding a new lab from me or something. He still listens to his mother, though. Please?"

I was about to pick up my hat and thank her for the root beer when she stopped whatever she was about to say and looked over my shoulder at the entrance. A second later, bells jingled and a breeze chilled us both.

"Sit anywhere you like," Sheryl said. "I'll be with you in a minute."

I turned my head. Two Asian guys in ski jackets stomped snow off their shoes. One's face was acne-scarred. Probably my age. He wore glasses. The other had longer hair, sharp face, pretty striking young guy. He was the one who spoke, very little accent.

"Thank you, yes. We actually were hoping to speak with Deputy Lafitte for a few moments. Deputy, is okay?"

Jesus, they knew me. They worked fast. Goddamn killers standing here being perfect gentlemen to the mother of the boy they killed. They unzipped their jackets. The practiced look of anticipation came easily to them, drawing in those who didn't know any better. But I was curious.

I led them into the time-warped dining room and sat at a table by the front window. The only cars in the lot were my cruiser, Sheryl's Subaru, a customer's car, and the Honda SUV rental of these two guys. Needed to trace soon as we were done.

They took off their coats. Underneath the older man's was a wrinkled flannel shirt. I also noticed he was trying to grow a beard but wasn't very good at it. The younger man wore a Vikings sweatshirt, loose-fit khakis, complicated sneakers. Like he'd walked right off a rap video shoot. But it was a front, trying to fit in. Might have worked if they weren't together. They sat down and Sheryl came over, asked for their orders.

"Water. No ice." The older one.

"A small salad and water, no ice." The younger one.

Sheryl didn't bother to write it down. She turned for the kitchen, bypassed the salad bar.

"What can I do you fellows for?" Twanging it up, playing the bad-ass charmer.

"We want some information."

"About?"

"You. What you do. What you do that you don't tell your sheriff."

Pretty direct. I said, "You boys know what the term 'wired' means?"

They laughed. The younger said, "That's not us. We're not your police. We have friends who speak highly of you."

"On which side?"

"What?"

"Well, do they speak highly of me as a cop, or as, maybe, just a regular guy?"

The older one spoke softly to the younger in their native tongue, I supposed, getting a nod. Then the older said in not-so-perfect English, "What he means, you are smart. Want what's best for your people."

The younger said, "We have been told you could help us if we played by your rules, and we do not want any interference. We regret the misunderstandings that have occurred."

I leaned back and waited until Sheryl returned with two waters and a fully prepared salad that had definitely not come from the salad bar. They bowed their heads at her as she stepped away. When behind them, she mouthed, *What's going on?* I winked at her. No worries.

"Those misunderstandings. How do you plan on resolving them?"

The younger man ate his salad while the older spoke. "Two have been resolved. We take care ourselves. The other, maybe you help with?"

My stomach cramped. They wanted me to get rid of Ian.

He said, "Our business, very well. Good money for everyone. Would be glad to pay for our error if it would help."

I had to ask. "How much?"

Another blast of their language. Nothing recognizable.

The older one said, "Thirty thousand."

Expecting me to go up? That's what it felt like, holding back just enough. Like I said, I knew how to think like the dealers. "Fifty."

Quiet. He fought a grin. One of those *As we*

expected things and I'm thinking the same but not letting on. Just a dumb hick cop in bed with the meth folks, willing to do anything for money.

That bothered me the more I thought about it. A good businessman wouldn't have done what these two just did. Walk in and proposition a lawman? Murder for hire within five minutes of meeting me? Throwing around just enough money—they could afford more and had they offered six figures, I'd be on my way to top the kid immediately—but low-balling to begin with? Apologizing to me for their error?

They weren't pros.

The younger man took over. "For fifty thousand US dollars, you take care of our loose end?"

This sucked. The dialogue would barely pass muster on *Walker, Texas Ranger*. I laughed. It started like a cough but spread all over until I teared up. Reached for my hat and stood, tossed a fiver on the table. "I'll get your lunch. Let's go outside."

We stood next to their SUV. I said, "What you two just did was pretty stupid. I want to crack your skulls and drag you into the station, but that means a lot of other things might get exposed. You understand?"

I didn't let them answer. Kept going, "You killed a couple of people under my wing. Granted, they weren't smart themselves, but if I had their bodies and some proof, you gentlemen would be dead already."

"You do not frighten us, Deputy Lafitte."

"Good, because if you're not scared you won't see me coming. Like I said, today's your lucky day. I'm in a cooperative mood, want you to learn something from all this." Truth was I didn't want my connection to Trigger and Spaceman exposed, or to incur revenge from whomever these two were working for. Personally, I planned to hunt these bastards down later and smoke them, but I needed more time, more intel. "I'm going to follow you out Highway 212 for a little while, get you started towards The Cities. When I stop following you, keep going. Don't come back."

The younger one said, "What about the money?"

The older man hissed and shot a few words that caused his partner to shrink.

I said, "I do nothing for you. You do nothing

for me. We don't know each other. Whatever it takes to erase your memory of this place and what happened here, do it. Climb in your vehicle and keep it at the speed limit. I'll be in your rearview."

They took it well. No sneering or vows of *We'll be back*. Instead, nods and straight faces. I jotted down their plate number as we eased through the sludge-filled parking lot to the Highway, and I followed them about twenty miles outside of town before pulling to the shoulder and watching their Honda fade to a speck.

SEVEN

The message light on my cell phone was blinking. Good time to check it out. Drew's number. Always good to hear from her, heartbreaking as it was. I dialed back and she picked up on the first ring.

"Oh my god, Billy, it's like the *best* news. I don't believe it."

"Let's hear it."

"We've got a gig! A real gig."

"Here? Or Marshall?" They had a few more bars than Pale Falls, but I wouldn't think they'd go for psychobilly.

"No, it's The Cities. Minneapolis. All I know is that Adam got a call from some guy saying he'd heard of us through some college students who were over there, and that he'd had a cancellation. Tonight! Isn't that, like, just the coolest? You know, it's short notice, but he said as long as we're there by eight to set-up, it's a ten o'clock show."

"He paying you?"

"Adam said it would cover gas, dinner, and maybe some pocket money. Who cares? It's a friggin' *gig*, man, at a club and all that."

I checked my dashboard clock. Four-thirty. "You in the car now?"

"I told Adam to take the stuff over and I'd meet them there. I just pulled out of the driveway."

Some cars passed me, and I was aware of being in the wrong county. So I swung a U-turn and headed back to Pale Falls while calculating—about three hours to Minneapolis, closer to two if I were to take the cruiser and fly. Maybe I could catch most of the show if I hurried up taking a photo of the brand on Ian's ass.

"Tell me where. I want to see you guys."

"You don't have to," she said, but I knew her cheeks were glowing when she did.

"Who's the guy at nearly every show you play? Come on, you know I'm coming."

She gave me some directions, an address I memorized and would plug into Google Maps later. The dive was called "Gilligan's".

"Like the TV show?"

"That would be cool if it was. I mean, not the real Gilligan. He's dead." Her signal faded and garbled her next few words.

"I've never heard of the place," I said.

Garbled. "What? It's new. Be there. I'll streak my hair purple just for you."

I smiled. She knew I was a fan of the LSU Tigers, purple and gold. "Stay safe, and I'll be there on time. Might even force a few drunks to buy your CD."

I had the Elvis Antichrist demo on MP3, so I played it as I drove back to Marshall in the cruiser near sundown. The corn and bean fields were peeking through the snow in spots, but we still had a long way to go. The wind kept trying to force me off the road. I was getting used to it. Sometimes Minnesota could be devastating in its natural beauty, but the next minute you wondered if it had been a cruel trick of light. I'd been told that if you travel up north, you've got those ten thousand lakes and the woods and wildlife that will take your breath away. It's a shame the southwest part of the state looked like it hadn't been painted in yet.

Elvis Antichrist in one ear, listening for radio

calls with the other. The song was "Dig Me With Your Love Shovel", and I looked forward to seeing them do it live at a real club with a real crowd and real lighting. I was hoping Drew would be mighty buzzed from it all, and then maybe I could convince her to stay the night with me at a downtown hotel. The thoughts kept coming and my dick grew hard and I cleared my throat. Needed one shot of the Ian's pale ass and then I was outta there.

The road beside the dorm buildings was lined with students' cars, emergency blinkers on, a cheap way to park illegally while they supposedly unloaded laundry or went to knock on their date's door. I pulled in beside a fire hydrant and in front of a Toyota from the nineties, when they all looked alike. A girl smoking under the dorm's awning saw me and took off for her car, two spots down, blinkers flashing away.

I passed her and she said, "Sorry, sorry."

"Next time it'll be a ticket." Not that I had any authority here—Marshall was Lyon County. But to these kids a uniform is a uniform.

"Sorry."

I winked at her. Not bad. The voice was cute,

too. Not enough to keep my mind off Drew, though.

Back up to the sleepy guy's room. I didn't expect Ian to be here but hoped he was. If not, a quick call on my new friend Heather would help track him down. After our talk earlier in the day, I was pretty sure she would be glad to help in any way.

Pounded on the door. Heard more than one voice. Tried the handle and let it swing, leaned on the doorframe. Two girls, two guys, a pizza box on the bed, playing a fantasy game on PlayStation.

"Need to find Ian."

The sleepy guy passed his game controller to one of the girls. Dumb-faced. Got up and stepped out into the hall, pulling the door closed so those inside couldn't hear.

"He left a few hours ago because I had friends on the way over."

"I told him to stay here."

"Yeah, but, you know. Maybe he's in the library or the student center."

I leaned closer, spoke directly in his ear. "If anything has happened to him because of you kicking him out...guess what?"

"Don't be like that."

"Fucking kid. You stupid fucking kid." I walked away.

Back to Heather's. Didn't bother with the sneaking this time, just buzzed the front desk and told them I was supposed to escort a robbery witness to a deposition. Maybe the girl who let me in would get suspicious and do some research later to see if I was a liar, but I doubted it. She was in her pajamas, some fashion trend—lazy chic. A short freshman with messy blonde hair who smelled like cigarettes.

"Um, maybe you should sign in."

I smiled at her. "Next time. And I'll even take you for a ride in the cruiser if you want."

She bobbed her head. "Cool."

Up the stairs to Heather's door. I knocked lightly, wanted her to think I was another girl from the floor. No answer. No voices. No nothing. They'd skipped on me. Heather probably thought she was a rebel, liked the game. When I found her, she'd rethink the attitude. I tried the door handle. Locked. It wasn't goddamned funny. I wanted in that room. I wanted to see if she had a caller ID box, maybe grab a few of her buddies, maybe even her source for the dope, and apply a little pressure. The recipe for instant cooperation, I hoped.

Fuck it. I was probably obliterating evidence, but on the bright side, it was much easier to get a search warrant if you'd already found what you were looking for. Looked like these dorms had been built thirty, forty years ago. The locks built into the handles were simple to pick. The deadbolts only locked from the inside, just like mine more than ten years before. Never changed. But if Heather didn't want to answer, you pretty much had to either take the door off the hinges or go in through the window.

I took a walk out to the cruiser, grabbed the lock pick kit out of the glove compartment. Never knew when you'd need it. I told Miss Pajamas at the front desk that I had forgotten some paperwork. Then back up to Heather's door. I worked the lock, had it in about four minutes. I pressed down on the handle. Popped open like a can of soda. The deadbolt wasn't engaged. It was a wonder more kids weren't killed or raped with that kind of security.

Inside, the room was still. The bedsheets still tangled on the bed same as they were earlier.

The incense was stronger, but none was burning. Something felt off. No caller ID box, but that was a long shot in a dorm room. Her cell phone, though, was sitting on the bedside table. I picked it up, scrolled through recent calls. A couple from the sleepy guy's dorm room where Ian had been staying. Others from several campus numbers.

Sometimes it took a few moments to catch what you were not looking for, especially when someone has tried mighty hard to hide it.

They missed a smear.

On the far wall behind Heather's bed, someone had tried to wipe it off, but a stray hair glued to the wall by congealed blood. I checked the floor beneath. Another few drops further down. None on the carpet.

I checked the closet. All clothes accounted for, as far as I could tell, no evidence of a mad dash. I checked the stuffed dragon where Heather kept her stash. I slipped my fingers into its mouth, down his throat. The stuff was there. That's when I panicked.

The carpet ended near the door, became tile. I checked closer, saw a couple of drops of blood had been wiped into the grout between the tiles, absorbed. Nothing they could do without a mop and some bleach. They didn't have the time.

A clean scene. I wondered how they got both Heather and Ian out. One was hurt, maybe dead, and the other scared shitless? Or was there a body still here, one they would come back for later?

The second bed. I hadn't even thought about it. Hadn't seen the roommate earlier in the day, a detail I glossed over except when Heather had mentioned her—

"Did you forget your key again?"

The other bed was made up nice and pretty, lavender comforter spilling over the sides to the floor. I got down on my hands and knees, lifted it. A dead blonde girl's eyes wide, gray, looking back at me. No body, only her head. I scooted my ass across the floor until I thumped the wall.

I stayed curled up for a minute, trying to calm down. Steeling myself for another look because I thought something else was beside the head, under her hair. I'd seen dead people plenty of times, plenty of nasty situations. Never a young innocent girl dead all because of me. The open eyes accused.

When my nerves stopped jangling, I crawled back to the other bed and lifted the comforter again, took a closer look. Her mouth, open but not bloody. The neck wound looked sharp at first, then ragged. The first slice hadn't done the job. They had to saw through. But again, no blood. Her hair was wet. Made me think they'd killed her in the shower, but the girls' bathrooms here were communal. They had done this somewhere else, which meant they'd caught her much earlier, which meant they had been watching me when I spoke to Ian that afternoon.

There were two Polaroids under the head. I slipped them out, the head wobbling a little. One was of Heather and Ian in this room, sitting on the bed, bruised faces in a dark room. The flash made them wince. The other was the blonde girl, a different background. She was gagged, tied-up, crying. Behind her, visible from the chest down, her assassin, holding a hunting knife, same type I carried in my truck.

Cop 101. In this situation, you:

a) Continue your investigation alone until you have enough evidence to solve on your own.
b) Call the local police in town, confess

what you've done (because your DNA is all over Heather's bed) and what you know so far, most likely ending up in jail.

c) Cover your ass after suddenly remembering that your one true love is on her way into a trap.

"Drew." Son of a bitch, they knew about Drew. The fucking gig was a smokescreen. I checked my watch: eight-fifteen. Pretty sure she had been at the club for an hour or so by then. No fucking way.

I almost headed for the door at a dead run, but the blonde girl's eyes reminded me I had a decision to make. No time to waste. No idea where the Asian fuckers were, or how they got back into town. The blonde girl's body was probably in the back of the SUV already when I chased them away. Why the hell offer me money then? Maybe they expected to lure me out into the trees and slice me open. Just get rid of everyone who had any idea in one afternoon. Any other witnesses, like Sheryl, would say, "A couple of Asian guys" but not be able to add much detail.

Fucked me over. Here I thought I was the

smart guy.

Eventually someone would wonder what happened to the girls who lived in this room, but I was hoping not that night. Looked in the closet, found a fleece-lined windbreaker. It was good enough. I lifted the head, the skin foreign to the touch, wet and plastic. Laid it on the fleece, and zipped up to get that dead stare off me. Wrapped the sleeves around once, then tied the ends, pulled tight until I was sure she wouldn't fall out.

I took the back stairs out, put the head in my trunk, then entered the dorm building again through the propped-open door. I needed to show myself so the smart girl at the desk wouldn't get suspicious. So back to the desk, where she was doing homework.

"What class is it for?"

"Ethics," she said. "I don't get it."

"All based on the golden rule, isn't it? Do for others and etc.?"

She shrugged. "I guess. Hey, where's the witness?"

"His girlfriend hasn't seen him in a while. Guess he forgot."

She set her elbows on her book and leaned closer. "Maybe I can help. Who is it?"

She sees you're distracted, trembling. Calm down.

"Sorry, but that would break confidentiality."

"Hey, I can call the head of res life, you could talk to her. She knows everybody." The girl reached for the phone. I covered her hand before she could lift the handset.

I told her, nice low voice, "It's okay. Not that big a deal. No one's in trouble or anything. Someone will try again tomorrow. What's your name?"

"Michelle."

"Oh, that's a sweet name. Mee-chelle, my bell."

She giggled. "Quit it."

I thought of someone on the local police force that looked a lot like me. Several, in fact. Then I messed up one of the names just enough so she would be sure. "I'm Officer Van Dovercooke. You give me a call and we'll set up a ride along. I'll show you the exciting side of Marshall." Then a wink.

She melted. "I can do it Friday. I'm not going home this weekend."

I rapped my knuckles on the desk. "Give me a ring."

Maybe she would call, but she would get the name wrong. She would insist. She would be asked questions, and those questions would embarrass her. She would say she must have misunderstood and hang up. Or, more likely, forget about it by morning.

I didn't care. I fought to keep from jogging to my car, even tougher in the needle-sharp wind chill while I was sweating. Cell phone to my ear, getting nothing but voicemail at Drew's number. Once in and cranked, I U-turned and got on the highway as fast as I could. Faster still up to Pale Falls, burying the needle. At some point calling the station would've been a sweet idea, let the night guys call ahead to Minneapolis PD and have them check the club's address. Then maybe buzz Marshall PD to start the search for Ian and Heather. But I didn't do any of that. All I thought about was Drew.

The roads were still iced over. I felt the tires slide a couple of times but powered through the drift. I'd told Ian he didn't know anything about loving Drew. That I was the one who really cared. So why didn't I get someone on the horn to make sure she was safe? I justified it by saying I had more info than anyone else at that point, and that to confess one thing meant having to confess ten things, and I wasn't sharp enough that night to lie solidly about every step. I loved my freedom more than Drew. I hated myself for that. If I made things right, then I had everything I wanted.

Happiest fucking asshole on earth.

A couple of radio calls asked me to check in. They wanted me to pay a visit to some old folks who thought there was a meth lab in the woods behind their home. *You and everyone else*, I thought. Ignored the radio. Done it before, will do it again. Just another lecture from Graham.

I made the turn onto 212 and slid into the oncoming lane, nearly lost it. No cars on the road, my performance only for the folks behind the counter at the corner gas stations. The dash clock closed in on ten til nine.

You're too late. You're losing time. If they've got her, you've fucked up and the trail is getting cold.

Sometimes the right thing is too hard to do.

When three kids die on your watch, there's no place in the country you can hide.

I picked up the radio handset. Stared ahead while driving. Nothing oncoming, black except for the moonlight on the snow, glowing. Keyed the button and called in my sign.

"Where are you?"

"Suspicious activity on 212, checked out a van. Listen..."

You believe in coincidence?

"Billy, you there?"

My headlights shone on Drew's little car, snow-dirty, parked on the shoulder of the opposing lane.

"I'm here. Nothing to report."

"Man up towards Montevideo called again. Saw lights in the woods."

"Tell him to wait."

I keyed off and slid onto the shoulder, pushed the door open against the wind and slipped across the road to her car. Plenty of these little imports up here, the college students second car, usually. All-wheel drive good in the snow. I knew it was hers from the bumper stickers—Social Distortion, The Reverend Horton Heat, Guana Batz. Plus the dent on the rear panel caused by some asshole who claimed it was Drew's fault. I had to convince him, forcefully, to pay up. He did, but she spent it on her bass amp instead.

When I was closer, I saw that the right rear tire was flat. Drew wasn't in the car. Her guitar case took up most of the backseat, Taco John wrappers scattered on the floorboard. I tried the driver's door. Unlocked. Her keys were gone, but some warmth lingered. Where the *hell* was she?

I could've called in an emergency, suffered through the rigmarole in order to get help. Or I could call in sick. Head home. Ditch the cruiser. Arm up and go hunting in my big red pick-up truck. Thing was like a tank, seven years old, beat to hell but still running strong.

I dropped into my front seat and made a decision. One more time with the handset radio. "Must be something I ate, but I'm going to head home and take a shit."

EIGHT

I turned into my driveway doing sixty, faster still to the house before braking and skidding, inches from the side door. Out in a hurry, thinking of what I needed—pistol, but not my service issue. A shotgun, sawed-off. My revolver, .357 snubbie, good back-up piece. And my hunting knife. Wear all black and go after the little fuck who introduced Ian to the Asians, wake his ass up and make him show me all the places he'd met these guys. Cut off a finger every time he made a noise in protest.

The snow I'd kicked up drifted back over me as I rounded the front of the cruiser, reached for the screen door.

"Billy." A strained female voice. It was coming from the darkness behind the house. My pistol was already in my hands, a reflex. Finger on the trigger.

Again. "Billy!"

And there was Drew, stage make-up running down a pale, chilled face. Arms wrapped tightly around her chest, her satin blouse and leather mini-skirt not enough to protect her from the cold. She was running towards me. I dropped the gun into the snow and embraced her. She shivered, chattered her teeth telling me, "Th-th-they're all dead. Jesus-s-s-s, all dead."

"Who's dead?"

"Th-th-the band. Band. Killed-d-d the band."

"You saw them?"

"I walked in." She stepped back, stamped her feet, looked me in the eye. "Blood. Two of them didn't have…" She paused, swallowed. "Didn't have heads. Kyle was tied up, screaming. He saw me, screamed for help. I didn't know what to do. I heard people scrambling, gibberish, something foreign. One came out of nowhere, reached for my purse. I just dropped it. My phone, my money, just dropped it and ran. The car was a block up but I made it. They were so close. They tried to get me out of the car, tried to break the glass, but I was too fast. I think I jumped the curb and ran over some beer bottles, cut the tire. I kept going until the rims hit the road. I didn't know what to do."

"You should've called the police."

She looked at me like I'd just told her to swallow her fist. "I didn't have my phone."

"Then you should've found a cop. Do you know what could've happened to you? Jesus, girl, you could've lost your fucking head!" All I was doing was scaring her further. I lowered my voice, nice and easy. "Why didn't you stay by the car? You could've been hurt walking all this way."

"What if they were after me? What about that? I…I needed to keep moving." She started crying, sounded like she couldn't breathe. I was able to understand, "My god, Billy, what's going on?"

I took her in my arms again and aimed her towards the house, led her inside.

Her stage clothes were icy, the sweat and river valley moisture freezing in the wind. I gave her some sweatpants and a thick flannel shirt, helped her get into them. Then I wrapped her in my great-grandmother's quilt and eased her into my recliner facing the wood burning stove. After boiling her a cup of hot tea with honey, I knelt beside her and tried to get more details.

"It wasn't a club, was it? A warehouse?"

She nodded. "I went in the front. If I'd pulled around to the side like the band, they would've jumped me."

"So they expected you?"

"It was because I parked a block up—"

"Yeah, you said."

"I don't know why they didn't kill everyone and grab me when I walked inside."

"Maybe Kyle told them you'd be along closer to the time of the gig. They wouldn't be looking for you."

She shook harder, the thought of her drummer stalling on her behalf working its way in. "You think so?"

"What choice did they have? Kyle must've said he knew something they wanted, something about you, or they would've killed him much sooner."

"It doesn't make any sense."

I rubbed the quilt over her arm. She was right. If these guys had wanted her dead, she'd be dead. Maybe they didn't expect her to escape, though. No reason to keep the drummer alive unless it was to help put pressure on her.

Pressure for what?

What did Ian and Drew have in common besides each other?

You, Lafitte.

Which also didn't make any sense.

"You get a look at these guys? Any descriptions?"

She closed her eyes, made a face. "I don't wanna."

"It's important. Be a trooper. Fight through it."

A deep breath later she said, "One was Chinese. The first one I saw. The guy who tried to break my window was white. I think he had very short hair, but he was wearing a cap."

"See the cap for me, sweetie."

She strained, eyes shut tighter, nostrils flaring. "I don't know. It was…old. It was black. It had a gold French thing on it. I don't know what they're called."

"*A* fleur-de-lis?"

"Yeah, that curly thing. I think you've got one."

A New Orleans Saints cap in Minneapolis on someone trying to roust Drew.

"I don't want to say anymore. I'm too cold," she said.

I patted her arm and stood, told her I'd be right back. Something was clicking and whirring in my head. Something about the Polaroid of the college girl, which I'd left in the cruiser. As I opened the screen, she said, "Don't leave! Don't, please."

I looked back. She'd sat up, the quilt falling off, fingernails clawing the armrests.

"You're safe. I'm safe. No one's coming. I need something out of my truck, and I'll be right back."

"Hurry."

"You bet." I reached for my gun to reassure her. It wasn't in its holster. Then I remembered I'd dropped it. I saw it through the screen. My hand tremored but I shoved it into my pants pocket. "Like a hummingbird."

Outside I lifted the gun and shook the wet off it. It was freezing, aching my hand. I dumped it into its holster, then opened the trunk of my cruiser. The windbreaker and head had rolled around some, but was still a tight package. I found the photos and looked at the crying girl, the man behind her holding a knife that looked like mine. It had been passed down from my dad to me when I was ten. The night before he planned taking me on my first hunting trip, he'd shown it to me, explained how to keep it safe, how to hold it, how not to. Same with the little .22 rifle so I could shoot squirrels. He and his older brother would be hunting deer. Too bad I was coming down with the flu. I still wanted to go, but was too feverish and achy, I tried to hold it together and promised I'd be ready to go come four in the morning.

He didn't have the heart to wake me, so he left twenty bucks so Mom could buy me a toy instead. I had really wanted to go and kill squirrels. Maybe that's why I eventually became a cop—because I never went hunting with my dad. He was killed a year later in an accident at work, fell off a girder at the power plant he was wiring.

The knife meant a lot to me. I usually socked it in the bedside table at night. But I'd left it in my big red truck after getting duped into that ice fishing trip with Tordsen and Graham a couple months ago. Wouldn't be doing that again. Nothing like being out on the Gulf or up tiny creeks all over South Mississippi in a boat. Ice fishing was more boring than hockey. Even the beer tasted boring.

I punched the remote control for the first

bay of my garage. If I'd only checked the truck this morning instead of leeching off the county, using my cruiser for "personal use". The light flickered, never worked properly. I walked to the cab seeing everything in horror-movie strobe. The tiny triangle window on the passenger side, smashed. All it took then was a stick to hit the lock lever. I opened the door, glass pebbles all over the floorboard. I checked the contents of my glove compartment, the armrest compartment, saw the stereo. Everything still there. I leaned the passenger seat forward, opened the panel to the backseat of the quad cab. Lifted the bench seat to the space beneath where I kept the jack, the air compressor, a .22 pistol, and on this last occasion my hunting knife.

The knife and gun were gone. Even my truck was a crime scene. I couldn't report it, not with all the evidence I'd never logged in, all the leftover meth crystals from when I was holding onto some product as collateral until I got what I wanted from a dealer. I'd need to clean the fucker up fast if I wanted to cover my ass, but there was no way to be sure I'd get it all. I didn't have time. And whoever stole my knife and gun probably knew that, too.

I drew my icy sidearm. Reflex, anger, whatever. Thought maybe I'd left it in George's ice-house on that northern lake. But I hadn't used my knife that weekend. I didn't take it out of the truck, never told him I had it once I discovered "ice fishing" meant sitting around a hole, drinking, and talking about the weather.

Then I remembered those headlights at the end of my driveway the night before. The paranoid side of me must've been right after all. The headlights had been a distraction while these guys jimmied the lock on the back door of the garage.

Before I got too far ahead of myself, I closed the garage and headed inside to Drew. She wasn't asleep, but her eyes were very heavy. She'd had to walk pretty far without her jacket to make it to my place, only to find it dark, empty, and locked. Still, she waited. I was her only option, it seemed. Safer than going home.

Yes, I was proud of her, worried about her, heartsick. Guilty. I'd have to tell her about Ian. She would resent me for keeping that from her overnight, but I hoped not for long. Sleep was out of the question. I had two runners in my head—find Ian and Heather and the sons of bitches who took them, then figure out a way to come out of this clean.

I put my hand on Drew's shoulder. She was still shivering. "You can have the bed, sugar. I'll camp out on the couch."

Her fingers reached for me, coiled around my wrist. "Don't leave me alone, Billy."

I stood there with her nails denting my skin for quite some time, feeling waves of warmth off the stove, the chill of the drafty house at my back. I was standing right where they clashed.

"Okay, kiddo. You're with me tonight."

NINE

I didn't touch her.

Well, I *held* her, my arm wrapped around tight as she lay against my chest, needing the sleep. I wasn't even tired. Adrenaline, fear, like I'd been plugged into a battery. Almost like a meth addict. I kept vigil, ignoring my duties. When the phone rang at eleven, I grabbed it only to keep from disturbing Drew.

"You're still sick?" Layla. That night's dispatcher called in the heavy guns to scold me.

"I can barely leave the toilet before another run hits."

"What the hell did you eat?"

"Roast beef sandwich. Must be *E coli*. I'm sorry I forgot to—"

"Yeah, yeah, you're lucky Jason wanted some overtime. Go fix your bowels."

After hanging up, I stopped looking at the clock. The guys in the diner weren't very good at keeping a low profile. Why would they come to me in broad daylight, make a public bribe? And why go after the people close to me? Could be I was seeing it from the wrong angle. Drew came to me about Ian, but before I'd even talked to him, there were those headlights.

Did Ian *ask* Drew to bring me in? Did the Asians ask him?

Drew shifted her body. Her leg slid against my thigh, and I felt my dick shift, grow. She made a little noise.

"You up?" she said, a sleepy growl.

"No. Go to sleep."

Not another word. Her body sweating, breath hot on my skin. It should be like this forever. No chance of that, though. Protecting her meant giving up the Lone Ranger routine. That meant telling her the truth. That meant losing her.

I was a goddamned walking Greek tragedy.

A bitter drive to Marshall the next morning. After I told Drew my plan, she didn't say another word. I'd mapped things out as far as I could and hoped they'd be distracted enough not to tie up loose ends. I think Drew was beginning to hate herself for trusting me.

While Drew showered earlier, I had taken the blonde girl's head in the windbreaker and threw the thing into the middle of the Minnesota River. I thought about tying on two chunks of concrete from the foundation of an old storage shed, but if things went bad, I didn't want that thing anywhere near my property. As it splashed down into the slushy waters, I thought of all I'd forgotten—*Your DNA is on the head, too. And the cold water will preserve all the trace…*

I braced my arm on a tree thin as a skeleton. Took in a scared breath of freezing air and let it burn my lungs. May the fish find the head quickly and pick it clean. The girl's parents would demand a better answer once they found out she was missing. I wasn't going to help give it to them.

Earlier, while the cruiser's engine warmed up I admitted to Drew that I'd lost Ian. Had gone to find him, but it was too late.

She shrank into the couch. "Why didn't you keep him with you? What…why…is he…?"

"I don't know. I'm sorry. I didn't think anyone was looking for him, didn't think they'd get to him on school grounds. Jesus."

"But I *asked* you. I said he was in trouble."

"Not this much, though."

Her hands were balled into fists on her lap. The towel on her damp hair slipped to the floor. Without make-up she was like a girl from those old paintings, an innocent milkmaid. Her eyes betrayed just how shaken she was. I moved to take her hands but she jerked away.

"What do you mean, 'not this much'? What did you find out?"

"Some nasty guys tried to move into the area and merge some meth labs into one solid operation, bully the others." It was only half a lie. "Ian lost some product, so the brand was a punishment from their own country."

"They're not American?"

See? One little goddamn slip. Let's paint that one over, too. "Chinese, drug *tong*. Gang."

She hugged herself, then reached down for the towel. Her hair was a natural mess, the stage colors washed away. My chest ached. I didn't want to be in the same room when she figured out how much of this was bullshit.

After a long stretch, the only sound the wood stove popping here and there, she said, "There's no way he's still alive. That's what you think."

"Can't say that for sure. Maybe they want to—"

"He's dead." Tears. "My God, he's dead."

"Listen…" I didn't have an ending for that thought. "I'll tell you what I plan on doing in the car. Last night I made some mistakes but it was because of you. I realized what was happening and came to find you. I saw your car on the way to The Cities. You'll tell the cops what happened at the warehouse word for word except you leave out how you stayed with me last night—"

"Stop, okay? Just…not now."

I changed into my uniform from the night before. We waited for her hair to dry. Then we drove.

It got tricky from there. No more sneaking around. I couldn't afford to fuck it up any more than I already had. At the girls' res hall I had to pull the same stunt on the desk girl except that this time, I had to use my real name. It was a different girl, and there were more people around. I told her she should probably call the head of Res Life. So she did.

The woman was younger than I expected. Short brown hair with a perfect nose and mouth. She wore slacks, jacket, blouse, told me I'd interrupted a meeting. Not friendly. Neither was I.

"You shouldn't even be here," she said after hearing the edited story— I wanted to pick up Ian, he wasn't here the night before. I decided it wasn't worth bothering everyone in town. But since he still hadn't called or shown up at his friend's dorm, well, okay. She turned to the girl at the front desk. "Call Public Safety, tell him to call the local police."

I said, "Look, let's go knock on the door before we go overboard. Maybe it's just a false alarm."

"These kids have rights, you know."

"I'm not violating—"

"Don't *even* finish that sentence. I can't believe this."

The lobby was filling with girls in pajamas and sweats. Some with booksacks slowed down on their way out. I asked, "What's your name?"

She looked down at her name tag, then back at me. Stone-faced.

"All right, sure, sorry. Sienna. Okay. Can we talk in private for a moment?"

Crossed arms, a sharp glance at Drew, at the assembled girls. She told them all, "This is none of anyone's business. You need to get ready for classes."

Some cleared out. We walked away from the desk, near the couch in a central lounge area. I told Sienna, "You don't want to get all self-righteous when everyone knows the back door to this place is propped open twenty-four seven. How many guys spend the night here? Are you turning a blind eye?"

"I don't need a lecture from you."

"Oh yes you do, Miss. See, that same door lets in more than these girls' fuckbuddies. I'm sure you tell their parents that their precious babies are safe and sound in this fortress they pay so much for. Should we bring that up when the police get here? Should we wait for all the paperwork to be in order before checking to see if these kids are okay?"

The heat showed on her face. Tight lips. Eyes unblinking. She called over the desk girl, whispered something that I caught the tail-end of, "…close the back door. Get rid of the can. Make a sign that says that it must remain closed at all times. Tell Mr. Luverne to meet me at the room."

Then to me, "Let's take the stairs."

Sienna knocked loudly. Knocked again. "Heather? Grace? Wake up."

Nothing. Another knock. "I need you to open the door. I don't care who's in there. It's urgent."

Still nothing. Sienna almost knocked again, but then opened her fist, laid her palm on the door.

I couldn't re-lock it after picking it the night before. All part of the act. "Let's take a look inside."

"I don't know."

A very subtle move, that was all it took, just letting my fingers brush over the leather pouch containing my handcuffs, unsnapping the flap. She sighed and found the right key, slid it in. Looked confused. "It's open already."

Sienna turned the handle and pushed the door open. The room was exactly as I'd left it. I walked in ahead of her, stood between the two beds, turned in a lazy circle, hands on my hips. When I faced the door again, two more people had arrived. One was a strong bald guy with a thick neck. He wore a suit coat over a pale green shirt, no tie, and held a walkie-talkie in his hand. He said to Sienna, "This him?" Then to me, "Excuse me, sir? Could you come talk to me first?"

Behind him was Michelle, the girl who'd

worked the desk the previous night. Jesus, how'd she get here so fast? Jackhammers pounded my bladder.

I played my part, though. Turned on the voice of authority. "Let's get everyone to stay out of this room. We need to report these kids missing."

The security guy said, "You sure about that?"

My shoulders drooped. I wanted to sit down. "Yeah, pretty fucking sure."

TEN

Here's what I told them:

Ian was being pressured by some meth cookers to sell their stuff to college kids. He didn't want to risk it, so he came to me. I convinced him to get involved and keep me informed so we could nail the bastards. Problem was that Ian was kind of stupid. He lost a batch. They hunted him down, gave him a beating. I left out the branding. I left out Drew, too. You could see relief in her face when I did, but also some tension when she realized how easy lying came to me. I said that the beating was enough for me to go after the guys, but I wanted Ian safe first, to testify. He said he would stay on campus with friends until I could pick him up.

"After coming here last night, I went back to Yellow Medicine County and looked for him there, talked to a few people. I thought he was hiding from me, or partying, whatever these kids do. It didn't occur to me until this morning that maybe they'd gotten to him."

We sat in the lobby of the dorm, all the girls cleared out except for Drew and Michelle. I had already confused her enough on the way down from Heather's room.

"You said you were here to pick up a witness."

"Yeah, exactly."

"But that you were from the local police. You said you were Officer Van Dovercooke or something like that."

The fact that she nailed it meant she'd taken the offer for a ride-along seriously. Shit. I had hoped it wouldn't stick in her mind. Too bad she was turned on by cops.

The big bald head of Luverne had looked at me funny, spoke to Michelle. "Is that what he said?"

"No, no, you must've misunderstood. I told you to *call* Officer Van Dovercooke—actually I can't even remember if that's his name. We just got to talking at a bar. Anyway, yeah, you should always call the local cops if you need help."

"You said I could go out on your shift,

though." Michelle all frustrated, too smart for her own good. Great. Jesus. Now Sienna and Luverne and Michelle were looking at me funny.

I shrugged. "I'm always glad to offer that to a smart girl who's interested in studying law."

That got a headshake from Luverne. He blew out a long breath. "What an asshole."

On the couch, we waited for local police. Public Safety still asking accusing questions. "Did you even *think* of contacting us? At least tell me you were ignorant of the law rather than ignoring it."

And: "You knew something was wrong last night and sat on it? You think that was the smart play, Deputy?"

And: "Can *I* have Deputy Van Dovercooke's number? What's his first name?"

I fudged through, tried to make it look like I wanted to avoid extra paperwork. A couple of times, he asked Drew why she was here, and I shut him down fast. "She's also a witness. Can't talk without her lawyer."

"How convenient for you."

"Why don't you suck my cock, Mr. Clean?"

He smiled. "Would you like that, Deputy Lafitte?"

When the local cops tapped on the glass doors with their flashlights—just to make more noise—Sienna stepped over to let them in. Two uniformed officers, one a lieutenant, walked in that lazy way we all did with their hands on their belts. Bulky jackets took away from the power, but you had to go for warmth over swagger. They weren't alone, and I wasn't sure if that was a good sign or not. Right behind them was the sheriff, my fucking ex-brother-in-law. It didn't feel like we'd been sitting here long enough for him to make the drive, but there he was.

He nodded around. "Gentlemen, Ladies. Billy."

Sienna found an errand to get rid of Michelle, who was still looking at me as if I'd stood her up for prom. Her own fault, a fool for the bad boys. The lieutenant introduced himself, just another Scandinavian name I had no idea how to spell. He suggested we move this discussion to the police station while his officers secured the scene, scraped together some clues to the kids' disappearance.

Might as well get this part over with. "When you check the sheets, Heather's sheets? You're going to find traces of, um, me."

"You contaminated the scene? Looking for a

lead on their whereabouts? We can sort that out."

"No, I mean. I mean on the bed, around the room. My hair, fingerprints. I met Heather yesterday. I was here."

Caught Drew out of the corner of my eye. The angriest stone cold face I'd ever seen, like she'd crack her teeth if she bit back the tears any harder. She crossed her arms and walked off on her own.

I shouted after her, "Hey, we didn't do anything!"

"Unbelievable," Sienna whispered, shaking her head.

I wasn't listening to the lieutenant's reasonable admonishment about mixing my personal and professional lives. Public Safety wanted to break me in two.

"Lock this bastard up! There's your suspect right there!"

"It was just a talk."

One of the cops huffed. "From what I hear, you're a pretty active talker, Deputy."

I motioned the other officer towards me. He kept his face hidden from the others, flashed me a *Way to go* grin. I asked, "You've heard of me, right?"

"Shit, you're all we talk about."

"Good or bad?"

"How do you get away with it?"

"Do me a favor." I lifted my chin towards Drew. "You see that girl walking off? She's important. I need you to take care of her."

"You giving me permission?"

I lowered my voice. "You touch her, you get plowed under a soybean field. And I'll get away with it, too."

That rattled him. He tried to think of a comeback. Instead, he stood frozen in a staredown.

I blinked. "Go. Her name's Drew. Do your job. Don't disappoint your wife." I flicked his wedding band. He shoved the hand in his jacket pocket and went after Drew, who was now out of sight.

Graham was at my side a moment later, landed a helpful hand on my shoulder. "Can't say I'm happy to hear all this. We'll have to have a long talk after they've questioned you."

"Who says they'll release me?"

"I say. I'm not going to let them humiliate you. Go, answer some questions, and if they start playing games we walk. You can get a lawyer. Right now, let them find those kids. Tell them everything you know."

If I told them everything I knew, Graham wouldn't be so quick to pull my ass out of the fire. Still, I'd been wrong about him. Thought he would fold to procedure and properness at even the hint of impropriety, ex-brother-in-law or not. Graham might be a straight shooter, a by-the-booker, but I didn't realize how loyal he was. Almost inspired me to tell the truth.

Almost.

"I owe you one."

He whispered, "Don't be so sure. I've got more to say on the ride home."

Goddamnit. More lectures. I'd rather they brought out the paddle and got it over with.

ELEVEN

Long story short—*everyone* was pissed at me.

At least they decided to not tell Heather's parents about me trying to sleep with their little girl. In fact, a search of the room showed that Heather had really fallen for Ian, that it wasn't just some fling. She probably didn't even know about Drew. As far as she was concerned, Ian was all hers. God, made me feel pretty slimy.

These genius cops figured out rather quickly that I wasn't a killer. Not anymore, anyway. Not college kids. The rest of their questioning was aimed at learning if I was incompetent or insubordinate or both or neither or a plain old sociopath. Luckily I knew how to foil the tests on that end. Know thyself, you know?

By the time Graham and I left, it was nearly dark. I was told they still hadn't found the kids, had little to go on, hoping that might open me up. Fuck that. The head in the river, the

Polaroids stashed away safely in my enormous front yard. Those were my "Go Directly to Jail, Don't Pass Go, Get Ass Raped by Someone You Beat Up Last Month" cards. I wanted them ripped to shreds and in the wind, but not until I figured out what was going on.

Graham asked a Marshall PD officer to follow behind in my cruiser so he could have a chat with me. By the time we reached Cottonwood, he still hadn't said a word.

I tried, "I'm glad you were there today. Thanks."

"I don't know why I agreed to this. Jesus, when Ginny said you could get into trouble now and then, I had no idea." He stared straight ahead, hands at nine and three on the wheel. "Dig some and there are incidents referred to, but the paperwork is all lost. Katrina, they say. The stuff after the hurricane is mired in confidentiality. After today, though, I think I understand why my sister cut you loose."

"I don't understand." He's slitting your throat.

"Listen, I mean, we obviously *like* you. Charming guy, Billy. Southern accent and hospitality. Gets things done. Nice to my kids. But he doesn't like procedure."

"I'm right here. No need to pretend I'm

not."

A quick turn of his head, right back to the road. "Then there's that. You've got a way to make us feel guilty when we're suspicious. Like you never got out of fourth grade."

The radio babbled, and I also took to staring at the road, the flat dull fields on either side, stretching for miles until you hit a lonely patch of trees or a barn. It reminded me that I didn't have many places to hide up here.

"So tell me," Graham said. "How often do you use your badge to get in a girl's pants?"

"Nothing happened, okay? Nothing was *going* to happen. I was just trying to scare her." I didn't believe my own lie.

"Any of that going on while you were married?"

I didn't want to answer. Wanted to punch him in the mouth. Instead, I said, "No, never."

He shook his head. "You knew a crime had been committed and you sat on it because of some girl?"

"I went with my gut. I didn't want to get thrown off the case."

"Case? You're my deputy, not a detective. You need to learn some discipline."

No way I was going to strike back at that one.

"Yes sir."

"Stop calling me sir."

More quiet with radio bleeps interrupting. Without the job, I would have no other choice. If I hadn't signed up for Gulfport PD when I was twenty, I probably would've been one of the meth cookers I rousted daily.

See, it wasn't my upbringing, or at least not what you'd expect. My adolescence was spent in the upper-middle class, on track for college with "B"s and occasionally "A"s (English) and "D"s (Math). I liked classic rock and heavy metal, liked sci-fi comics and movies. My friends were the nerds in junior high who changed almost overnight around age fifteen and discovered that the girls who smoked and wore black were more interesting than the cheerleaders we had lusted after. Typical story. My dad was an electrician. My mom was an elementary school teacher. And *holy shit* I was bored.

When I was sixteen, one of my friends figured out who was selling the pot. So we moved up from diet pills and allergy medicines. We tried E. We thought the rockers on heroin were creative geniuses. And one of us got hooked on crystal meth.

Not me. Fucking needles? I'd had enough of that when I was a kid with chronic bronchitis. Pretty soon the guy was skipping classes, then weeks, and then he came around asking for money. Guy looked scabby and pale. When I told him I was broke, I watched from the front window as he broke into my mom's car and took the CD player.

That wasn't what made me want to be a cop. I thought it was kind of cool to watch this guy steal something. Thought it was cool to lie about it, tell my folks I had my headphones on and didn't hear a thing. By the time I was seventeen, I'd learned to shoplift CDs, porn mags, snacks, and single bottles of beer.

Too many stolen bottles one night, and I got pinched for drunk driving. I took a punch at the cop and he waylaid me. Here's what got me on the thin blue line—he kicked me when I was down. When I looked up at him, my insides racing to come out of my throat, he had this grin on his face. Not angry, not breaking a sweat. His balls were made of iron. He lifted me by my arm, nearly pulling it out of its socket, and said, "Son of a bitch, I love my job."

Later, while waiting for my mom to come

straighten me out, the guy sat beside me on the bench, gave me a Coke. "You don't ever try to hit a cop. Let's say you succeeded, right? Maybe you punch me out, take my gun, handcuffs, whatever. Maybe you kill me, maybe not. But then," he pointed around the room, "every cop in this building, and out on the street, and in every other town in this whole blessed country, will make your life miserable. I mean never let you forget. Might as well be dogshit."

"That's not fair."

"Fuck fair. *We* tell you what's fair."

I never stole again. I started watching old *Miami Vice* episodes my dad had taped which my mom kept after he died. I started working out and reading about hand-to-hand combat. I didn't tell my friends. I didn't tell my mom. I just...changed.

If you want respect from the badasses and psychos, become a cop. Then that's who your colleagues are.

After a few minutes, Graham said, "The college girl." He fought a grin. "Tell me about her."

"She was one of those arty types, pretending to be a hippie. Really raw, sensual. I thought we had a vibe going. Man, I felt so old when I realized…" Trailed off and stared at empty fields we passed. "Why did you want to know?"

He defeated the grin. "I love my wife. But sometimes, you know. It's nothing." He left unsaid *Don't tell Ginny.*

"We wouldn't be normal if we didn't."

"Just not on duty."

"Am I on duty? Back to work?"

A long sigh. "We can't put you out there right now. I'm taking you home."

Ten seconds before, I'd thought all was forgiven. Fuck. "What're you saying?"

He gave me his full attention this time as we passed the huge casino sign, the road widening to four lanes. "Look, I'm begging you. Take a couple of sick days. Whatever. But I don't want you leaving your house until we've figured out what's what."

I gave him a little laugh. Why not? At least I wasn't fired. "Guess I can finally unpack."

TWELVE

Four acres felt like a jail cell that day. But at least I had some cellmates. Assistant Chief George Tordsen showed up with a rack of ribs and some barbecue sauce. As usual, his hair was a perfect helmet, and his jeans were creased. Cowboy boots had seen wear-and-tear, but were pretty damned clean. His flannel shirt, ironed. Definitely not like me—I wore a pair of jeans until I couldn't stand the smell.

When he spoke, it was the soundtrack of Minnesota, heavy on the vowels. "I heard you've been grounded. So I thought you deserved a reprieve."

"I'm a baaaaad boy."

"Stupid, too."

"Admit it. You've been sent out here to babysit."

He shrugged. "I didn't know you considered yourself a baby."

Even with snow on the ground, we fired up the grill and tossed some Cajun sausages on with the ribs—I'd had them shipped up on dry ice. Damn glad that New Orleans was getting back on its feet so I could spend my paycheck on the flavors these people were clueless about. While the smoke drifted, the wind stoking it hard, I stood on the bank of the river and stared at the slow-moving dark water.

Nate showed up not long after, out of uniform and carrying a twelve pack of Leinenkugel Dopplebock, a fine brew out of neighboring Wisconsin. He came right out and said it. "Sheriff's orders."

We drank some beer, cursed the wind, traded stories. They were careful not to mention my woes the rest of the afternoon. I pretended not to notice. How could I think of anything else? I appreciated what they were doing—those ribs were damn good—but when I scratched a little more I understood they weren't really on my side. Sympathetic, friendly, yet more like prison guards than allies.

Everyone was pissed at me, but since they didn't know the whole story, they were pissed at me on *my* terms. That gave me breathing room. And if the powers-that-be thought I was going to sit in my crib like a good little toddler, wouldn't they be surprised.

We sat in my living room after the food, flipped around the satellite TV until we found some drag racing, and I was surprised when Tordsen said, "Do you have any plans for your next move here?"

Didn't like the sound of that. "What do you mean?"

"Well, just thinking that maybe you've messed up pretty badly. What are you going to do to make it right?"

"Sit tight, wait it out." Hoped I sounded sincere. Every word was a lie.

Tordsen was smarter than that. "It might take you a while before we can put you out on patrol again, but I'm not saying it won't happen. You understand? All is not lost for you yet."

I hung my head, thinking of how a sinner felt at the altar. I needed that look. He was handing out good advice and I knew it. A smarter man who was concerned about his career would've taken heed. Me, I felt there was more at stake than just my job.

Still hangdog, stirring in a little bit of remorse, I said, "Do you think I could have the rest of the evening alone? I…you know…want to call my kids. It's been a while."

They were on their feet in a minute. Handshakes all around. I wrapped up some of the ribs and sausage for Nate, saved him from another night of frozen pizza. Tordsen shook my hand on his way out the door.

"Billy, think about what I said, okay? It's going to be fine, you'll see."

As he climbed into his truck, I thought, Maybe one day I'll be just like you, George—careful and spotless. But only because the undertaker cleaned me up nice.

It didn't take long to figure out what the next step should be. I dialed Layla, said, "I'm going to get online, so if the phone's busy, that's why." Nobody had broadband out on the river.

"What about your cell?"

"Aw, shit. I probably left it in the cruiser." It was on my bedside table.

"What do you need online? Can't it wait?"

"None of your business, honey. Unless you feel like stripping for me."

"Oh, come on, Billy." She gave up after that.

I wet down the grill flames and tromped back to the house in my steel-toed CAT boots to arm up and go find Tracy Vis, the son of a bitch who'd gotten Ian involved in the first place. Right before I left, I turned on my old PC and fired up the Internet and navigated to a porn site dedicated to goth girls. Might as well keep up the illusion—God knows they can track all that shit nowadays.

Locked the door, checked to see that the shotgun and .357 were loaded and ready, the carried them out to the big red truck. Would've slipped the hunting knife in my belt but the big bad Asians had it. They'd cut off the girl's head with it, I was painfully certain. Reminded me of those hostage tapes from Iraq and Afghanistan. Thinking of that got me in the zone. Ready, set…

Going after Vis would be a piece of cake. He'd probably cave quickly and I could run down the Asians before the night was over. All I had to do was find him at his granddad's farm house north of town, which he'd inherited but let go to hell, or at one of his three labs. The wind pushed me into the left lane and I nearly rammed head-on into a black Suburban that wailed on the horn until I shook myself and jerked back into line. Verging on a fishtail. Held it, slowed, braked, and pulled off on the shoulder. Forehead on the steering wheel.

If Ian died, I could count out ever being with Drew. I could count out the job. I could turn again to too much red wine and a bullet in the revolver, playing Spin the Chambers until I won. Last time I tried that, I'd already lost twice when Ginny called, this about a day or two before I got the Minnesota job.

"I worry about you," she said. "If only, you know. It's not about me anymore. I'd probably stick with you if not for the kids."

"Maybe you should have told me before we had any."

"You don't mean that."

I gave her a drunk laugh and said, "Shit, you don't play fair at *all*, you bitch. You hand me loaded dice and a stacked deck and I play along. Are you just calling to rub it in?"

She didn't speak for a while, and I was about to apologize when she cut in. "It's not about love. I can't help love. Whatever else it's about, I wanted to tell you. Don't give up on me yet."

I hung up on her, but she had saved me. I put the gun down and went to bed. Give up on her? I did that the moment she mentioned divorce. Every touchy-feely thing she had said afterwards didn't stop her from delivering those papers. Fuck that double-speak bullshit. She saved me because I decided not to give up on me. I wanted to fuck more women and screw over anyone who ever doubted me again.

When facing the unwinnable a second time, odds are there won't be another escape hatch.

A speeding semi hauling tractor parts shook the truck and scared me silly. I gripped ten and two on the wheel until my fingers ached, then pulled back onto the Highway.

I found Vis at the second lab. The sun had already set after two strikeouts at his house and a lab outside of Olivia, a small town to the east. This other one was damn near the South Dakota border, about fifty miles west of Pale Falls, so I was sure my "on the internet" ruse had run out of juice. The deputies were out looking for me, I supposed, but quietly. Graham wasn't going to put it on the airwaves. All I had to do was stay away from my colleagues until I called in and made up some excuse—just wanted to get away from it all and go fishing. Or whoring. Yeah, the second one made more sense.

And if I delivered good intel from Vis, all might be forgiven.

The place had once been a hunter's hideout, a double-wide trailer that had been nicely furnished although a little dusty the first time Vis had shown it to me. Apparently the owner died and had never told his wife about it because he'd been using it as a love nest to fuck his wife's twin sister. Damn thing had furniture, flat-screen TV, DVD, queen-sized bed. After a season of meth-cooking, all of that except the mattress and the TV were gone, replaced by beakers, coils, hotplates, plastic jugs of foul-smelling chemicals, empty Sudafed boxes, and dirty syringes.

I pulled up with my lights off, parked a quarter-mile down the trail and walked, revolver leading the way. The only sounds were wind and the light crunch of my feet on brittle dead leaves and ice, some patches still solid enough that I slid across the top. Vis's car, a Ford Probe that had been repainted canary yellow, was cold, engine off for quite a while. The trailer was filthy with piles of dirty snow still covering most of the vinyl siding that bordered the bottom edge. The wooden stairs to the front door had been replaced by a stepladder. Lights burned from somewhere inside. I wasn't close enough to tell from which room. I had told Vis that first time to install motion sensor lights, but it looked like he hadn't taken the advice. Dumb boy. Good boy.

So why sneak up on him? After all, he was in my pocket, right? I thought if he had helped the Asians find ways to get to me, then being scared shitless by me was the proper antidote. Quiet steps around the trailer to get a feel for who was inside, where they were. No one in the front room, dark through the cloudy window. The room was empty, the TV was gone. Vis had hit bottom again.

Around back, the light shone yellow through the kitchen windows. I heard scuffling but no voices. He was here alone, I guessed. He didn't know how to cook the stuff, so I didn't know what business he was up to, unless he'd learned. I cringed, thinking this joint might explode at any moment. Better to take him now than wait for it.

The back door looked like it hadn't been used since the hunter had descended to scout out some bucks while his sister-in-law slept off the sex. The stacked gray bricks didn't look steady, but I just needed them to hold for one strong motion.

Crouched. Climbed. Twisted the knob. It

wasn't locked. Figured. Still possible that I'd need to shoulder it. Counted to three.

Banged hard into something right inside, banged again, crashing a makeshift table to the floor, sawhorses scattering left and right. Glass shattered, bottles emptied, and the thought flashed too late—*It's probably more dangerous now than when you thought he was cooking*. Vis was too stunned to grab the rifle in the corner near the door to the back hallway. He stood over the sink, upending a bottle. The air was poison, acidic. Smelled like piss and dead animals. His thick jacket was bleached spotty all over the front. His toboggan cap leaked out strands of his mullet that hadn't been washed for weeks, and the beard was patchy, full of white. One glove was missing a ring finger. The finger was a scary white and blue.

I stuck my gun in his face. "Not one move. Got it?"

He hummed affirmative and then sucked in breath. Said, "Shit, Billy, don't freak out on me."

"Fuck freaked. Let's go with angry."

"I didn't do it. They knew already. I led them along, thinking there might be money in it, ya? That's me. I'm not crazy, Billy."

I floated an arc around him, checking the doors to the front room and the hall, everything else in the trailer dark and cold except for the kerosene lamp beside Vis on the counter. When close enough I picked up his rifle, a .22, and pulled back the bolt, emptied the chamber. "You thought this would protect you?"

"It's all I've got."

I tossed it to the ground. "What happened to the Glock?"

Shrugged. "Pawned it. Pawning a lot these days. I was going to tell you soon as I had the goods."

"What are you pouring out over there?"

"Ammonia. Just…stuff."

That explained the piss stink. I didn't want to ask about the dead animals.

If he was shutting down this lab, this particular one and not the others, this must have been where Trigger and Spaceman were killed. Could be it was the only lab the Asians knew about.

"Business on the skids?"

"Please stop pointing the gun at me. Please." Chattering teeth.

"How could they know about me unless you told them? I don't get it. They're all over my people, my friends. Better tell me something that makes more sense."

"But I swear, I thought you might already—" His eyes flicked over my shoulder. Shit. I hadn't heard a thing.

I mean, was he psyching me out? Trying to distract me? Should I turn around?

I had no time because a second later, I was lashed across the back by pure steel.

My whole body tightened and I spun on my heel. The girl was swinging back the dog chain for another shot. Aimed for my face. Saw the gun at the last second, tried to switch. I held up my arm and the chain snapped on the skin and wrapped over, the loop on the end thumping my skull.

She pulled back. The chain raked. She said, "Grab him, will ya?"

No arms from behind. Vis wasn't as stupid as I thought.

My arm throbbed but I lifted the gun and was going to fire, I swear, but she got her aim right. The chain split the skin across my hand and I dropped the gun. No way to hold on when it felt like that, like a goddamned buzzsaw. Fell on my ass and cradled the bleeding hand even though my inner voice screamed *Gun gun gun gun gun!*

She moved for it first. I reached out and came up short. She kicked my arm and lifted the revolver in both hands, finally lifting it enough that she'd blow my foot off with a lucky shot.

I slackened, took a deep breath. "Okay, okay, take it easy. I wasn't going to hurt him. No one's going to hurt you. We're all going to be just fine."

"Shut up, asshole! Stay right there, don't fucking move!" All TV talk. I got a good look finally. She wore filthy tennis shoes and long thermal underwear. A thick Columbia jacket over that. I guessed nothing beneath. She had a thick neck. Her face was pitted with acne and scars. Brown wiry hair. She'd been in the back bedroom.

"Baby, come help me," she said. "We need to kill him."

Vis groaned, crossed his arms. He stepped over beside her, took a weak glance at me, then shook his head. "Haley, how many times do I got to tell you? You can't shoot the police."

Haley kept the gun on me while Vis tied my hands and feet with a nasty god-knows-what-stained sheet he tore into strips. I should have exerted a little more intimidation— walk over, take my gun, tell the girl she shouldn't play with dangerous toys. After Vis cocked the hammer and told her the trigger would be easier to squeeze that way, I kept my mouth shut. I'd seen accidents happen from much less stress.

I was tied tight, but had held my hands together in a way that gave me a little wiggle room. I started working on the knot as soon as Vis shoved me against the wall and down to the floor.

"What are you doing?" I whispered to him.

"Don't talk, all right? I don't want her tweaking any more than she already is. It's just for show."

"It doesn't feel that way."

"I told you to *shut up*." He wiped his face, shook his head all agitated. The girl was pointing the gun at the floor, the weight of it defeating her.

"Why can't I shoot him? He knows our names and everything."

I spoke up. "Who? What? I can forget everything, look the other way. Ask your man. I'm good at that."

She glanced over.

"Yeah, he's solid, babe."

"So if that's the deal, then why was he pointing that gun at you?"

Vis was fidgety. "You know, those guys. Those *guys*. They stepped out of bounds. I don't understand it."

"Me neither," I said.

"Can't you shut up?"

"Where are you going to go? You have money?"

Haley lifted the gun another few inches but gave up and let it slide. She said, "Course we do. Still some left. Baby, there's some money, you said."

He lifted his shoulders, pinched them, made a cramped face. "Some."

"What money?" I said.

"They gave me money. Listen, it's easy. They don't want to deal with you. All this stuff happening to you? Just a warning. Scare you away from their operation."

"Fucking *warning*? Didn't you see them *kill* Trigger and Spaceman? Ian puts you right there."

"They shouldn't have followed him. It's business, that's all. A rough business."

I got loud. "They murdered Drew's whole band! She's the only one survived."

Vis paled. Haley's eyes grew wide. She said, "Elvis Antichrist?"

"God. Damn."

Haley's tears ran black from her mascara. "No, that's…no."

Vis said, "Um, the guitar player is Haley's brother."

He wrapped her tight in his arms while she cried and babbled, saying it wasn't true and she needed to call him and I was lying. Vis knew better. I had assumed he knew about the band. If not that, what else did these bastards have in store for me?

"I need your info, man. I can help you both if you'll give me the guns to bring them down."

Haley broke away and got her strength back. The gun up. The barrel in my face. She stood over me and I nearly pissed my pants.

"You! It's all because of you!"

"I didn't –"

"Fuckin' cop thinks he's one of us, but he's not! And you killed my brother!"

"I loved your brother! All of them! Their biggest fan."

"No, liar! You're a liar!"

The finger on the trigger was moving. She was going to do it. All the meth in her system clouding her judgement, the sleeplessness and the paranoia and the grief and the power of the gun—

I shouted "Vis! Jesus!"

He grabbed her arms and pushed them to the left just as the muzzle flashed, detonated, and I threw all my weight to the right. One painful note rang in my skull. Hurt to breathe. Opened my eyes again. Vis gripped Haley in a bear hug. She was screaming, but I couldn't hear it. She squirmed and fought. He held fast. My gun was on the ground.

The slug had ripped open the wall a couple of feet above where my head had been. I took another deep breath. My jaw ached.

Vis was telling me something. I heard muffled words, no sense to any of them. Noise is all. A minute later he lifted Haley under his wing and grabbed one kerosene lamp, extinguished the other. Said something else to me, but I only caught "Sorry…if you…but I can't. I have to think about myself."

"What?"

"Good luck. I'm sorry."

He left with Haley still bawling and weak-legged. They went out the front, left me in darkness, the smell of ammonia and deer rot making me gag, stinging my eyes. I admit it—I was scared. Worked one wrist out of the rag, desperate to get the hell out of these woods. No telling what tweakers and fucking loons would soon be breaking in looking for a place to sleep. They'd strip me bare, shoot me without any of Haley's hesitation. Maybe even cook my meat if things were that bad out here. I struggled while listening to the Probe come to life, rev a few times, and then take off too fast down the dirt road. I hoped he wouldn't slash my tires or set the truck on fire.

My hands freed, I worked on the knot around my ankles, much tighter than the wrists. The cold was getting to me. I hadn't shook like that since I'd kicked cigarettes cold turkey. Fumbled, couldn't loosen the rag. Tore a fingernail trying to wedge it into the knot. Useless. I searched for something sharp, or a stick, or anything. That's when footsteps echoed on the stepladder outside and then thumped across the front room. They were coming. I had five bullets left now.

I reached for the gun, had to stretch out for it, footsteps closer. Once it was in my hand I swung around just as the steps stopped and I felt someone staring down at me. I aimed at a familiar tall black man. Rome, head of security at Jackpot Harvest.

He was aiming back, a chrome automatic.

"Well, well," he said. "And here I thought I was going to find you dead."

THIRTEEN

Rome cut me loose with his pocketknife. I relaxed, felt suddenly very tired. Still too much to do before I could sleep.

"Were you following me?"

"Perfect hiking weather. Cold as my ex-wife and black as my skin."

I'd only ever seen him dressed to the nines at the casino. Here he was decked out in black jeans, black jacket, Timberlands, also black. He knew a thing or two about blending in.

"I would say thanks, but since I'm a little pissed that you didn't catch those bitches and didn't rush in when you heard the shot—"

"Again, thought you'd already be dead. If I hadn't heard the conversation, I would've probably killed you myself the way things have been heading."

"What things? What have I ever done to you?"

He stood from his crouch, held out his hand. I took it and he pulled me up. Knees aching. The big bad-ass going soft. I shoved my gun into my waistband and crossed my arms. Waiting.

He said, "How about I take you home? Pretend this was a dream."

Shook my head. "Not going to happen."

He sighed through his nose and tapped his gun barrel against his forehead before slipping it back into a shoulder holster. Yeah, that was a surprise. People with shoulder holsters usually don't play well with others, especially me.

"Some sort of fed, right?" I said. "DEA?"

He started laughing, strong and long. I smiled but couldn't join in. I didn't get the joke.

"You're not going to tell me? Would you like me to arrest you for trespassing or something?"

He laid a hand on my shoulder, wiped away the water in his eyes with the other hand. "Damn, you're a hillbilly. You seen that movie *In the Heat of the Night*? Poitier and that other guy…damn I forgot his name."

"The fat white guy?"

"Yeah, but he was a big star, too. He was in *Oklahoma*. Anyway, you've seen it?"

"I like that movie."

In his best Poitier, Rome said, "'They call me Mis-tah Tibbs!'" Another burst of laughter.

"What about it?"

Rome squeezed my shoulder. "That's pretty much this right here, except I'm smarter than Sidney and you're not stupid enough to call me 'boy'."

I shrugged his hand off and turned for the back door. "I'm not your fucking punchline, so you'd better get your ass far away before I stop being gracious, *boy*."

He pointed a finger in my face. "I knew it! I knew you were going to do that. Son of a bitch, you're predictable as Old Faithful. Look, come with me for a minute. I want to show you something."

"I don't have time."

"Yeah, you do. You're not going to find any Asian gangsters out in these woods tonight, and you're not going to find that little runt Ian and his hippie girlfriend either. But if you come with me, I'll show you what you *can* find."

I was stunned. Guy I thought was a simple security guard at a shitty casino in the cornfields knew the whole score. Or thought he did.

We passed my truck. The tires were fine.

Tweakers too lit to think of details like that. Real life ain't like TV. Once we made the asphalt, I saw the same black Suburban I'd nearly sideswiped when I started searching earlier in the day.

"Didn't I nearly—?"

"That was me." He led me around back, clicked a button on his keychain to open the tailgate. Inside was an Igloo cooler. "Take a look."

Things were moving too fast for me to step back and think things through. I didn't need what happened next, though. I really didn't.

Slid the top to the side. Resting on a bed of ice was a wet, dead, blonde girl's head. I stumbled, fell, kicked myself up again and made a noise like a burned baby. "Th' fuck? What? How did you? *Fuck!*"

He replaced the lid and said, "I didn't know what you were doing. Soon as I fished it out, I couldn't believe it. This was Heather's roommate, right?"

I nodded, numb.

"So at first it looks like all my fears were confirmed. You definitely had something to do with what these cats were involved in. Either as the clean-up crew or the killer himself, I wasn't able to tell. But *something*."

"No, that's not it. You've got it all—"

"Easy, man. I got that now. Nothing sinister. It ain't right, you more worried about covering your own ass than letting the law do its job, but from what I heard later, and then what you just said to the dealer in there, you're clear on the serious stuff."

Since I'd basically admitted to being in on Vis's operation, I had to ask, "What do you mean by serious?"

Rome fingered his chin for a few seconds, showed his teeth. He loved his job, whatever it was. Then, "You haven't looked up that brand on Ian's ass yet, have you?"

"How did you know?"

"About the brand or you not looking it up? Doesn't matter. I'm all psychic and shit. It'll make sense in a minute." Rome reached into the Suburban again, pulled out a briefcase. He clicked it open and searched through papers until he picked one. A computer database entry, it looked like. A lot of foreign writing on it, not Asian characters. Most of those looked alike, right? This was familiar in a different way. Stuff I'd seen on the news. At the top was the same symbol I'd seen on Ian's ass. A moon. One of those foreign characters, kind of like an "F" but not quite.

"That's the one," I said. "So this writing here?"

"Arabic."

"These guys are Asian."

More teeth, more gums. Cheshire Cat Rome. "Keep going. Asia's also got Afghanistan, Pakistan, Other-stans, you know. It's got India, huge Muslim population there. Down into the Philippines, Malaysia—"

I stopped him. "They're into meth now? In the midwest?"

Rome bobbed his head. "That's the crazy part. We didn't think so, but here they are. Not very good at being gangsters, either, so we know they're not some Chinese mafia."

"Then what do you think they're doing?"

"Wrong question. First ask me who they are."

"Fine, good, who are they?"

Soon as he said it, I had to ask that he say it again, make sure it wasn't a bad dream. Too bad. I was awake and the wind was cold and the ache in my knees spread to all my other joints.

What Rome had said, who these guys were: "What we've got here are some Islamic terrorists, via Southeast Asia."

We sat in the cab of the Suburban with the heater thawing our skin while I let this sink in. Terrorists on the prairie. Made no sense.

"I could understand The Cities. But here?"

"Not all that strange. Who'd suspect a few Orientals coming into a small town to be up to no good? Over there, you're right. Closer scrutiny. In Yellow Medicine County, they're just looking for work."

"Or dealing crystal meth."

Rome scrunched his face. "Yeah. They need the money because they're not part of a larger organization. This is the grassroots stuff, a mixed-bag. Some Asians, Saudis, Pakistanis, maybe even a few Turks. They're really bad at it, though. We think they want to do some smaller ops, like blowing up post offices, dumping anthrax in reservoirs. Know what that would get them?"

He watched me like he thought I had an answer.

"I'm just as confused as you are."

"I'm starting to get that. But I'm not confused. You caught our eye, but it looks like we suspected you of the wrong thing."

"Who's *we* and *our* anyway? What are you?"

Rome reached into his breast pocket, pulled out an official-looking leather thingie, spread it and let me take a look. One card ID'ed him as "Franklin D. Rome" of Immigration and Naturalization Services. The second card, same name, issued by the Department of Homeland Security.

"Motherfucker," I said.

"No. That's Bin Laden. I'm a good guy."

He explained: small groups, mixed race memberships, looking to gain attention from the big boys, which in turn would give them money and status.

The heat passed over us in waves, and I felt nauseous and uncomfortable in my skin. I rubbed my palm on my clammy forehead.

Rome grabbed a peppermint from the ashtray, handed it over. "Helps with stomach shit and dead bodies. A miracle candy."

I sucked on the mint a while. There wasn't much to say. I replayed everything in my head and wondered how these guys decided I was worth terrorizing. My friends, my loved ones. I hoped not my family down South. I'd have to give Ginny a call and check in.

"Don't get too freaked out, man," Rome

said. "Truth is these people are all over, in places you don't expect. The ones you think are a hundred percent guilty turn out to be regular folks, no ties to anything crazy. Then out of nowhere—" he thundered his hands together "—somebody we dismissed as pure snow tries to blow up a school."

"That's a bit much."

"No, really. You don't hear about half the sons of bitches we stop. That'd get the whole country panicked."

"You pretty much think Ian and Heather are goners already."

"Unless the terrorists think hostages would help them. For that to be the case I think you'd get a message soon."

"They didn't hold Drew's band hostage."

"The first time I'd heard that was when you told that dealer. I'm sorry, man. Think of it this way, though. If they'd caught her, I bet she would've been the hostage. These guys don't do 'Plan A' and then 'Plan B'. They do it all at once to scatter our resources, lead us down some dead ends." He shifted the Suburban into gear. "Now go get your truck and follow me."

"Where are we going? What's the next step?"

"Ain't you supposed to be home? I'm sure

the sheriff wants to know why you're off the map."

"You'll be my alibi?"

"Been a rough day. We needed a couple drinks. We're pretty good friends, you and me."

"We are?"

Another one of those wide smiles. "We'd better act like it from now on. I almost didn't save your life, after all."

FOURTEEN

I sat in front of Graham's desk like a high school class clown who'd gone too far. Slumped, not willing to look him in the eye. My ex-brother-in-law was pissed at me forcing him out of the house this late at night looking for my sorry ass until 11:45, when we showed up at the river house. Two cruisers had been waiting to drag us both to the station. Rome now leaned against the side wall, still undercover as a casino security chief and my drinking buddy.

"All you had to do was ask, or just let him bring the beer to you, for Pete's sake."

I shrugged. Rome mumbled an apology. I'd never seen Graham this angry. I'd broken his trust and didn't expect to earn it back.

"You have witnesses to this, right? Other guys at the bar?"

Shit. He didn't believe the story anyway. I said, "You'd have to go pretty far. Cactus Jack's, halfway to The Cities. It was a busy night. I don't think they'd remember."

"They can try." Graham lifted the phone. He didn't get as far as dialing information. Another deputy knocked on the doorframe. Graham hung up. "You need something?"

"We just heard. There's a lead on the missing kids around Wood Lake. The Marshall cops need you to go check it out."

Graham twisted his lips, then said to me, "You'll behave, right?"

"Promise."

"I'll be watching."

We stood. Rome pushed off the wall. Graham held out a cautioning hand.

"If you can stay put until I get back, I'd like to have a few words with you."

"I'm coming along."

"I don't think so. This doesn't concern you."

My turn. "Rome had better come along. He can fill you in on the way."

Our sheriff was full of surprises that day. Saved my ass when I thought he wouldn't, and then he didn't get angry when Rome revealed his real profession. In fact Graham was impressed. Instantly got all respectful, calling Rome "Sir" and "Agent Rome". At one point he said, "I'm so proud of the job you guys are doing to protect us, anything you need, just ask."

I took in their conversation from the backseat as we sped down dark county roads with the flashing lights on, no siren. Wood Lake was about ten miles south of Pale Falls, another one of those places where you'll be driving past miles of cornfields, then suddenly you see a neighborhood of nice tract homes. A few rows, no more, and then more cornfields. Eerie.

We avoided the subdivision and headed right through to one of those fields. A Lyon County Deputy was waiting for us on the roadside, a line of eight police cars—Marshall, Lyon, Yellow Medicine. We took our place in line and were escorted through the empty, ice-slick field to a crowd of uniforms with flashlights and a spotlight trained on the ground. It wasn't looking good. I wasn't sure I wanted to see it.

Graham caught me clearing my throat, said, "It's not your fault."

"If I'd said something earlier—"

"They would still be dead. Agent Rome's right about that."

Some of the cops on the crowd saw Rome and looked confused. Most of them had been to the casino on either business or their downtime. Graham made the introductions, blowing whatever cover the man had left. Rome took it like a rock, but I didn't think he expected to be outed so soon. Like he said earlier, he'd expected to find me shot in the head.

"What've we got?" Graham said.

One of the deputies flicked her flashlight beam towards the earth. A half-assed grave, loose soil on top of a leg pulled out of the hole by deer or something. They'd nibbled at his ankles. Dirty khakis. I crossed my arms, not feeling like a cop anymore.

Someone else carefully brushed the dirt off the rest of the body, skinny like Ian, wearing the same clothes as our last meeting. Brushed off his jacket and then his neck. But there was no head.

"Someone you know?" Graham said to me.

I didn't answer for a long time. Maybe he asked again, but I didn't hear him. Finally, I took a step closer, even though the cops were warning me off, talking about contaminating the scene. Fuck that, this wasn't *CSI*. All I wanted to do was tug the kid's waistband, look at his ass.

One of the cops said, "Hey, what's he doing?"

I crouched beside the body, said, "It's easier when they can't run, ain't it?" Then I checked for the brand.

Somewhere in the crowd, I heard a low, "Jesus, I'd heard he was a psycho, but *shit*."

It was there, the puckered skin around the "F" and quarter moon.

I looked up at Rome. "Ian."

He nodded. "I'd better get some Feds on the way."

The cops buzzed around each other, excited. This was bigger than their day-to-day small town duties for sure. Might even catch some murderers if they got lucky.

They could have the thrills. It looked to me that my part in the case had dried up—I was personally involved and at risk, so no more free range roaming for Lafitte. I would be guarded twenty-four seven. I would be an embarrassment. I would be pitied by my protectors. Shit on that. No matter what it cost me, I wasn't going to be a rat in a cage.

Rome was on his cell phone, calling in the big guns while also telling the local cops to not touch anything else. They'd already brushed away enough dirt to reveal another torso, this one a girl's. I didn't need to see it to know. I sidled up to Graham and said, "You know, I should probably be the one to tell his girlfriend about this. We've known each other a long time."

"That doesn't sound like a good idea."

"Honestly, she's a friend. Please."

He clucked his tongue while thinking. "We don't even know for sure if it's him yet."

"It is."

"But DNA—"

I stopped him with, "Can't I do *something* good right now? One little thing, that's all I'm asking."

The poor guy. If only I was another deputy, someone he had a little more influence over, someone who actually respected his tight-assed leadership. Graham knew I'd never leave him alone if he turned me down.

I sweetened the pot. "I'll tell his folks. Save you that one."

He shook his head. "No, it's my place. The girl's parents can wait, too."

Damn, I took one step over the line. The man seemed to be growing some balls. I said,

"I can't just stand around here doing nothing."

"That's exactly what you need to do. I can't babysit you right now, and I can't put you on the case. As long as I'm out here tonight, you're out here with me."

"Might as well slap the cuffs."

"Enough."

I turned and walked back towards the road.

He caught up. "Hey, what do you think you're doing?"

"If I'm not on the job, I'm going to sit in the car. I can't stand this goddamned wind."

"You'll do what I tell you, Deputy Lafitte. Is that clear?"

Kept walking. "Either arrest me or let me do something, Sheriff."

Come on, come on, give in. Don't shut me out.

He stopped walking. I kept going about ten more paces before I stopped, spun, hands on my gun belt. "Well?"

He called to the crowd for Nate, who was talking to the new female cop from Marshall, a strong blonde girl. Nate excused himself and ran over to Graham. I swear, way too eager to please. A puppy.

Graham told him, "Take Deputy Lafitte to my car. Put him in the backseat. Lock it. Do not let him leave. You need to stand watch over him. Understood?"

The kid was freaking out. "Is, um, he under arrest?"

"Look, watch him, please. That's what I need right now more than a bunch of useless deputies giggling over a couple of bodies."

"Do I cuff him?"

"*No*, you don't cuff him." Graham raised his voice, squeezing Nate down to two inches high. "Just…do it!"

The rookie looked at me, then the sheriff, then "Yes sir. Right away." He fast-walked up to me, took my arm. "Sorry Billy, you heard the man."

"Nate, if you don't let go of my arm, I'll break every last one of your ribs."

He let go. "That's uncalled for."

I walked ahead of him. "Not to me it isn't."

After I convinced him to crank the cruiser and turn on the heat, I knew Nate would be easy. He might have been almost a friend and fishing buddy, but he believed all the rumors about me regardless. The false ones had me as some sort of TV antihero, a mean fuck with dirty hands and a vigilante heart. They liked that. They feared it, too. Everybody wanted to be my friend.

Nate complained about the Feds, thinking he was supposed to live up to the stereotype.

I said, "I don't care. They're more qualified. We don't want to get tangled up in this mess."

"We're as capable as they are. This is our turf."

I leaned towards the cage. "Did anyone tell you what's really going on?"

He looked over his shoulder, not expecting me to be so close. "It's drug stuff, isn't it?"

"Yeah, that's it." I relaxed into the seat and thought about what I planned to do. A career-ending move. A criminal act. What would the next step be?

That same TV show the rookies loved would have the antihero pull some sort of shenanigans at the very last minute to avoid being fingered. Or he would catch the bad guys first, thus absolving his sins. Not realistic at all. We lived in a country where criminals could sue the people who arrested them for being a bit rough. I mean true criminals, caught in the act, winning lawsuits against the guys trying to protect the public.

I didn't have a chance of surviving this either

way because whoever was cutting heads was probably doing it with my hunting knife. I didn't have an alibi for when the murders took place. I had even covered up evidence that helped me in order to cover up *more* evidence that painted me guilty as sin. Oh yeah, I was screwed and the Asians knew it.

Time to sneak out of the house under Daddy's nose.

"Who was that lady cop out there? She new?"

Nate smiled. "Out of Marshall, yeah. Her name's Colleen."

"You, uh, were chatting her up. She's single?"

"Wide-open. Okay, so she's a little older than me, but that's cool these days. It's not like I'm looking for a *wife* or anything."

Sure he was. I could tell.

"You getting anywhere with that?"

"I only met her waiting around here. Who knows? She seemed sweet enough."

"Dude, you need to be out there getting your groove on. Those other guys are going to move in, but she's going to wish it were you. You were kind to her. If it were me, I'd find a replacement and get my ass back out there."

He stared off into space as another van pulled up. The Feds wouldn't be here that quickly, so I guessed it was the coroner.

Nate said, "Maybe I could ask her to come help me. Maybe tell her I need a break."

"No, man, she'll see right through that. And *I'm* here. That'll really spoil the mood. Better get out on the field."

Leave me alone. I know my way out of the backseat. I know how to jimmy the car. I can disappear and let them eat your ass instead of mine.

"I don't know. What are you going to do, meditate?"

"Take a nap."

"With the heater running?"

Shit, he was scared of Graham. I could understand that. Pussy boy. I would have to take it up a notch.

"Your loss, that's all I'm saying. Your alternative is watching me piss. Like, right now. I need to take one."

"Can't you use a cup?"

"Do you *have* a cup? I don't. Jesus, it's after midnight in a cornfield. I need to take a fucking leak!"

"Hey, cool it. Okay, okay. Give me a second here."

He was about to climb out and open my door, at which point I would knock him silly, shove him in the back seat. Take away his gun. Take off his shoes so he couldn't kick the window out. Cuff his wrists behind him. Then hit the road with the cruiser and not stop until I was in Canada. If I tried to stick around and do things on my own, I wouldn't last a day. The problem with the wide open spaces was that there were fewer roads. But I wanted to see Drew first. I wanted to tell her how sorry and miserable I was.

That was the plan. I was ready to pounce. Turned out I didn't have to.

Nate was startled by the sheriff thumping a knuckle on his window. The kid lowered it and Graham leaned in, rested his arms on the door. "Everything okay in here?"

I gave him a thumbs-up. "Peachy."

He nodded, looked at the ground. "You know we towed your truck, right? Just to be safe. We noticed the broken window. You lock your keys in?"

"It was a bad day."

"Yeah, well…" Tapped his fingers on the frame. "You promise to be good?"

"Depends."

"If I send you to bed without supper? Promise to be at my office tomorrow morning at eight-thirty?"

"If I don't?"

A long sigh, a cloud of breath obscuring his face for a second. "Please, Billy, it would be a mess if we had to lock you up. Agent Rome's the only one keeping the Marshall police from taking you in right now. If you've got nothing to hide, let us help you."

It didn't feel like the perfect answer. I'd still be useless and trapped. However, it was better than going to jail or getting shot by eager coppers on my fugitive tail.

I said, "I promise. Cross my heart."

Graham told Nate to get me there, no detours. Nate's "Yes sir" was a little mumbly. I'd just stoked his lust and now he had to leave? I felt bad for the guy. Graham turned away, but then back to tell me, "Oh, please make sure you've got your shield and sidearm tomorrow. Very important."

I hummed affirmative and watched Graham walk back to the field with another cop at his side.

Nate shifted the car into Drive and U-turned. "Man, that sucks. I'm sorry."

Even unsaid, every cop knows to carry his shield and sidearm on duty. If the sheriff was reminding me, it was because he wanted them. Suspension. Or worse.

I said, "Take me home."

FIFTEEN

Another sleepless night. Another bottle of red wine. Every plan I worked over in my head ended with me in jail, Drew hurt, my kids without child support, all the rumors confirmed.

The revolver was on my lap. One bullet in the cylinder. I spun it once, waited. Yeah, I had played this game before—the first night I stayed here, and then again on New Year's Eve. I lifted the barrel and shoved it under my chin, against my Adam's apple. Pressure, pain, but nothing like what was going on in my skull. They say most suicide attempts are simply cries for help. The real deals will fool you until you find their cold bodies hung, shot, sliced, or suffocated.

If that was the case, what to you call it when someone gambles?

Cocked the hammer. Took a deep breath.

Closed my eyes. Squeezed it easy.

Click.

Didn't win the grand prize. If you ask why I fooled around instead of gritting my teeth and doing the deed, it was because I liked the drama. Even I didn't know if the next snap of the trigger would be the end. More fun, like a roller coaster. I didn't have the strength to try again that night.

I was facing the end of my career in disgrace for a second time. Maybe being a cop was a bad choice after all. Goddamn Katrina. Before the storm I was bending rules but not snapping them in two.

The wine was the best I owned, a French Cabernet I was saving for a special occasion. I wasn't sure what that might mean, exactly, but in the back of my mind I saw a speculative snapshot—me, Ginny, the kids, together at a grand dinner table, a fried turkey the centerpiece, with Gin's cornbread dressing and dinner rolls.

At the halfway point of the bottle, I wasn't at the table anymore. The kids were sullen. Ginny had bags under her eyes. The turkey had been replaced by Spam on white bread. Every mouthful of wine made the scene that much worse.

Spam into Hot Pockets. Hot Pockets into the cheapest frozen pizzas, the ones that taste like ketchup on a cracker.

Then the headlights appeared at the end of my driveway again.

It wasn't that these were distinctive, that I could tell those particular headlights from all others. But they paused the same as those others had. Another excuse to freak me out? Was I supposed to trudge out there and plead for mercy? Give myself over to the fuckers who killed three innocent college students?

I stood from my chair, set the bottle on the end table. Headed for the door with one bullet in the gun and no jacket. Only jeans and sneakers and a white T-shirt. If this was the final showdown, then I'd go down after taking careful aim for one of their eyes.

Outside. The wind at my back. Instafreeze. I couldn't even shiver.

The car didn't stay still. This time it rolled up the driveway, crunching the remaining snow and fallen branches. I couldn't make out the driver because of the headlights. No clue if he had passengers. I lifted the gun with one hand and held it there, waiting. I'd at least let them get out of the car.

The car eased to a stop ten feet from my toes. The lights died and left ghosts and blobs in my sight that I blinked away. The driver's door opened, closed, and a man in a long black coat approached. The top of his head and ears were covered by a hat with flaps. A scarf tight around the mouth. He was unarmed, his hands in thick gloves. Like me when I first arrived, he didn't seem to function well in the cold weather. Closer, daring me to keep the gun trained on his eye. The chill caught up with me. I lowered the gun when I realized the eyes weren't those of an Asian, but a Caucasian.

I thought I knew them.

Then he spoke. "My guess is you've got one bullet in that gun, and you didn't win again."

I thought I knew those eyes but I was sure I knew that voice.

"I never won either."

The voice dug up a face from the past, something I'd repressed. Yeah, I knew this man. He had been my partner on the Gulfport Police. He had saved my life a few times, and I had saved his. Together, we killed a gangbanger and covered it up.

I said, "Paul Asimov."

"So, are you going to invite me in or shoot me?"

Inside, he shed himself of the winter garb. It had been nearly two years since I had last seen Paul, and the time hadn't been good to him. He was thinner, and his hair was speckled gray. He was only thirty-seven. I made a pot of coffee and we pulled a couple of chairs closer to the wood stove. His posture was closed up, but he wasn't shivering as bad as I expected from someone new to the area. How did he hunt me down?

He shouted at me while I poured two full mugs in the kitchen. "Not doing so bad for yourself, Billy."

"The house is falling apart. I can't hide as much of my rebel side here as I could on the coast. It's too goddamned cold."

"It's still a life."

I walked to the stove, handed Paul a mug of black coffee. Mine was sugared and creamed. "Sounds like trouble in your world."

"We backed you because you backed us. But then the bottom fell out. It was like everyone got a chance to start over except guys like us. All goodie two shoes and shit, those hypocrites." He took a sip. "Still making it strong."

"Doesn't pack the same punch as French Market."

"You can have that shipped up, you know."

"Trying to forget it as best I can." I stared into the darkness. "How'd you get the address?"

"You get mail here, so there's a trail. Mapquest draws a line right to your front door."

"That was you the other night, stopping and then leaving?"

A devil's grin. "Maybe I tried once before, couldn't get up the stones. I'm here now, buddy. Happy to see you."

He gripped my neck, a real good buddy vibe coming out of him. Back in the old days we got along, saved each other's ass, but we were never as brotherly as other teams. We could drive for a half-hour without talking. On calls, though, we were in sync. More like twins or something.

"So life isn't easy street for you?" I said.

Paul shook his head. The hair was cut short, scars on his scalp like borders on a map. He kept the sides high-and-tight. Lost his goatee. Lost a couple of teeth, too. "Maybe you didn't turn, but someone still had my strings. The brass waited until you were gone a couple of months before bringing me in for questioning. On that nigger's shooting, on the Katrina shit, on our side action."

"How'd they know about that?"

"You tell me." Eyes locked on. Leery? I couldn't tell. Heard a voice in my head: *What if he's wired up?* I didn't want to believe it, but I had to find out.

"You need anything? Want something stiffer in that coffee?"

He lifted his mug. "Bring it on."

I started towards the kitchen. Set my own mug on the table before grabbing my revolver and turning back. I wrapped my arm around Paul's throat and stuck the gun in his ear. Whispered, "Don't say a word."

Felt through his shirt, chest and back, then his legs, his balls. Couldn't find anything obvious. I wondered how small mikes had gotten, if he could have a wireless bug smaller than a dime in his pocket.

"Jesus, Billy."

"You swear you're on your own? Not trying to trap me or anything?"

"Yes, yes, I swear."

"And I mean fucking *swear*, man."

"On my grandpa's grave, I swear. On his good name."

I could accept that. The man worshipped his grandpa, who practically raised him. I eased the gun away and stood back. He had spilled his coffee on his jeans.

"Got any sweats?"

He might have been suspicious, but he had been my partner once. "You can have the bed. I'll take the couch."

It was just good manners. The guest deserved the bed. I wasn't sure I could sleep anyway.

I refilled his mug, poured in too much scotch, and he caught me up on his life. I was careful with every word of my responses. The whole thing felt weird, the timing either way off or perfect.

"My girl, she left." Paul had been engaged to a blackjack dealer for half a year. She was good for him. Tempered his dark side. "Just left. Before everything came down. She told me she was evacuating to her parents' house in Birmingham. Three weeks later I hadn't heard from her, so I called. Her mom told me Viv'd only been there a week before she went on to Nashville with an old boyfriend, already found an apartment."

"That's tough."

He shrugged. "I needed to do something to make use of my skills. I knew who to talk to. I'm not proud."

I had already guessed where he was going. That could have been me. "Yeah?"

He nodded, eyes on his mug. "They needed me in Atlanta. I spent the winter collecting old debts, enforcing new deals. Jesus, I hated it. Used to crack these niggers' heads and now they treated me like the hired help. Goddamn hard to turn down a monthly bonus that was your choice of a PT Cruiser or a Mustang. Hard to turn down free rent in a loft apartment."

"But how much real money did you get?"

That got a nervous twitch. "Couple thousand a week. But it went fast."

"You're broke?"

"Mostly. I've got pocket money. And I found some new people to work with once Atlanta went sour."

I sighed. "Shit, what did you do?"

"Motherfucker got pissed because I roughed up his cousin. It was sort of a test, they didn't tell me. Trying to drag me in deeper, to make up for my *trespass*, that's what he called me being a cop. I shot his kneecap. I walked out without a scratch on me, and even stole his Hummer."

His grin spread, then a smile, and I couldn't help but join in. "His fucking Hummer?"

"All pimped, but still, you know."

"You're driving a piece of shit Toyota. Where's the tank?"

He rubbed his neck with his fingers. "Left it behind in Detroit. That was the next stop, only spent the summer there. Laying low, doing a little work-for-hire so I wasn't anybody's bitch."

"Never figured you to be."

He was quiet a long moment before saying almost too softly for me to make out: "We did all right on the Coast, right? We were solid cops."

"Cheers to that."

We clinked mugs. Another minute of listening to the wind, not so fierce any more as Spring started to win out.

Then Paul said, "I knew where you were before Detroit. It wasn't until then that I figured out a way to reconnect. Something I thought we could do together."

I laughed, barely, hoping he would tell me some crazy plan—start a private eye business or fake our IDs and run off to Mexico, join the police force down there. Learn all about grift from the masters.

It sounded like he said, "I'm sorry."

"Excuse me?"

"Sorry. For it not working like it was supposed to. I've come to make it right if I can, explain myself."

"What did you do, Paul?"

A drunk grin. "Hey, remember when you called me Asimov instead? Like we were tough guys—"

"No, back it up. What did you do?"

He said, "It was just, you know, a good looking deal. Some guys looking for a good place to make some quick money, and me thinking of you out here in this vast untapped resource."

"Jesus, don't tell me this."

"They're out of my control. Goddamn slant-eyes have no idea about good business."

My head hurt worse than it had since losing Ginny. I was blacking out, wanting to ask if he knew what they really were, how much shit he'd sunk us all in. Paul kept going, "I told them you were the man, but they needed to wait for me to touch base first. They didn't want to. I tried, I swear."

"Shut up, Paul. Go to bed. Just…shut up."

After that, dreams mixed with things he had said or might have said while I was losing consciousness. I thought of the Asians, of Elvis Antichrist, of a blond man in a Saints cap attacking Drew. Then drifted into dreams of the Coast, of zombies coming after Ginny and Paul and me in the middle of a thunderstorm. Zombie dreams were the worst. Every time I had one, I woke the next day thinking the world was more dangerous than I had first thought.

SIXTEEN

Waking up was a bitch. Something in a dream I couldn't remember startled me conscious. I fell off the couch and banged my head into the coffee table. Last night's mugs half-full of cold coffee crashed onto the floor. Shards and puddles, my revolver right in the middle of one, wet and sticky.

I was sweating. The dream came back to me—a zombie nightmare, another one. I'd had too many of those lately. This time the Asians were the zombies. They had gotten to my kids. My kids wanted to eat their mother's brains. I was helping lead them to her. Don't know why. All I know is that zombies creep me out. Maybe dealing with all the scabby tweaking meth fiends triggered my subconscious to dream about zombies. Single-minded and dead to the world.

Another ten seconds and the details of the

night before came to me: careening over to the couch seconds before I passed out, pushing Paul out of the way and telling him to find the bedroom, we'd talk come morning. Then it got worse - the white man who tried to get Drew in Minneapolis, could that have been Paul? If so, then how did I play this? Goosebumps. Chilled from the sweat, cramps and hunger pains from too much booze. Checked my watch—six forty-five, the sun working its light into my front room. Time for coffee and toast.

I was too wiped out to tackle the mess I'd made. Cheap table, anyway. I started a new pot of coffee dripping and checked in on Paul. He had ended up fully clothed, on his side in a fetal-curl. Hardly a sound from him. I listened until I made out a breath, then retreated to the kitchen. Didn't look forward to confronting him over collaborating with terrorists, killing my citizens, thinking they could infiltrate American society through our weak spot—our addictions. It would have been a brilliant plan if they hadn't picked up all their info on running a drug ring from B-movies.

My cell phone light was blinking. I couldn't get reception for shit in the house, so I stepped outside to listen to my messages. Needed open sky. I peeked into Paul's car on my way to the mailbox at the end of the driveway. There was a Saints cap in the passenger seat. My stomach cramped up. I listened to a couple of useless calls from when Graham and Layla were hunting me down the night before.

Then one from Rome, after the dig: "I'm sorry about this, man. It looks like we're taking over from here, so I will need to talk to you again soon. We can protect you should any charges come up, so don't worry."

Sounded like code for "Kiss life as you know it goodbye."

The next call. Drew.

"Listen, I know it's not your fault, but I'll never understand why you lied to me about Ian. I…I don't get it, Billy. I thought you of all people…"

I checked the time of the message. Three in the morning.

She kept on: "We probably shouldn't speak to each other anymore. I just…I can't trust you. I guess I never really did, but I wanted to. Please don't call back."

The robovoice said I didn't have any other messages.

The mailbox was full of bulk-rate circulars,

bills, credit card offers, and an unstamped envelope with only my initials written on it.

Inside were photos on cheap copy paper. Probably from a digital camera and an ink jet printer. Heather and Ian, beaten, their mouths taped, eyes dead even though they were still alive at the time. The next picture, Heather being forced into oral sex. Her face bruised. My heart broke. Poor kid. I hoped she had fought back, bit the guy's package clean off, something, anything. I wanted the motherfuckers to suffer. I flipped to the next one. Ian, his captor standing behind him, hooking his fingers on the inside of his lips and stretching them to a horrific smile, the lips split and bleeding. If only I'd acted faster, taken him with me instead of going back for a piece of tail. I choked down a scream.

The next, holding a knife against Heather's neck. My knife—the white "X" my dad had marked on the handle so obvious this time. They wanted me to see. Since his hands were gloved and his face hidden, the man with the knife could have very well been me.

I felt that it *was* me as I turned to the final photo, exactly what they wanted. Typed neatly across the bottom: *If you're not with us, you're against us.* The photo showed Heather and Ian's heads, cut from their bodies, side-by-side on a table.

My stomach lurched and I heaved sweet coffee and wine and bile onto the pages and then the ground as I knelt down, too weak to stop myself. Another wave of nausea, eyes tearing up. Like gravel in my throat.

"Jesus, Billy!" Shouted from up near the house. Asimov ran towards me. "You okay, buddy?"

The anger steeled me, helped me choke back the acid. When he reached me I landed a fist in his crotch. He dropped like a bomb. I grabbed the wet photos, held them to his face.

"Was this part of your fucking plan? Was this how you were supposed to get me to play along?"

He babbled, but I kept those pages in his face, gripped the back of his neck

"Fucking murderers! Not drug dealers!"

"What the hell are you—?"

"Goddamn it, they're *terrorists.*"

Paul shoved a palm against my chin, the pressure getting me. I fell away. He kicked me. He tried again, but I rolled away, crouched. We faced each other like wrestlers under the spotlights.

He was breathing hard, hands out and ready to strike. "I didn't *know*, okay? Why would I get you wrapped up in something like that?"

"They've killed five people in two days. You were *there*! You went after Drew!"

"I swear, I wasn't going to hurt her. I was trying to scare her away. Man, I had no clue they were going to kill those guys. Listen to me. I came here last night because I need to stop them. It was a huge mistake, I know. But it's out of the bag and we need to shove it back in."

I was too tired to keep up the pose, sat my ass on the rocks and dirt, tried not to cry in front of Asimov, but the floodgates were open. I dropped my head to my knees.

"I'm sorry," he said.

"Why did you play along?"

"Fuck, I don't know. I haven't been all there the last few weeks. These guys are freaking me out. I escaped, Billy. Out of it. We can beat them."

I rubbed my eyes dry. "This is what happens to you? Digging a hole in your gutter? Jesus."

I brushed myself off. My jeans were soaked with morning dew and melted snow. Helped Asimov up. I picked up the photo pages, knew

I'd need to hand them over to Graham. Still wet. Talk about tainted evidence.

"So now what?" Paul said.

"There is no 'now' for me. The sheriff wants my badge. I'm a two-time loser. I have no clue what's next for me, but I can't afford to fuck it up any more than I already have. I still send checks to my kids."

"But we got into this, maybe we're the best to get us out."

I shook my head. Fucking moron. "*We* didn't do shit. This is all you. And we're not Starsky and Hutch. We're half-assed adrenaline junkie cops. I'm done with it, that's all."

I left him standing in the yard as I trudged back to the house. The coffee was waiting for me.

The meeting with Graham was pretty much what I expected. He tried to make me feel comfortable, keep up the brotherly vibe. He offered coffee. I was floating in it already. A glass of water, sure. I could deal with that. Layla set it on the desk between Graham and me, and I lifted it for a long pull, all down in one shot, so he couldn't see that my hands were shaking.

Rome was the hard-ass. Soon as he saw the

first shots, he began to pace. The way he looked at me, something shifting.

Graham said, "It's terrible, all this. You live out here, think you're isolated from all the world's problems. The meth is bad enough, but, wow."

I nodded. Rome must have filled him in on the full story. I wondered how long it would be before the local newspaper got hold. Then the national news. Then I would be center stage in what looked like a conspiracy.

He said, "I mean I know how it looks to the Homeland Security guys."

"How's that?"

"It's more than just what you know. They think you really had something to do with it. Like you were at least a middleman for the meth operations, but more likely one of the cell members."

"Oh, fuck no. That's what they want you to think, but that's crazy."

Rome spit a laugh, kept pacing. "Is it? Because if that's the case, these bastards are doing one helluva job making all the dots connect."

Rome was hoping I'd confess. Graham was praying I'd give him solid proof I didn't have anything to do with the Asians. As soon as I turned over those photos and told him what Paul had done, thinking he could work with wannabe terrorists and keep clean, I had my chip in the game. But not as a cop. No, as soon as I spilled on Asimov, he could roll right back over on me about the gangbanger I'd killed in Mississippi. If I were him, I would've done it to me. And that's a friend talking.

I wanted him to get to it. "You want my shield and sidearm, right?"

His face wrinkled a bit. Squirmed. "Listen, it's procedure. The right thing to do for now."

"I suppose you also plan on telling me the Feds would like me in protective custody because of my first hand knowledge."

Raised a hand to Rome. "That's not up to me."

A long moment passed, me looking at Rome, wishing he could give me some hope. The agent said, "You guys make it hard for someone to help you. We had planned to take Deputy Lafitte in last night until you, Sheriff, cut him loose."

"Take me in for what, exactly?"

"How about murder? Conspiracy? Treason?" Rome counted them off on his fingers.

Whoa, that didn't sound good. It hadn't really occurred to me just how bad this looked. Why not just give up Paul, then? It had been an easy choice before the threat had ballooned like this. Why weren't the words spilling out, then? Jesus, what was wrong with me? Asimov surely wouldn't be a fountain of truth when faced with a horde of Fibbies. Telling them he had sold out to terrorists was pretty much the same thing as wrapping a towel around your head and waving an AK-47. What it felt like was that I needed to hear it from him first. I didn't care how bad it looked right now. No way I was throwing him to the lions without making sure he was beyond redemption. He was the one telling me we could be a team again. Doing that would feel better than giving in to the suits in sterile rooms.

It occurred to me, too, that Graham wasn't putting on as much of an act as I assumed anyone in his position might. The guy really thought of me as family. It was an obligation to him.

I had to clear my throat. "I appreciate your help, Graham."

"No problem. You deserve that much

respect, at least. I know some good lawyers from The Cities who might be willing to take your case. You should get one, let him push for a deal if you'll cooperate. They'll do it. Terrorists are more important than mobsters."

"Don't go filling his head with that shit." Rome stopped pacing, braced his arms on Graham's desk. Stared into me. "There's one deal and one deal only—you tell us everything you know, and maybe you get put away in a minimum-security prison, one of those country clubs."

"I don't deserve that. You know it. I want to keep my job, stay here."

"That's a pipe dream now. Not an option. Think about it. What's the alternative? They'll put you in a real jail. You'll never even see a trial. It's my way or you're toast."

I didn't want my kids thinking their father was a traitor, carted off to prison. Not like I was being Superdad anyway, but I liked thinking that one day I could be a part of their lives again. Maybe even regain some sort of friendship with Ginny. Hope is what kept me going through lousy winters at this shithole backwater department. Hope that the exile was only temporary.

Graham was right. I didn't get to choose anymore, so I had to ask myself what was the better option.

I took the dried but crinkled photo pages out of my jacket pockets and handed them over to Graham. "These arrived at my house. Probably yesterday. I didn't get them until this morning."

He flipped through. "This is the girl you were with?"

Almost said, *You know I wasn't*, but was sick of arguing about it. "Heather, yeah."

"And we know Ian."

Rome peeked in from the side as Graham made a bad noise. "See what I mean?"

"My God, that's awful." The sad turn of his lips signaled his vulnerability, something that would drive him out of this job eventually. He would take in more and more darkness and then have to make a decision—live with it or exorcise it. You could read his decision with each new photo.

"Did they arrive in this condition?"

"I threw up on them. Sorry. Shock to the system."

He let go of them. They floated to his desk, scattered. A solemn nod, a pastor giving counsel. All I had to do for absolution was say

That knife? It's mine. Someone broke into my big red truck and took it.

Someone. One of those Asians. Stealing an insurance policy. Then I wondered if maybe Paul had been the one... Shit, no. Then again, I had left him at the house alone while I was wasting time getting lectured. It was fine, I assured myself. Paul wouldn't have come to warn me if he was out to get me. It just didn't make any sense.

"If that's all, I should go pack a bag," I said, already pushing up from the chair.

"Okay, sure. Get someone to drive you home."

"I want to come along," Rome said.

"Can't I just use my truck? One last time?"

"Are you completely insane?"

Graham stood, clamped a hand on Rome's shoulder. "Give the guy some breathing room, all right? You'll have plenty of time together later on, kids. How about it, a favor for me?" His expression was stone. The voice was level. He didn't wait for Rome to answer before turning to me. "Get someone to drive you home. Be back in an hour."

I sat on the edge of Layla's desk and said, "He

told me I could use Big Red. They don't need it anymore."

That same stone expression I got from Graham.

"Come on."

Layla unlocked one of her desk drawers, pulled it open just a bit. "I always forget to lock that one. You want some coffee? I feel like a cup."

"Okay."

She took a slow motion walk to the break room. Why she liked me enough to risk her job, I had no idea. Sometimes the blessings fall and you don't question them. In the drawer, right on top, were my keys.

The truck was parked out front. Graham hadn't bothered to impound it or anything. Maybe if I asked nicely he would fix the window for free.

Not after you steal your own truck.

Funny when you think of it that way. Having to steal my own truck. That's exactly what I did.

SEVENTEEN

I wanted to race back to my house and beat Asimov to a pulp. My head was filling up with brutal pictures—it was *Paul* holding my knife. It was *Paul* thrusting his dick into Heather's bruised mouth. Maybe not, but it was the only thing I could think about. I had to know for sure. Did he really sell his soul on this one? After all, he had been a guest in my *home*. Both of them, now. He'd hugged my ex-wife, held my kids. That's the guy who was setting me up to take the fall for *terrorists*?

No, I got it - it was to take the fall for Asimov, let him fade into the background noise again, a ghost, so that when I tried to blame him they'd think I was not only a traitor, but batshit insane as well.

Fuck that. It wasn't going to happen.

That was the plan anyway. Only one thing could run me off the rails.

The cell phone rang. I looked at the number.

Drew's. I nearly swerved off the road, held steady and opened the phone with my chin.

"Hello? Hello?"

"Billy," she said. Her voice shook.

"Are you all right?"

"Jesus, what's going on? I just...somebody else tried to run me off the road. Tried to *kill* me, Billy!"

"I'm coming. Tell me where you are."

"I'm driving in circles. I don't know where to go. Why are people trying to kill me?" Drew coughed, cleared her throat. It wasn't fair, what she was going through.

"Don't the police have someone watching you?"

She said, "They don't send the bodyguard until sundown."

"That's all?" What assholes. This is how they treat a murder victim's girlfriend, one of my close friends, who'd already been targeted once? She only rated part-time security? "Meet me at the Falls. Five minutes. If you see anyone suspicious, take off." I pulled into the parking lot of the nine hole golf course near my house, spun around, and headed out towards the Falls.

I pulled up just as she parked her Toyota, the

hood dented over the left headlight. She climbed out, hugged herself, and stared at me. She wore a U of M sweatshirt and old jeans, her hair pulled back into a simple tail. Sunglasses too big for her face, amber lenses.

I parked beside her and hopped out, glancing this way and that to see if she'd been followed. Seemed we were clear.

"What happened?"

She waved her hands angrily. "Fucking Chinese guy tried to run me off the road! Whole truckload of them. I had to pull onto the shoulder. Then he gets out with a *gun*, Billy."

"You're okay? He shot at you?"

"Are you insane? I hit him. See the car?" She turned back, pointed. "He bounced off and I took off. I called you."

"Is he dead?"

"No, he got up. Just bruised him."

"What type of vehicle? An SUV? Where?"

"Stop, stop. Too much. It was…that, um…Suzuki. Yeah, SUV." She looked at me, cocked eyebrow. "You know who they are, don't you?"

"Tell me where. I need to know."

"I'm not saying another goddamned word until you tell me what you know."

She stood her ground. I was going to lose.

I just said it. "Ian wasn't involved with drug runners. These guys were terrorists."

Something changed in her, one short blink behind her sunglasses. "I don't understand."

"That brand on his ass was the mark of some homespun terror group. They wanted to raise some quick money by taking over drug operations in the Midwest. Meth, heroin, smuggling across the Canadian border, lots of stuff. They wanted to do it from behind the scenes, make it look like Chinese organized crime."

"You're shitting me, Billy. I don't like it."

"No, babe, really. I'm not kidding."

"But why me? Why Ian? Our *band*?"

I let out a breath, looked away. "They thought I was going to help them. So they're trying to set me up in order to convince me to do what they want. If not, I get locked away for a long time.

She stared at the Falls, a manmade dip of about ten feet, lots of ducks swimming around at the bottom of it. The rush of it was intoxicating, even if it wasn't all that impressive. I had to snap my fingers to bring her back.

"Oh. God. I'm going to throw up."

"I don't really know what else to say."

Drew said, "Terrorists in Pale Falls? We're not, like, New York or anything. Why us?"

"It's all about the money. They came from Detroit."

She turned her face to me. I wanted to kiss her glossy lips, let her know I'd protect her. I'd massacre the guys who killed her band, who had tried to kill her. I'm talking pliers and fingernails, screwdrivers and eyeballs, nails and balls. If she'd only give me a chance. *Go ahead, say it: give me a chance.*

She said, "How do you know they came from Detroit?"

Did I want to lie again? "Look, don't worry about that."

She dug in her jeans pocket, came out with a keychain bottle of pepper spray. "No, it sounds like you must've screwed them over and now they're taking revenge."

"I had no idea about any of this until *you* asked me to help Ian."

"Fine fucking job you did, too!"

I stepped towards her, too fast, too mad. She held up the spray but couldn't bring herself to blast me. She winced, waiting for me to slap her, I guessed. Instead, I gently took the bottle from her fingers and dropped it to the ground.

"Drew, I swear I didn't want any of this. I messed up big time, but I'm trying. You've got to believe me. I don't want anyone to hurt you. I don't want anyone else to get hurt at all."

I reached for her arm, a light touch. She grabbed hold, pulled me into her embrace. After a long minute, she pushed me away. "No, don't do that. You can't expect me -"

"Sorry, no. You're right. It's okay."

The quiet stretched on, us close enough to feel each others' heat, but with a force field between us. She lifted her chin, a Mona Lisa smile on her lips. "They won't get us. We're too smart for them."

I liked that. She was a tough one. She'd be fine. The ducks and the rush of the falls soothed our fears for the moment. Nothing out there in the big bad world could get to us right then and there. For the first time in days, a little glimmer of happiness. Not just the high of a good fuck or a bottle of wine, but true happiness. Drew had forgiven me for my mistakes on this. She had found the right people to blame for Ian's death. With her on my side again, what was to come next didn't seem so overwhelming after all.

I said, "Look, right now you need to get to the sheriff. Tell him what happened. Don't stop on the way. Fast as you can to the sheriff. I need to pick up someone, bring him in. I'll meet you there."

"Can't you just follow me?"

I thought of everything Asimov could be doing at my house to drag me deeper into this. "I don't have time. We need to move fast."

"You know, I still don't trust you. But I do think you'd do damn near anything to protect me. "She leaned over, pecked me on the cheek. "Thank you for that."

I was dying to kiss those glossy lips. I bet they were cool, like mint. I hated mint. But I wouldn't have minded right then. "Get out of here. I'll catch up."

She climbed in and drove away, the look on her face one I'd never forget, like the memory of my fourth date with Ginny. That night on the beach, mid-summer. One of her sandals washed away in the surf, us laughing as she waded out knee high trying to get it. It didn't work. So I tossed one of my sandals in after it. We kissed with the waves lapping around us, one shoe apiece. A permanent mental photo. So was Drew and me by those falls during the spring thaw in Minnesota. Maybe not romance, but that girl brought out the *want* in me.

EIGHTEEN

On the way back home I imagined what it would've been like asking Drew to run away with me instead. Just grab her and go. Send one big lump check to my kids right before I set out on the road. It made for a sweet distraction, singing along to George Jones in the radio along the way: "Oooooh…White Lightnin'". Felt like a love song to me. I thought about telling Drew she should cover it with her band, then remembered her band was dead.

Well, hell, that's what we'd do—start a new band. I could be the manager, muscle some nightclub owners. Sure, we could pull it off. Find a joint in Vancouver that would let the band do half-psycho and half-lounge, whatever the customers wanted. What would they call themselves? I liked the word "pirates". Maybe "Psychopirates" or, hell, why not "The

Decapitated Terrorists"?

I turned into the driveway and saw an unfamiliar vehicle parked behind Paul's. End of the fantasy, back to reality. It was the Suzuki Drew had described. Guessing who had rented it was easy enough. And me without my gun.

I thought of what they'd just done to Drew, so I didn't slow down. I slammed into the SUV's bumper. Rattled the fuck out of me. It wasn't going anywhere unless the driver wanted a demolition derby. I climbed out, figured at best they were waiting to talk to me, at worst were waiting to finish me. Quick peek in the front room windows—the older of the two guys I'd had lunch with was standing, watching. Paul was seated on the couch and the younger one was in my favorite chair, reclined, legs crossed and head back.

That was my only advantage.

I stepped inside. Paul couldn't look me in the eye. The other two could. The younger one twisted his neck to face me. "It is about time."

"For what?"

"For us to come to an understanding. And now you owe us a truck."

I crossed my arms. "You know, I never asked to be involved in the first place. Didn't I run you two out of town? But here you are, and I hear you‘re still putting the pressure on my friends."

"No matter now. Asimov says you're involved, so you are."

Paul shook his head. "I never actually said that, remember? It was only a suggestion."

Two steps. I grabbed the chair and pulled hard until the whole thing flipped backwards, the twerp with it. He kicked and tried to push himself up. I put a boot on his throat, held it. His buddy started towards me. I held up an empty hand.

"Another inch, I crush him."

The big guy shouted loudly in his own language and I didn't know what the hell was going on except this kid beneath me choking, trying to pry my foot off his neck. Then, more noise. Off to the left, coming from my kitchen. I looked up in time to see a couple of other Asian men, bearded, both in black T-shirts and khakis, rushing towards me. I retreated quickly to the door but not fast enough. They were on me—one grabbing hold of my arms while the other punched me in the face and stomach. Each pop connected, my skin giving way, sounding squishy. He was hitting me with brass knuckles.

Paul was up, coming to my rescue. "Hey, that wasn't the deal!"

I took another punch and felt the skin tear over my eye.

The Big Man took out a pistol, took aim at Paul. That shut him up, sat him down. The twerp I'd choked was on his feet, spewing like a chicken thrown through a jet engine.

That's a cute comparison, the sort of shit you think up when you're about to pass out. Which I did.

I wasn't out for long. Barely a few minutes. It was getting dragged outside across the gravel and rocks of my driveway, around the garage into the wide backyard that bordered the Minnesota River, that woke me up. The pain was coming at me from all sides and it was cold.

When they dropped my legs, I opened my good eye. Five men standing over me. The sky gray-black behind them. More snow? No, spring was finally poking through. This would be the wind moving in.

The younger man was still holding his throat. The knife was in his other hand, held low, fingers tight on the handle. He looked as if he would slice out my intestines and leave me to hold them in if the others allowed it. That might be the better option, considering what they did to Elvis Antichrist.

"Who are you?" I said. "Really."

The older man smiled. "I'm Wally. That's The Beav."

They all laughed except Paul, standing at the edge of their circle with his arms crossed.

The two bruisers damn near fell over laughing. One said, "Eddie Haskell!"

Paul crouched beside me. "The whole thing's fucked, man. These guys, well, I should've told you first."

I pushed up on my elbows, whispered to Paul, "Did you know what they were? Really?"

He turned his face to the river, finally saying, "Maybe. I needed something, you know? I needed guidance, meaning…"

"You're not, like, *them* or anything."

"No, no, I mean, you run into some guys living in my apartment complex, ask them some questions. They sound like they have commitment, honor, like they have a real fucking cause, you know. I'm no fan of the government myself after what happened on the Coast. Maybe I wasn't thinking straight."

"They recruited you?"

"Didn't feel that way at the time. I just needed a place to fit in. It's not like I pray to Mecca. Couple of Saudis introduced me to a couple of Malaysians who needed help getting things." He looked down on me, hand resting on my shoulder. "On my own, I'm pretty good. But I thought with us working together…you weren't supposed to know about these guys."

"What was I supposed to do, then?"

"Get a system going, protect it, and look the other way while the money funneled back to Detroit."

"You thought I'd want to be under someone else's thumb?"

Paul shrugged. "For the money, maybe."

"I thought you knew me better than that."

He leaned closer, whispered. "I'm sorry, I really am. I had no idea."

"You've got to say something to them. Come on."

"Listen." He swiveled his head, checked out the Asians. Then, to me: "In case this goes bad, I left you something."

"What?"

"Just trust me, okay? You still like brunettes more than blondes, right?"

He was talking nonsense. "Paul, what are they going to do to us?"

He started to say something else, but the big man said, "Enough talk, all lovey-dovey. Plan didn't work, so you two no longer needed. All evidence points back to Lafitte. We make it look like he killed the drug dealers, killed the band, and those students, then killed you, too. Next, he'll have risen from the grave to kill his redneck Sheriff. And his niece, his nephew."

Paul looked over his shoulder. "Hey, this isn't our fault. If you'd just let us do what we do best—"

"No, not anymore."

He had the gun in his hand before either of us could react, an auto with a silencer, pointblank at Paul's temple. I watched the bullet exit, spew blood and brain across the sky, rain down on me as his body collapsed in slow motion, going to land on top of me. Please, not Paul. I needed Paul. I was supposed to be the one saving his life. I couldn't beat these guys alone.

My body reacted: Roll, roll, roll!

I did. Paul's body missed me. I glanced over my shoulder, willing him to *move.* Maybe I had seen the whole thing wrong. That wasn't his brains. Yeah, he would pop right up and help me kick some terrorist ass.

No movement. He was gone. And it looked like I was next.

I swept the legs of one bruiser. He went down, and I was up. Another bullet aimed for me took out the bruiser's shoulder. He let out a wail and I started running. A big open yard. Too far away from the garage, the driveway. Shit! The closest place to hide—the river.

The embankment was steep and the river was still low, the Spring melt only just beginning. Dead tree limbs had weaved together a wall.

Another shot. A sting on my side and then a fire. The bullet split the flesh under my arm, between ribs. Adrenaline overpowered it enough for me to reach the bank and jump.

Midair.

Falling fast.

I missed the water and was nearly impaled on broken stumps. Bruised, gashed, shot, beaten, but I still had sense to start rolling towards the water. The icy chill was a shock to the system—thought I was going to stroke. But I slipped under, the pain dulling. I kicked. Bullets plopped in around me, missed my head by inches. I kicked. Kicked hard. Kicked and didn't know if I'd live or die but I sure as hell wasn't going to die at their hands, for their twisted reasons, for their cause.

I can't say I blacked out in the water. More like froze out. I would either drown or wake up in a hundred years, a psycho Rip Van Winkle. My mind was protecting itself, sending me towards the light. But then I hit a tree branch, the naked limbs scratching my face, my eye. I thrashed and grabbed at the branch until I was fully awake. My hands were nearly frozen, my fingers numb, but still alive. Which meant pain. Lots of it. And I was still seeing my old partner fall over and over again, an endless cycle. Damn it, it wasn't fair. None of this. If we'd both just played by the goddamned rules. I blocked out Paul as best I could. Didn't want to join him in the afterlife quite yet. I needed to get my ass in gear.

I was sitting in a foot of water near the shore, seething through my teeth, my side throbbing in the icy flow. This looked like an area without easy road access, but I had to believe those guys were on my tail.

I crawled to the bank, not as steep as it was near my home, but still a muddy five foot climb into the woods, which didn't offer as much protection in March as it would only a month later. Everything was gray, stripped. I had climbed out on the opposite side, so at least we were separated by the river, but that didn't stop bullets. I forgot about the wound under my arm until I started walking upstream. I'd never been so cold before, aching whenever I flexed my fingers. My face was ice, stinging worse every time the wind blew. And I could barely see, the skin around my eye caked, swollen, causing me to see double. Hypothermia coming on fast. I had to hurry. A hand to my right side showed me that the bullet had cut across thin skin, leaving a massive cut that pulled wider with every step. I yanked the sleeve off my right arm and tucked it under my arm trying to cover at least part of the wound. Complete failure. But I left it there anyway to soak up new blood.

Walking upstream, yes. Back to the house, back to the truck, back to the only way I knew to get out of there. It was slow going—my clothes were saturated, ten pounds heavier, freezing to my skin. Shoes were like waterlogged sandbags. If the bastards were waiting for me, I wasn't in any shape to run. I would have to hide out until the middle of the night and do some damage with tools from the garage, then take their car. Probably drive to the hospital. Probably tell the sheriff everything I knew, go ahead and tell the Feds the same. Anything. It was the only way left that I could fight back.

If I wasn't dead, that is.

Thinking of home drove my steps. Shivering, aching, bruised, but moving forward. My mind wasn't playing fair: Tell them everything? Okay, sure. All the evidence points to you—your knife in the photos, your old partner vouching for you with the terrorists, your connection to Ian and Heather, the blonde girl's head fished from the river. Tell them your fairy tale, but you're the one going down.

Wait, the Feds knew it was our little terrorists. Rome knew.

No, he knows someone is working with them. Why not you? If it fits, it fits.

Sharp pain, rocketing from side to shoulder to brain. I fell. *Fuck!* I rolled onto my stomach and tried to push up. My chest wasn't having any of it. I wanted to scream out the hurt, but that would give the bastards a blip on the radar to hunt me down.

I held it in. Let the air out slowly. That's

when I decided to stop worrying and get on with it. One step at a time. The house was the only destination. After that, I had all eternity to make up my mind.

I rolled onto my back, feeling the skin rip wider on my side. Anywhere I applied pressure, a rush of river water stunned my skin numb. The throbbing wouldn't stop. It was a steady rhythm of pain, disorientation, my heartbeat shaking the doubled-vision trees. I had to keep going. Sat up, more tearing. Just grit my teeth and did it. Caught my breath for several minutes before getting too cozy, wanting to drift to sleep rather than continue hurting so much.

I slapped my dead face with my dead hand. Another, harder. The new pain dulled the old. I grabbed the nearest tree and pulled myself up. I had promises to keep.

NINETEEN

I woke again. I was looking up at Drew and Graham. Drew sat on the side of the bed—*my bed, I was in my bed*—holding my hand. Graham was over her shoulder.

"Can you hear me?" he said. He snapped his fingers in front of my nose.

"Shut up."

A few more snaps. "What was that?"

I pulled my arm out from the sheets and grabbed his fingers. My grip was weak. He slipped away. To Drew, "Same old self."

"You should see the rest of him."

Graham nodded, a sad grin on his mouth. "I'm just glad he's not dead."

I said, "Are you?"

He stepped around to the other side of the bed, knelt down. "You know there's a dead man in your yard, and the gun that probably killed him is on your living room floor. There's a bunch of files with plans of some sort, some in Chinese or something."

I remembered what Paul had said. Couple of Saudis had introduced him to Malaysians who needed help. "Not Chinese. Malaysian."

"I can't read either. Photos, a list of names. Mine's on it."

He watched my eyes. Casting aside all the gut feelings and good faith, instead relying on his training, thinking of all the suspects he'd ever questioned.

"Graham, I didn't do it."

He took it in, squinted just so, and then looked down with a shrug. "Yeah, I know you didn't, Billy. I wish that were enough, though. I don't know what we can do."

He stood, adjusted his hat. All decked out in uniform, there was nobody I trusted more at that point. He pulled a warrant from his back pocket. "I was supposed to serve this on you if I found you first. Arrest warrant. Agent Rome is pushing hard for it."

"He's crazy. You think that's me? Have you ever seen anything that would make you think—"

"It's not that. It's the money. Rome says someone offered you some money, and that you took it. All cash."

"I turned them down."

Graham raised his voice. "How am I supposed to know that? You know good and well you're hiding a bunch of stuff from me. I've known about the protection money you're getting from meth dealers for a while now. I didn't call you on it, though. As long as you keep sending checks to Ham and Savannah, I was letting it slide. Now I'm supposed to trust you're clean on this all of the sudden?"

I had no clue he'd been onto me. Smarter than the average bear. Not so goody-two-shoes as I first thought, either. The only thing I could think to say was, "If I'd accepted that money, I would've been under their thumb. And if there's one thing you *know* about me, it's I don't like working for anyone but myself."

Another moment, Graham slowly nodding. "One of the things Ginny said to sway me was that at least you'd be low maintenance. Able to amuse yourself. But she also said that's how you get in trouble. I admired that."

Flashed back to what the Malaysians had told us right before they shot Paul: *kill your redneck Sheriff, too…*

"They're coming after you next. Your whole

family. *My* family."

Graham stepped closer. "How do you know?"

"They out and out said it. Said the redneck Sheriff and his kids were next. They wanted to kill me, but still make it look like I had killed you.

"Rice pickers want to call *me* a redneck? You're the Southerner. Why the kids?"

"Anything to get their way. They want me. I said no. That's enough to rile them up."

Graham crumpled the warrant into a ball, threw it across the floor. "I don't believe you deserve this sort of treatment. None of us. The Feds can't help. We need another way. Fast."

I coughed. "When you think of it, let me know."

He turned for the door. "I'm going to get rid of that gun, those papers."

"The papers," I said. "That's evidence."

"Evidence against you. Right now I'm just worried the Feds are about to railroad you." He stopped. "So, who's the guy in the yard?"

"Asimov. He was my partner in Mississippi. He's the reason we're in this mess."

He clapped his hand on the doorframe a couple of times. "If I didn't think your kids needed their father so much…" Then a sigh.

"That man out there was my friend. Not perfect or anything, but I owe him one. I couldn't save his life, but we can at least make his death less, you know, pointless. No one needs to see him like that."

It took Graham a few minutes to let it sink in, but he finally said, "Okay, I'll deal with that, too.

When he left, Drew squeezed my hand.

"What happened?" I said.

"You tell me. You didn't show up. So the sheriff and I drive over, no one's here."

I shivered a little thinking of what would have happened if the terrorists had hung around. I had gambled on them leaving because of all the gunfire, thinking it might draw attention. Not here in the boonies, it wouldn't, but they didn't know that. Drew thought I was cold, lifted the quilt to my shoulders.

She said, "Your truck was in the driveway, the front end smashed and the tires cut to ribbons. I got scared, started shouting for you, looking around. Then the dead guy in the yard." She closed her eyes. I didn't know if she was remembering or erasing. "Which, for just a second, I thought, you know … but then we heard you down by the river."

"I'm not dead yet."

Drew smiled. "I'm starting to think you're a superhero."

"Yeah. My special power is making the world bad for everyone I know."

"At least you can't fly. Then you'd be a *real* ass."

After another hour of recovering, I struggled off the bed and into sweats and my boots before walking outside to watch Graham get rid of Asimov. I could walk but it hurt like hell. I needed to. I still had a little trouble with the eye—hard to judge distance, and I really had to concentrate to focus. The sun had warmed the air just enough so that I didn't want a jacket, being that time of year between winter and spring that made you hate the changes until it had all changed already. Deadly wind. Nearly all the snow had melted in the past couple of days. The ground in the river valley wasn't quite as hard as it was on the prairies.

When I caught up with Graham behind my garage in the acre of yard bordering the river, he was trying to dig a grave in that cold dirt.

"What're you doing?" I said.

He kept shoveling. "Don't worry, I can handle it. We've got time."

"No, I mean, 'why'? A fresh grave might draw some attention, you think?"

He set a foot on top of the blade, leaned the handle against his shoulder, hugged it. "Mm hm."

"What?"

"I don't see another way." He turned his head, looking at me over his shoulder. Me, hobbling. Me, bruised and barely able to speak for the pain, only able to see out of one eye. Me, saved by Graham. Even then I still challenged him. It's just that he hadn't spent enough time in his life thinking about ways to lose evidence and bodies and witnesses. I had.

"We can put him on the burn pile."

Graham nodded. I was surprised by how he was taking all this. "That won't take care of the bones, though."

"We'll get rid of those later. Right now we've got work to do."

"Are you able to help drag him over there?"

Again, I had to hold my tongue. Finally said, "I've got an axe and some tools in the garage. I'll do what I can, but you'll have to carry my load."

He dropped the shovel. "No, wait, no."

"It's the best way. Smaller pieces burn much faster."

"Jesus, Billy. He was your partner."

I looked down at Paul's bloody face, eyes frozen open. The thick blood made him nearly impossible to sympathize with. It could be my own son, Ham, and I'd probably build the same wall—it just wasn't him. I didn't like that about myself, but it wasn't the time to make a change. "Exactly. I'm doing him a favor. Let's go."

A hand ax. The shovel. A rusty saw. We spent the next hour dismembering Asimov. Gagging, turning away. We both stopped two or three times, said, "I can't do it," then got our shit together and started again. When I swung the ax, my sore muscles flared. The best I could do after that was pull the arms and legs taut while Graham hacked and sawed through muscle, ligament, bone. We had to twist the limbs from the joints like you would a chicken wing. Paul's joints made the same sounds. That's what you remember when you chop up your friend, the weird noises and the surprise at finding just how well we're put together. The worst was when I had to bash the teeth out of his skull with the back of the ax. Had to pick them out of his mouth one by one.

No funeral, no words, not even a moment of silence. We carried the pieces two at the time over to the pile of tree branches, dead leaves, cardboard boxes, broken furniture, dead squirrels, and used charcoal from the grill, threw them on. We kept looking around like we expected to get caught, but there was nothing but an abandoned house next door, a deserted boat launch, the river, and Drew occasionally looking out the window for a few moments before disappearing again.

When all of Paul was scattered on the burn pile, Graham soaked it with lighter fluid. I flicked a match and tossed it on. Then another, another, and another. The flames spread, caught the rough breaks on the branches, the leaves that weren't wet. The dampness caused more smoke than you'd see when we burned leaves in the fall, but eventually everything burned low and steady. The wind chilled us and we stood closer to the fire, shoulder to shoulder.

"Were you close?" Graham said.

"Close as partners." I hunched my shoulders, tried to zone out the aches. "Loyal, but definitely different. We didn't hang out much off duty, and while I was the type who'd bend the rules, you know—"

"Hm," he said, then he chuckled, grinned.

"—yeah, yeah. Well Paul just out and out broke them. A lot of my bending had to do with protecting him. Because of that, I guess he trusted me more than he should have. Always thought I'd go along."

"And did you?"

"To a point. Too far probably." I waited for him to ask something else. He didn't. But I felt a need to spill. Maybe it was the "nearly dying" thing. "I killed a drug dealer who was blackmailing Paul. Guy had already been busted, was trying to make a deal, but figured it was more important to have the upper hand inside. Protection, right? A cop in your pocket, you're a king in the joint."

"Pretty smart."

"Except that he wanted money, too. Wanted a bribe to keep his mouth shut. Wouldn't budge. We told him over and over that having us on his side was enough. But the fucker kept rubbing his fingers together, pulling this 'all about the Benjamins' shit he'd seen on TV. No business sense at all."

"I see."

"We think it was a cop show, with the bald guy? Some sort of gangsta godfather had him by the balls. Asimov told our guy that the difference was on TV, they had to stretch it out for more shows. In real life we just end your ass."

"Then what?"

"Well, we did it. Boom. Guy was threatening our families, our jobs, all that."

He grunted. Both of us still watching the fire. The hypnotic effect of the flames almost made me forget it was a funeral pyre until I focused on Paul's finger bones. I let it blur again.

Graham said, "But I thought you said you did it. Not 'us'. You."

I shrugged, didn't like the feeling. "For both of us. I was the one with the shotgun. We'd taken it from the scene of a robbery, kept it just in case. As far as anyone knows, our godfather was shot with a stolen twelve-gauge. I've never told anyone else this."

Another chuckle from Graham, a much less funny joke. "I can see why."

"So you want to take me in? Get this over with?"

"Is that what you want?"

My swollen eye burned. I covered it with my palm. What *did* I want, anyway? "As long as Drew is safe—"

"Geez, you're like a broken record. Shut up for a minute, all right?"

I shut up. I don't think I'd ever heard him be so direct. Maybe it had been there all along, but religion or the wife or the kids had kept it in check.

He said, "There were rumors about the shooting. I heard them when I called around before hiring you on. But at the time, I had someone else telling me to trust you, and I was willing to hear her out."

"Ginny." It wasn't a question.

"You already know she went to bat for you big time. When I asked about the rumor, though, she said if it were true, the scum deserved it."

"Wow." I'd assumed all this time she hated me for what I had done as a cop. Never once thought she was on my side. I didn't know what to say.

"Anyway, the point is that I knew you weren't the cleanest cop out there, but I also knew you were loyal, sort of. And I knew you didn't want to lose your job because of your kids. I mean, that's my niece and nephew we're talking about, too. If I believed for one minute you were screwing around with terrorists, well..." He trailed off, waved his hand towards the fire.

The grass rustled behind us. I turned my head. Drew was easing up to my side, covering her eyes with the sleeves of a sweater. "Is it safe to look?"

I tried to put my arm around her. It hurt way too much. She stepped away.

She said to the sheriff, "I'm so sorry. That was terrible. I don't know how you could do it."

"Had to be done," Graham said.

After a while I said, "So why help me? Just curious, you know. Why not go by the book?"

"Because you won't get a break from the Feds. They'd pretty much drop you in a hole you can't escape from, question you fifteen hours a day even though you don't have any answers." He glanced at Drew, then me. Back to the flames. "I heard the way they were talking about you that night. Even Rome. You're as bad as Osama himself."

Drew rubbed my back. "He's the most honest liar I've ever met, at least. I don't know why I still trust him, but I do."

Graham said, "I think it's charisma."

"Or my pretty face," I said. "So what next?"

"I hope the Malaysians left town. Maybe they think you're a loose end already taken care of."

"I doubt it. They'll assume Paul told me everything, so they'll need to see me dead with their own eyes."

"Did he? Tell you?" Graham said.

My turn to grin. Asimov had gotten me into trouble, yes indeed. But he also gave me a ticket out as a parting gift. "Sure as hell."

TWENTY

The wounds would have to heal along the way. I had Drew stitch the slice under my arm as best she could with the first aid kit from Graham's cruiser. It took nineteen. I powered through it. She bandaged the cut above my eye. Otherwise, I'd just have to fake it until my focus came back. Then, dirty jeans and black boots. A bowling shirt, two pins with devil tails crossed on the back with a foxy femme fatale right in the middle. Leather jacket.

Combed and slicked my hair back like Gene Vincent Reborn. Shaved the mustache. I was ready.

We were invading Detroit. Taking it to the Malaysians' backyard where the orders were being shouted out. On their own, our terrorists were powerless. We wanted to find the source, arrange a "final meeting" on our terms. Graham's idea. This whole business and the threats against his family had lit him up in a way I hadn't expected. I wondered what he would do if I weren't involved—let the FBI run with it? Go home and line his windows with heavy-duty plastic, buy bulletproof vests for the kids? Move farther out into farm country than he already was? I'd thought of giving up just hours earlier. Not worth it. But whatever he saw in my false front was feeding him courage.

The Malaysians had taken Paul's rental car, but I thought about what he told me right before they shot him. Said he'd "left me something", then asked if I still preferred brunettes over blondes. Maybe he hid some evidence in a place his keepers wouldn't suspect. Graham, Drew, and I needed a place to start. We each took a room. Only took twenty minutes for me to get into Paul's head, notice a box in the office, three from the top of a four box pile I still hadn't unpacked. The tape on one side was loose. I moved the other boxes, found that the tape had been ripped off across the top. If Paul had looked in others first, then he did a good job backtracking with new tape. Inside were back issues of Playboy from the eighties, some of my dad's that had been passed down to me, collectors' items.

So…which one?

The top was too easy. Bottom was the same principle. Paul must've thought it through. He remembered what Ginny looked like. Brunette. Most of the girls I went for. Drew, too. Maybe he chose a deadringer? I didn't think there were any. My fingers walked through the pile. He was in a hurry. You want it to be loud.

It was plenty loud. Bright red, too.

"Women of Canada." On the cover, a drop-dead brunette in a red mountie uniform. A cop.

I yanked the issue from the stack, flipped, and found folded pages, some emails, all coded but easy to crack once you knew the players. The others were handwritten notes, some in Paul's careful block letters the same as his reports, but others scrawled as if written in a big hurry. Then, a Mapquest printout of four addresses in Detroit. I guessed our little wannabe terrorists moved around a lot. I hoped we weren't too far behind the curve.

"Found it," I shouted. Graham came in from the kitchen, then Drew a few moments later. He took the pages, looked through, nodded stiffly the way he always did.

Soon as the fire died to ashes and embers, he would be right beside me bagging the bones.

We would spread them along the roadside wilderness on the drive from Pale Falls to Detroit, some sixteen hours east. One day I'd make sure Paul's family found out what really happened to him, sort of. By then I'll probably say he went hiking alone, never returned. Attacked by a bear, most likely.

I told Graham, "You're in charge, Sheriff. It's your call."

Drew looked nervous. I didn't know what to say to her—I wanted her to come along, and so did she, but how do you break it to Graham? He flipped a couple more pages, glanced up—me, then Drew, then, "Your tires are flat, and there's no way we can take the cruiser and be conspicuous. I guess that leaves us looking for a ride."

Drew said, "Mine's good on gas."

"Kind of old, isn't it?"

"They last forever."

Another official head nod before saying, "Well that seals it. Let me call George, tell him to get a few deputies to keep watch at my house."

"You can't tell him where we're going, though."

"I'll just say something came up in the case."

He grinned. "I'll tell him it's classified. That'll do it. Then I'll call home, see if the kids can't skip school for a couple days."

He stared at the cell phone in his hand another long moment. I wished I could say something to help, or tell him to go home, protect his family. But I was being selfish. I needed his help to get a little revenge.

When he left the room, Drew said, "I'm scared, but I'd feel worse sitting at home. I hope it's okay if I come along."

"It's better than okay. It's the right thing to do."

She giggled, suddenly turning on her stage persona, then said "Let me doll myself up. Never know who you'll meet at a truck stop."

TWENTY-ONE

We were in a working-class suburb outside of Detroit. A not-too-dirty row of townhouses. Graham and I stood at the door marked 4 and knocked. We heard shuffling. We leaned against the door on either side of the eyehole. He could still see us, but not as clearly as he would've liked.

"Who is it?" Heavily accented. Arab.

Graham said, "Friends."

A pause. He was checking us out. "You have the wrong house."

"Are you sure? Paul told us otherwise."

"I don't know anyone named Paul."

I said, "He said you would say that. He also said to tell you 'I like Disney cartoons. Let's rent one.'"

It had been in his notes. This address, the name "Aziz", and the secret phrase.

Aziz, if that's who this was, waited another half a minute before finally unlocking the door and opening it as if were made of stone. We had to look down. Short guy, maybe five four. He had a close-cropped haircut, no beard. Tiny wire-rimmed glasses. And he wore an Italian soccer jersey over jeans.

"Paul sent you?"

I nodded. "He's had some trouble, didn't have your number handy. We're going to help him but he wanted us to clear it with you first."

"Me?"

Maybe we'd fucked up. Paul had jotted down "contact" and a couple of other words we couldn't make out—written quickly, probably on his knees. The words curved down, letters spaced out. Still, the door was open.

Graham looked out at the street, the neighboring townhouses. "Not on the porch, man. They'll get photos of us."

Without waiting for an invite, he stepped past Aziz, who was still thinking about the imaginary surveillance. We had staked the place out for a few hours. He didn't know we were watching, and we knew for damn sure no one was watching him. All the better for us. No telling when the Feds might pop up along this trail, but we kept the radar on.

I followed Graham. Aziz closed the door and jittered. "Really? Paul did this? I'm being watched?"

A tight hallway, empty of adornment. Off to the left, a narrow living room. The furniture looked stock. Probably furnished when he moved in. I caught a flash of movement, blonde hair, and a woman's whisper: "Oh shit!"

She reached for a headscarf that was draped across the armrest. I caught the side of her face. A white girl, maybe eighteen.

Aziz stepped over to her, held up his palms. "No no no, is okay. Americans, see?"

She wrapped the scarf around her hand like a boxer taping his knuckles, grinned shyly at us. Not like the rest of her was modest anyway—barefoot in lowrise jeans and midriff-baring tank top. I made a wild guess that Aziz was in college, was enjoying the attention of American girls and culture. He leaned over, whispered in her ear. She leaned her cheek against his and made a kissing noise before settling back onto the couch and turning to the flat screen TV. Maury was on. More paternity tests.

Aziz led the way into the kitchen. Again, the furniture and appliances were functional, cheap, clean. A few dishes in the sink, the faint smell of cinnamon. We sat at the table.

Graham leaned towards the young man. "Why did Paul tell us to come to you if you can't help? This is getting ridiculous."

"Hey, I can help. I can. It's a surprise is all. I haven't talked to him in a long time."

"What's a long time?"

"I don't know. Three, four months?"

I played along, a sarcastic bark while starting to stand. "Let's get out of here. Let him play with his Barbie doll in there."

Graham nodded, and Aziz got a little louder.

"Sit, please, sit. It's fine, really. I can handle this." He didn't hide fear well. Good.

I shook my head, fists on my hips, then sat, faked being over all this, the little boy playing American for the cause, but becoming all "corrupted". Anything to redeem himself.

"Did Paul say why he needed help?"

Graham said, "The Americans were already on his trail. He didn't pick up their scent until our friends provided them with bait. You've heard?"

"Yes. I know."

"That was a bad mistake."

"I said I know." Stony stare. He was on our

side after all.

I peeked over my shoulder towards the sounds from the living room. It sounded like she'd turned the volume down to listen in. Maury shouted, "You are *not* the father" and the audience whooped it up.

So I got conspiratorial. "You know what this looks like, right? Your woman in there. You might have reasons to hold up our plans."

"She's a friend. I'm supposed to be a part of the culture."

"Looked like more than a friend."

"That's none of your business." Then he said something in Arabic, slowly, playfully, in my face. It seemed to satisfy him. So Graham grabbed him by the scalp and yanked him half a foot off the chair.

"Is that smart, what you just did? Is it smart to think you can play both sides and get away with it? We've got to clean up a mess that shouldn't have been spilled, and we've also got to think about why it was spilled in the first place. If you aren't the man we're supposed to talk to, then point us the right way. Maybe we'll keep our mouths shut about you know who in there."

The volume on the TV went back up. Aziz

was breathing through clenched teeth, eyes on Graham until the sheriff let him go.

The girl called out, "Is everything okay? You want some Bacardi and Cokes?"

"It's fine! Don't bother us." Aziz seemed more embarrassed by her than by Graham's rough treatment. To us, he said, "It's very hard sometimes. They…they just throw themselves on you. The clothes they wear. It's very hard."

I played with the salt-shaker, spinning it in the air, catching it, salt grains flying across the table. "Don't tell us. We're Americans. We're just in it for the money."

He thought about that for another minute, looked confused. "Then maybe you would like that drink after all."

I smiled. "Sorry, no rum for me. I only drink the blood of Christ."

Aziz turned to me, eyebrows crunched together, but whatever he wanted to say faded before he opened his mouth, his gaze rising to my swollen eye. "What happened to you, anyway?"

Graham cleared his throat, said, "We don't have much time."

"Did Paul tell you exactly who I should ask?" Aziz sounded confused.

Actually, Paul *had* told us. The notes contained a chart, a hierarchy. Aziz was the bottom. He was the least important and therefore would've been the last to find out that Asimov was already dead. The only reason to come to him first was to get the new clearances that were surely in place now since Paul had written his notes.

Graham shrugged, made an act of it. "Guess we're on a 'need to know' basis. What do you think?"

Aziz thought it over. Checked his watch. I did too. We'd been there fifteen minutes. Maybe too long, probably not long enough. But every minute wasted there was a chance we'd get nailed for this. Graham's wife already thought he was having an affair after she called Layla and discovered there was no prisoner transfer. The department had called him at least a dozen times, left messages. Rome had left seven for me, all of them loud and full of "assclown" and "lunatic" and threats of charges I'd never heard of before—"conspiracy to inhibit a government investigation via treason through mental incapacitation"—so I knew he was making shit up. He'd called Drew's mother, too, and was threatening to take her into custody.

Drew's reaction: "Mom's the toughest bitch I know. She'll be fine."

We'd been planning on Aziz's hesitation. That so I could say, "Listen, let's skip the hoops and go right the source. Forget the phone. Come with us."

Another glance at his watch. "Now?"

"You got other plans? Is Dr. Phil on after Maury?"

For a moment I wondered if we'd bungled the research, got the Muslim "call to prayer" times wrong. Five times a day. Maybe our watches were slow. Again, we thought we could force him into quicker action if the pressure was on. It would either work or backfire. Coin flip. That was all we had on such short notice.

Aziz finally nodded. "Okay. Let me get a jacket."

He stood and we followed. The girl asked where he was going.

"Business. Just business," he said. We stayed close as he opened the closet by the front door and reached inside. He was taking a bit too long. He brought his arm out of the closet too fast, but not fast enough. Graham had already caught hold of the guy's arm, thrust it up. Aziz squealed, dropped something. I grabbed it. A snubnose thirty-eight revolver.

Graham body-blocked Aziz against the back of the closet, clothes stretched on their hangers, some snapping off with a *ping*. The girl rushed in from the living room, her head covered this time. I didn't have time to second-guess. Grabbed her at the waist from behind. Gouged my arm with the steak knife in her hand. I held on. She kicked her heel into my toes over and over. Didn't phase me. Steel-toed boots versus bare heels. No contest. She struggled and shouted, but I slipped my arm around her neck, applied pressure, cut off the blood to her brain. After thrashing some more, banging her elbow on my stitches, she shut up for a minute and I got the knife out of her hand, dropped it on the floor. I ripped the veil off and used it as a gag.

I asked Graham, "You got him?"

"Yes indeed. You got her?"

"Almost."

I dragged her into the kitchen with one arm wrapped around while I rooted through drawers with my free hand. No rope, no appliance cords long enough. I found a box of plastic wrap. It would have to do. I pinned the girl's arms behind her back, shook the tube of wrap from the box, and bound her wrists with it. Then sat her in a kitchen chair and wrapped her tightly around her chest and the back of the chair. A temporary fix at best.

"So," I said, kneeling in front of her. I was breathing hard, wondering if any stitches had popped. Something sure burned. Three of her floated in front of me. I had to blink a few times to bring just one of those into view. "Your boyfriend has you trained pretty well."

Her breath through the scarf was loud and wet. She swallowed hard, inhaled through her nose. It whistled.

"If I take this out, I only want one thing from you—the name of the group you and Aziz belong to."

She stared a long moment, her gaze trailing off towards the blood on my sleeve where she'd cut me. Then, a nod.

I tugged the gag down past her chin. "One thing."

"Burn in hell." Not even a second to think about it.

"Your loss." I forced the gag back in place while she tried to bite me, then took off my shirt to examine where she'd pricked me. Nasty bugger, but nothing compared to what I'd been through already. I grabbed a paper towel, folded and placed it over the wound, and rolled the plastic wrap around my arm. Then I checked on Graham.

He'd moved Aziz from the closet to the carpet in the hall, face down, Graham's knees on the twerp's back and neck.

"Anything yet?"

"Paul had told him about you. Even showed him a photo. Without your mustache it took him too long to figure it out."

"Son of a bitch."

"At least he didn't know, you know."

"About what?" Aziz said. It was muffled in the carpet.

"Shut up." I tapped his nose with my steel-toe. "Hey, I need to borrow a shirt and jacket. You won't mind."

He said. "I'll sacrifice myself before I help you. They'll kill us all."

As I started up the stairs to search for clothes, I answered, "They already tried."

It had taken over a day to get to Detroit. We switched driving duties while the others slept. We ate at truck stops. We pissed and shit at truck stops. We bought truck stop coffee. Kept mostly quiet. Listened to talk radio, set our cell phones on vibrate and ignored them most of the time.

Once in town, we holed up in a Holiday Inn Express, enduring the raised eyebrows of the desk girl when we said we only wanted one room and wanted to pay cash. It was my first visit to Detroit, and I was overwhelmed by industry—left, right, everywhere you looked from the interstate once you hit the outskirts. I'd been more surprised by Michigan on the way over—the woods, trees in bloom, the hills. I'd expected the whole state to be industrial sludge. Live and learn.

Armed with Asimov's notes and no earthly idea what to do first, or what to do once we found who we were looking for, we talked strategy and ate fried chicken from the gas station next door to the hotel. We debated who to target first. We tossed out the full bore approach because we guessed the Feds and the terrorists both might be on guard.

"It seemed like a good idea at the time," Drew had said. She was stretched on her side across one of the beds, hand propping her head. "Somewhere around Chicago, though, I didn't get it."

Graham and I started to answer. We both stopped. Hoped the other had a better answer. He said, "I don't want to fight on their terms. I just want them to leave."

What was the point of going after them? Better than sitting at home to wait for two underlings to rain down death again. Better than watching our little slice of Midwest heaven, as much as I hated it most days, become infected with fear and pointless death. Religion? Politics? Fuck it. It came down to something much more primal—control. And the best way to do that was to manipulate the players. Why else would 'Roid Ragers listen to the little man in the striped shirt? Who made up these rules, anyway?

I turned to the window when I answered, getting a view of the parking lot, a Burger King, the gas station, an overflowing dumpster. "When I was a kid on the Gulf Coast, all we worried about were the communists. I said something once like, 'Oh they won't bother nuking us here. We're nothing to them.' And my teacher said, 'That's where you're wrong. We're very important—a Navy shipyard, an Air Force base, and one of the busiest ports in the country, not to mention spitting distance to

New Orleans, plus all the oil fields in the Gulf. We're one of the first strikes.'"

Graham nodded. "Makes sense."

"But do you tell that to a seventh grader? Freaked me the hell out. It was on my mind up until the Wall fell, and then Yeltsin took over, threw out the commies. The thing, though, was that until the teacher told me, I thought I was safe."

"I know what you mean," Drew said. "Kinda how I feel about terrorists."

"Exactly. They don't bother with small town Americana. Not the best use of their resources. Then my goddamn partner, looking for anyone anywhere to give him some attention, tells them all about us. You wonder if they would've ever bothered otherwise."

Graham laughed. "My money's on these guys having spread all over already. They're just biding their time, doing things the right way. Patience, planning, invisibility."

"How does that explain our Malaysians?"

"Could've been their first assignment. Go check out the podunk meth dealers in Minnesota. They got overeager."

"Maybe, but how does that help us?" Drew said.

My turn. "I don't know. We'll figure it out later."

I hoped I could keep my word.

We made sure Aziz's girlfriend wasn't going anywhere for a while - upstairs in the bedroom closet - then dragged Aziz out the door. An advantage if the next flunky was a weakling like Aziz.

Graham told him, "You're going to help us climb the ladder."

"You can't. I won't."

"What's the girl's name?"

It stopped Aziz a moment, eyes flicking back and forth. "Lake."

"Lake? Like a pond?"

"Like a lake."

"You love her?"

He nodded once. Involuntary. He caught himself and held his chin straight, teeth clenched. Swallowed hard before he said, "Not that much."

Graham looked at me, said, "Billy, you want to go do something to make her cry?"

Damn, he even shocked me for a moment. I played along. "Be right back."

I wasn't halfway up the stairs before Aziz

folded.

"Just, wait, just…it won't work, so there's no need to…look, I'll take you, but we'll all die."

I came back down, tense but ready. "We heard you the first time."

It was a dumb play. We didn't have anything to gain. Aziz was right. Not a chance in hell. Guess it was appropriate we were in Detroit, then.

TWENTY-TWO

What was it we wanted? After the first day in the hotel, the stakeout, the planning, well…we couldn't put it into words.

Drew said, "I just don't want Ian to have died in vain."

"Amen."

Could've been anyone. At first I thought we just had some entrepreneurs coming into Yellow Medicine to build on the meth trade. Now look at it. Whoever it was, they shouldn't have killed Ian, and Heather, and her roommate, and Elvis Antichrist. They shouldn't have shot Paul. I didn't really care about terrorists all that much. Seemed far away before this. I mean, watch suicide bombings on the news, watch nutjob leaders slag America, you shake your head and say, "Fucking morons." What's the point?

Let's say they get their way. Worldwide Islamic State, okay? How's that going to suit them? Nothing left to do but install their theocracy and find out very quickly that without the infidels to kill, their only enemies will be each other. Corruption will set in. Different sects will splinter and mutate and grow anew. Terrorists who don't get their way will bomb the rulers, take control, so on and so on.

Seriously. History itself backs me. You still think it's all America's fault?

I asked Graham while we sat outside Aziz's townhouse the night before we approached him. My ex-brother-in-law voted for democrats. Blame his big heart, wanting to believe that everyone could make everything fair if our country would just stop being so damn selfish and arrogant.

"Tell me," I said. "You still conflicted about all this?"

I liked his answer, though. "If we're not, then we're pretty much the same as them."

Aziz took us to a video store. Not in Paul's notes. It wasn't a chain, more like an abandoned convenience store—you could still see the outline where the gas pumps once stood. Only one other car in the lot. The sign was a homemade paintjob: *Tricky Video & Games.* Faded posters covered every space of the glass front wall, layered three thick in spots.

We climbed out of the car, looked around at the blight. Broken bottles, broken houses, broken apartment complexes. The only brightness came from the more recent posters and the orange, blue, and green pop bottles crushed on the concrete.

"Before we go in, we just wanted you to know about our back-up plan."

Aziz's mouth moved, no words, all confused.

Graham keyed the chirp on his cell phone. "You there?"

It chirped back. Drew's voice. "All set."

"Make her say something."

A rustle, then Drew saying, "Talk."

Our little blonde terrorist screamed out, "*Fuck you!*"

Then a loud slap, more rustling, and Drew's voice again. "Done."

Aziz still hadn't closed his mouth. He finally whispered, "You are stupid men. You don't understand how this works."

I said, "Seems to me you kill people to impress God. Genius, I'm telling you."

He ignored me, spoke to Graham. "We speak to Umar inside, and Umar tells us who we talk to next."

Inside, all my expectations flitted away. I had expected a craphole front, barely enough movies to make it a real store. Instead, it was packed wall-to-wall. And not just your standard American Hollywood "culture killers" either. Mostly these were imports—Mexican, Bollywood, Iranian, Egyptian. Their customers were definitely immigrants hungry for a taste of home, a language they understood. It was a damn good idea. And that definitely made the place look legitimate in the eyes of the law.

The guy behind the counter was a skinny Pakistani, maybe a few years older than Aziz. He was watching a Bollywood musical on a TV that hung behind the counter. He didn't register us at first, just a quick wave at Aziz, then back to the movie.

"This is the one where she gets kissed. You heard about that, right?"

"Unbelievable."

"Only here would that not rate at all. You should see the stuff we get from Mexico."

The clerk finally turned away long enough to see that this wasn't a private conversation. He looked geekish, one of those computer hacker types. Rumpled white oxford shirt. No smile, plenty of anger as he stared at us like we were dogs. Too late, I realized our disadvantage—he could have guns under the counter, or guys waiting in the back with swords. The whirling dancers on the TV felt like a bad omen.

"Can I help you?" he said.

Graham and I pretended to browse the new release shelves, waited for Aziz to do the talking for us.

"These men are friends of Asimov. He needs our help but couldn't contact us through normal means."

"That's because he's dead," I said, cutting our puppet off. The clerk was probably in the loop. Had to be. If he was the one we came to before going up the ladder, then he already knew Paul had been eliminated. "So what are we going to do about it?"

Wide-eyed Aziz looked as though his mouth had gone dry. Croaked, "I didn't know."

"Your friend here did, though. And we need to talk to someone about this."

Graham had made his way to the side of the counter. Neither one of us wanted this guy grabbing a gun.

The clerk grinned, wrinkling his cheeks. "I know you now. You're the guys from Yellow Medicine County." The words were dripping. Then he laughed.

"Something funny?"

"Yellow Medicine. You know, like piss. Like you're all piss drinkers."

He laughed louder. I caught Graham's hand sliding towards his pistol. Jesus, I didn't need a firefight. "Funny shit. Real funny."

Distract, distract, don't pay attention to the man sidling up to you.

Maybe my eyes flicked one too many times. The clerk's followed. He moved.

Ducked under the counter and came out with a shotgun. Full-sized awkward son of a bitch. He would have to adjust to get it on his shoulder, pump the action.

Graham's gun rising.

"No!" I jumped across the counter, knowing damn well my stitches couldn't take it. Searing pain across my ribs as I grabbed the stock and the barrel, but fuck it—I held on. The clerk jerked me back and forth. I got a knee up on the counter and slid over to his side, pushed him against a shelf full of DVDs, trying to brace his neck with the gun. I wasn't strong enough.

He kept jerking. Left right left. Finally got me off balance, my hand slipping off the stock. The clerk swung the wood, popped my face and sent me reeling to the ground. Spinning, dizzy, heard the shift of the pump.

I waited for the explosion. I expected it.

And when it came, I didn't feel anything. Heard glass shattering. Opened my eyes to Graham struggling with the guy from behind, gun pointed towards the front windows. I climbed up. Pebbles of glass, a hole in the center of Sandra Bullock's head on a *Miss Congeniality* poster. A scream from outside, a woman, just visible through the hole. A couple, now jumping back into their car, the windshield cracked and scratched with shotgun pellets.

I shook away the pain in my face, stepped up to the melee and punched the clerk in the nose. It bled and he let go of the gun. Graham yanked it away. The clerk slid to the floor.

Time was short. Cops would show up. I pointed at the video cameras in the corner. "You can get that?"

Graham nodded, started searching for the recorder. I looked around until I found Aziz on the floor covering his head. He wasn't going anywhere. I turned my attention to Umar, the clerk with the broken nose. Goddamn. It hurt to breathe, hurt to move. The whole thing was supposed to be a nice talk, some persuasion. I was getting tired of fighting. But not quite yet. Umar was mumbling, staring at me and mumbling.

"You got something to say?"

More mumbling. Louder, in his own language, Chanting, it seemed. No…prayer. He was praying.

"What, you want God to strike me down? Want God to punish the filthy American?"

He didn't blink. Full on stare, still chanting. Chanting. Chanting.

"Stop it," I said. "That's enough."

He kept it up. Louder. Grinning, even, broken nose and all.

"I said that's enough." I towered over him. He still didn't stop chanting, louder still. "Shut the fuck up already!"

The chanting turned to singing. Louder and louder.

I searched for something to shut him up. Pointing guns wouldn't work. He knew we needed him. I grabbed a DVD case off the counter, opened it and removed the disc. Umar kept singing. I knelt beside him, held the disc to his throat and shoved hard. He coughed but kept singing.

"I'll slice your fucking throat. I'm sick of it! Slice your fucking throat!" Very nearly ready to do it, too. They sit around and plan to kill, kill, kill, and then think God's up there giving them the thumbs up. I wanted to slice his jugular, wanted to watch him die, see how he reacted when he knew death was coming for him, not as a martyr but as a helpless video clerk beaten up by two white guys. Keep up the pressure, start sawing into the skin.

Graham came back into the room from the back, saw what I was doing, and shoved me away. I tossed the DVD, slammed my fist on the counter and let out my frustration. Sounded like a lion, but much less confident. I couldn't take these guys much longer. They would drive me over the edge, and it was bad enough I already had two wheels dangling.

He grabbed the front of my shirt. "What the hell? What are you doing?"

"I'm tired of it, all right? Fucking tired! We just wanted to talk!"

"You think this *helps*? You think he's all keen to cooperate now?"

I pulled away from his grip. "None of them

want to cooperate! Goddamn it, they loathe us. We're talking passionate hate. I'm sick of trying to win over someone who won't budge."

He turned to Umar, now sitting up, staring at the floor. At least he'd stopped praying.

"He's not even Arab," Graham said.

I nodded. "I know. Might as well be."

"But you…*you're* why they hate us, that sort of shit."

I laughed. "You really think that, don't you? I'm not why they hate us. They hate us no matter what. They always will. Why else would they lie, hide, infiltrate our cities? Pretend to be just like any other immigrants even though they're really planning to kill as many of us as they can? Innocents!"

"Come on—"

"Ask him." I stepped past Graham, knelt beside the clerk, grabbed his hair and forced him to turn his head to the sheriff. "Just ask him. You're trying to protect him, but I bet he still hates you as much as he does me."

Umar said, "Want to bet?"

I let go, wiped my hand on my pants. "You know what? One thing that might take the wind out of your sails?"

Looked like he wanted to tear my throat out

with his teeth. He kept quiet.

I said, "Everything you believe is a sham."

I didn't feel justified. I didn't feel ashamed. I felt numb, that was all. Didn't need a goddamn lecture from my boss in the middle of it all either. He wasn't the one trying to save himself from a life in prison. I had to remind myself that he was trying to save his kids, though, and I was the reason they were in danger. I didn't know if doing what we were doing would help clear my name or not, but it felt like a better way to try than kneeling down before Rome and his type.

Later that evening, back in the hotel room, Drew eased up behind me as I stood at the window, crossed her arms. I was a little more at ease, having crushed and snorted a couple of the pain pills Drew had rounded up for me before we left home. Half-bottle of Vicodin from her aunt, leftover from back surgery. Hard to believe anyone would leave half a bottle. She must have a nice life.

Graham was in the bathroom. He'd told her the story of our day, including the video store debacle.

"He's not really mad at you, you know. More like at himself," she whispered.

"You weren't there." I wasn't in the mood for diplomacy. A few shadows passed by on the curtains. I tensed up, then took a deep breath as they continued on down the walkway.

Drew said, "He reacted the way he knows he should. But you've got no filter, so it's all the same to you. Didn't even stop to think. You're all instinct."

"I thought instincts were supposed to protect us, like in animals."

The toilet flushed and she gave my shoulder a quick squeeze before retreating to her bed. "There's always survival of the fittest, too. You've got nine lives."

"I've used up six, at least."

Shadows passed outside the window a second time. Then the three men they belonged to. Maybe Drew was right about my instincts. I knew we were in trouble. I knew then that following through on our plan after the video shop had been the wrong choice, a miserable failure.

I said to Drew, "Get under your mattress. And grab my gun."

TWENTY-THREE

What happened after the video store was that we took the clerk and Aziz to the car and got the hell out of there with the videotape that had captured the whole mess. I kept the pressure on Umar in the backseat, choking him on-and-off until he started to crack, Aziz begging him to keep his mouth shut.

"What, like you did?" He lunged at Aziz. "The same way you didn't tell them about me? You are the lowest! A traitor!"

I tapped his broken nose and he fell back in a coughing fit. Graham was driving, scanning for a nice secluded place. There had been witnesses, after all. The plan sucked, the way we pulled it off sucked, what we hoped to accomplish sucked.

We finally pulled into the parking lot of a packed megastore and I laid it out to Umar. "Aziz might not be in the loop, but I'll bet he knows more people like you, one step up. And maybe those people won't be as committed as you."

"I have nothing to say."

I tapped Graham on the shoulder. "Let's go, boss. Time to baptize him."

Umar said, "What?"

"Find a little pond or ditch, let my friend here consecrate you to Jesus Christ, and then I'll drown you. My friend's a Lutheran lay minister. He's qualified. God answers his prayers."

"Lies."

"You think this is worth dying for, right? That there's virgins waiting for you and all the pleasures you've denied yourself down here? What if it's all true, right to the letter, and we have the power to take it away with our little ritual?"

"It doesn't work that way. I have to accept it. You can't force me."

I shrugged. "Fine. At least it'll be fun for us. And we'll take pictures. And we'll mail them to your leaders and your family. How do you think they'll react?"

"I'll fight you. I won't let you."

"Yeah, you will." I took out a sandwich bag filled with the crushed up Vicodin I'd been snorting when needed. “Hold him down.”

“What are you doing?”

“Just a little bit of chemical persuasion. You won’t feel a thing. Literally.”

Graham opened his door, stepped out, closed it. Stretched his arms, making a show of it. Then we watched his torso slide past the windows, stop at the back door. Nothing for a long moment, Umar breathing too hard.

By the time Graham had reached for the handle, the clerk was whispering to me, “I’ll tell you where to go. Don’t get my family involved, please. They have nothing to do with this.”

“They have as much to do with this as three murdered college students from Minnesota.”

“Please, I beg you.”

I pretended to think about it. The decision was already made, of course. We weren’t evil, weren’t even close. I was capable, but respected Graham too much to seal the deal.

“We need a name, an address, and a guarantee we’ll get in and out alive.”

Umar took a long hard look at the baggie in my hand, then Graham’s imposing frame outside. Then, “Yeah, I’ll tell you.”

We drove to Ann Arbor, the manicured college

town that was the exact opposite of everything we hated about Detroit—it was everything we hated about the suburbs. Cookie-cutter homes too damn big for their lots. It was nice, really. Clean, beautiful, like a Disney park or a country club. Maybe that was why it got to me. It was all a little too manufactured, all slick surfaces and pleasantries.

If we were going there, it meant the terrorists had the exact same reaction. It was a good place to blend in because no one expected bad people to do bad things there. It was full of smug types who didn't realize how smug they came off. Low-key materialism, taken for granted. Then a cell moves in and acts like they're international students, but who are actively plotting attacks that take years to perfect. These guys weren't the smartest, we guessed. The offshoot plan to take the wilds of Minnesota was a terrible move, and the violence inflicted by the Malaysians certainly didn't help keep them invisible. To make this short: we had no idea what to expect. A respected cleric with a perfect beard, or a young hothead with a chip on his shoulder? Maybe a handful of young hotheads?

We pulled up to the curb of a two-story McMansion with a three-tiered roof. Light brick façade gave way to beige vinyl siding. In the driveway, a Camry and a Tahoe. Funny—they tried to fit in by hitting both extremes. All around, lawns in transition from winter brown into yellow and green. Just a typical, upper middle-class neighborhood in Ann Arbor. Umar told us that there were usually fifteen men here, so I slapped him and told Graham to find us a pool. The clerk then said, "No no no no no" and adjusted it to five. He was one of them. Three of them were students with jobs. The other two hung around to head up operations. That sounded more like it, but I only believed half of what these guys said.

We marched Aziz and Umar through the yard to the front door. They looked defiant but powerless. If they only knew how we felt. No confidence at all. Total sham. All we knew is that we wanted to get out alive, go home, return to normal.

The clerk knocked. A few moments later, someone shouted in Arabic. The clerk looked at Aziz, who nodded and answered. It hadn't occurred to me that Umar might not know Arabic. I thought all Muslims did. But we'd already seen that they had Arabs, Malaysians, and Pakistanis in the same cell. So they communicated in English.

A voice came through the door. "That's right?"

"Yeah," Umar said. "Salesmen."

A few minutes later, the door opened. A young, strong Arab-looking man. Short hair, no beard, in khakis and a red-striped shirt. Half of him was hidden by the door. Smart move. He looked us over. We stared him down.

"Why are you here?"

"We're here to see whoever's in charge."

"Why?"

"We need to ask him something."

The man nodded. "I'll need to make sure you're not armed."

"Oh, we're armed." And just like that, I shot Umar. Pointblank against his shoulder. The blood cascaded across the threshold, onto the door and the tile in the foyer. I shoved the screaming clerk aside and blocked the door with my foot, my gun an inch away from the greeter's face. Graham was snapping at me, harsh whispers that I didn't pay attention to. I hadn't told him I was going to shoot anyone. It was the stupidest thing I'd ever done. None of the bullshit I'd pulled down South compared. I was a target. I was endangering the sheriff's life.

But it had to be done.

"You get him down here and no one else gets shot. Drop your gun right now. I want to hear it hit the floor."

After a long pause of us listening to Umar bitch about his shoulder, I heard the clatter. The greeter backed up, hands empty and high. I wondered what he must be thinking.

He said, "Will you come in?"

"Why, so you can pin us into a corner?"

He held out his palms towards us. "No, I give my word. Safe. Everybody is nice."

I looked back at Graham. He could barely look me in the eye, realizing just how low I could go. But he gave me a sharp nod, then rustled Umar to his feet. We stepped into the foyer, waited as the door closed behind us.

Our greeter took the clerk by the elbow, asked, "I take him? Make him better?"

I waved him off. "He stays here until we're done. Bring a towel."

The greeter went into the back of the house, leaving us alone in the foyer. He was gone before we could think better about it. Graham and I looked at each other.

He said, "Wanna follow him?"

"One of us should."

We stood still.

I said, "Okay. Next time, we should do that differently."

Graham took post at the foot of the staircase while I kept an eye on the hallway to the great room. Manufactured class—a mass-market chandelier and fake marble tile, framed prints of famous impressionist paintings that must have come with the house. It was strange, looking at a Manet while Umar yipped in pain. Nothing in the house was distinctive to the occupants, which was the point. There was nothing to notice. Most people wouldn't think of the absence as a warning sign.

Graham said, "It's a nice house."

"Too soulless for me."

"Really? I don't get that."

"All these new houses, all the same. They've got no character anymore. Your choice of three styles, two colors, that's it."

"Home is what you make it."

I shrugged, wasn't listening. We only spoke to fill the silence. I said, "Yeah, it is."

Sounds from the back of the house, echoing Arabian. Nothing to stop these guys from coming around the corners with guns blazing, drop us just like that, with the only concern being clean-up. I glanced at Graham, could tell our thoughts were synched up. We lifted our guns and waited. We wouldn't shoot first, wouldn't be able to dodge the bullets, but we'd damn well do *something* to make our country proud before we shuffled off.

Instead of a grand warrior, the guy who came around the corner with our greeter looked more like a yuppie. Polo shirt and Gap jeans, Adidas sneakers. Hair was nice and short. No beard. The greeter was carrying the towel for Umar. They saw the guns and raised their hands like this was a John Wayne western.

"Please, no need for that, okay? You're safe, okay? My word." He patted his hand against his chest. "Please."

We didn't lower the guns. We didn't waver. The clerk had shut up, paying attention to the confrontation. Aziz had flattened himself against the wall.

I said, "I'm Deputy Lafitte. This is Sheriff Swoboda. We're here on behalf of Yellow Medicine County, Minnesota, and Paul Asimov."

His hands were still open, careful, and slow. He couldn't speak without gesturing. "And how is Paul?"

"You know goddamn well…" I took three big steps towards him as Graham yelled at me. My gun nearly touching his nose. He didn't flinch, didn't stop grinning. He had our number, and that was the worst feeling of all. Even worse than what I had to say next. "You're in charge here? You're the leader?"

He raised his eyebrows. "Allah is the leader. I simply follow the path he lays out for me. I am good with strategy, plans. I can visualize. They ask me to make plans, so I make plans."

"Who are you?"

The grin widened. His face was elastic. "I am a servant of the One True God."

I nodded. He believed every word he said and was amused at us for doubting. Nothing we could do would shake him. I couldn't admire that no matter how hard I tried, not in any religion or political system, not in love or war. The truth is only as real as what you see in front of you, and here it is: truth wavers. The only constant is change. Even in faith—people want what they want and believe they can have it in spite of what their faith tells them. So they either justify what they want or change their faith to fit it in.

Just like Mr. Servant of God here, following the path. And if one of his followers decided one day next week that Allah was telling *him* that the plans had changed and the cell needed new leadership, I wondered how confident he would be then. How willing to let Allah lead the way, even if that meant losing his status.

It was never about religion. It was about being selfish, which was the most powerful and convincing faith of them all. What we desire for ourselves. What makes us feel good inside.

The only difference between these clowns, Homeland Security, Graham's church congregation, my ex-father-in-law's bible thumping and myself was that I had no trouble admitting it.

I wanted to blow the cell leader's brains out. But then the greeter would take over. If I blew the greeter's brains out, I'd have to face another one vowing revenge within a week. Tit for tat. Neverending. Same as the Israelis and the Palestinians, the Catholics and the Protestants, the Commies and the Capitalists.

I said what I had come to say. "We would like to ask you for a favor."

The elastic loosened, lips drooping somewhat. "You ask *us*?"

"Are you listening?"

He exchanged a few mumbled phrases with the greeter before blinking several times, face more serious than before, arms crossed on his chest. Then he said, "I'm listening."

"You came out to Yellow Medicine County because Paul told you I could help. That I would pave the way for your fundraising through crystal meth."

A slight nod. "That's close enough, yes."

"He made a mistake. I don't want to help you. Your people caused too much trouble. We can't afford a war, neither of us. You would eventually lose, and in some ways so would we."

"How do you mean?"

"Whatever your plans are, blowing up post offices or poisoning the water, all that terrorist shit, someone's going to find out if they haven't already. But what you did out in our woods, that wasn't helping you at all. We don't want to be part of the battlefield, don't want to lose any more kids like those your people butchered."

The grin started to climb again, so I smacked his cheek with the gun barrel. His eyes went dark and narrow, hand pressing hard against the cut. The greeter grabbed my wrist.

I was shouting at the leader, who was bent over, wiping the blood from his face, sliding his hand against the wall rather than ruin his clothes. "I said, are you *fucking listening*?"

The greeter was going for something in his belt—knife, gun, no clue—but Graham was there in no time flat to bean him on the back of the head. He spiraled down, unconscious.

The leader had squatted, bloody hand on the wall to steady himself. I crouched eye level with him, waited until he lifted his chin.

I said, "It all comes down to this. Leave us alone. That's all we ask. We can't take you on, and we're not going to let the government ruin our lives over you pussies. Just stay away. Pull your people out. Don't come back. You want to sink a ferry or make a couple hundred people sick, go for it. You won't get far anyway. But stay the holy hell out of Minnesota."

He didn't respond at first. He breathed at me, wiping his face once the blood began to drip onto the tile. Then, "You will die for this."

"I'll retire to Florida and eat too much fried seafood. That's how I'll die."

"Your family, your friends—"

"Like you haven't tried already? What was Ian? Or Paul? Are you really stupid enough to threaten me when I'm giving you a free pass?"

"You insult us."

"Dish it out, but can't take it. Is that what type of bully you are?" I looked up at Graham. "Jesus, no wonder we can't win. We're dealing with seventh graders."

"Yes," the leader said. "You can't win."

"This was a bad idea," Graham said.

I nodded. It was.

A truce. Just ask the fuckers for a truce and hope they realized how serious we were about it.

I whispered to the cell leader, "Come on, man. Roll this over in your head. We've made our point. We shot your guy. Maybe he lives, maybe not. That's a fighting chance. More than you gave the people you beheaded. Now we're willing to leave you alone if you'll agree to stay off our turf. Can you be reasonable for once in your life?" I tapped his forehead lightly with, "Just? One? Time?"

He stared at the ground. Shaking. More hate than fear. I stayed there, inches away. He could've torn my throat out or head butted me, but he didn't. The shaking subsided and he said, "Okay, yes. We give you what you want."

"Tonight. You call those two bozos you've

got working over there and get them on the road tonight. You pack up the butchers in Minneapolis who killed my favorite band. And if you planned on dumping anthrax in the Mississippi River, I'd suggest rethinking that, too."

"I said I understand." A little testy. "Minnesota is off-limits."

"Now, swear to Allah."

That burned him. His face grew tight and dark.

"Come on," I said. "Say four little words and everybody's happy, okay?"

It took him a few swallows to get down all that pride, but he finally squeaked out, "I swear."

"You know what I want. Almost."

"Okay, yes. I swear to Allah."

Was it satisfying? Not at all. I had a sour taste in my mouth, didn't know how to react. Stayed there beside him. Should we shake on it? A hug? I loathed him. I'd sold out to him.

"Good. That's fine." I stood, waved my gun towards the clerk. "Get him cleaned up."

Shook his head. "We have our own way of handling this situation."

"What?" It was Umar. "Please, I beg you."

I wanted to laugh. Big shots in killing, but not so much when it came to sacrifice. Their Middle Eastern brothers would have been ashamed of these clowns.

I backed towards Graham, still ready for anything. I chirped Drew on the two-way.

"I'm here," she said.

"We're good. You can leave the girl now. Our boy did his job." I suspected that Aziz wouldn't be going home to her, though. He looked relieved for barely a second before realizing what this meant for him.

Graham gripped my shoulder as we walked back-to-back towards the door, but it wasn't enough for me. I watched them all, knowing good and damn well we'd just shown them that we didn't have balls the size of theirs. So, fine. We just wanted some peace and quiet. Being heroes took something we didn't have.

But I could be myself. "And just in case you didn't think we were serious, how's this?"

I took aim at Umar, shot him in the face. No chance of living through that one. Graham screamed. I took aim at the cell leader, was going to give him one, but Graham jostled me, made my shot go wide. The guy ran back into the depths of his house.

The greeter pulled a pistol from the towel in his hand, but Graham grabbed my collar and dragged me out of the house before he could get off a shot. We sprinted to the sidewalk and into our car. The sky was darker, purple clashing with gray as night fell. No one chased us or took potshots as we drove away, Graham in the driver's seat again.

As soon as we started rolling, Graham was frantic. "What were you *thinking*? Oh man, oh God, oh Jesus."

"Calm down. They would've killed him anyway." Fell out of my mouth nice and casual, but my chest was thumping double-time. I pictured him praying on the floor of the video store. Contrasted that to his fear on the floor back there. Yeah, what had I been thinking? Some ridiculous idea that I'd scare them off by killing another one of theirs? I was too used to dealing with meth dealers, good ol' boys who just wanted the easy life instead of the backbreaking work their fathers had slaved over. I'd crossed the line.

Graham was still breathing too hard. "I need to call home. Oh god, Billy, you know how they work."

"They're not going to hurt your family, all

right? It's gotten too hot for them now. Don't worry about it."

I didn't believe it, not really. Wanted to. I'd acted like the gung ho cop again instead of thinking for a moment, not remembering until it was too late that it's always tit-for-tat with these guys. Shit. And they would feel a lot less bad about it than I did right then.

"Hey," I said, "I'm sorry, really. I just couldn't let what they did to Paul stand without…you know. Still, we got the point across. It'll be fine."

When he finally spoke again, it was a whisper while exhaling. "Jesus have mercy on us."

"On you," I said. "How do you know Jesus didn't want us to smoke 'em?"

Hands tight on the wheel, eyes on the road. "Call it a hunch."

TWENTY-FOUR

An icy and quiet drive back to the hotel, Graham not speaking the entire way. His shoulders were hunched. He kept glancing at his cell phone plugged into its charger. Desperate to call his wife, kids, Tordsen, anyone. I wished he had, too. If I'd brought on another massacre, might as well load six bullets into the revolver next time I played my game. Stack the deck in my favor. We planned to drive back to Minnesota the next morning because we just couldn't think of anything else to do.

Graham had eventually said, "I'll call Agent Rome in the morning, tell him what we've found."

"He's not going to like it. We probably sent those guys into hiding again."

Graham shrugged, said, "Doesn't matter. It's over. We're screwed. We tried, and now we've got to get out of the way."

"It's not that easy for me. He wants my head."

"I'll back you the whole way. You'll be just fine. Maybe we'll get in a little trouble, but then again we might get a medal out of the deal. I just want to go home and never do anything like this again." Then he headed for the shower, leaving me alone with Drew.

We never really expected our little terrorist wannabes to keep their word and pull out, leaving our citizens to worry about simpler things—new breeds of corn, pesticides, preparing the fields for spring planting, helping their kids get summer jobs or waiting for them to come help out on the farm. Anything else but what we had dealt with the past week. It might take months to dull the image of the college girl's severed head and the bodies of Ian and Heather every time I rested my eyes or tried to fall asleep. Longer for Graham, I imagined. Killing Umar wasn't going to do a damn thing except add another shot of gore to the slide show. This wasn't justice. This was a nightmare.

As I stood at the window, the nasty yawn in my stomach quieted down and it seemed as if I might get a few decent hours of sleep. I lifted my shirt, found that a few stitches had popped and bled through, but it wasn't as bad as I expected. Still stung dully through the Vicodin buffer zone.

Then, those shadows outside the window, stopping in front of our room. It hit me before I even knew who they were—they weren't taking it out on the family, but on *me*.

Drew followed my instructions, tossing over my pistol and hiding on the far side of the far bed, ready to climb under the mattress.

I called out, "Graham? Maybe you'd better get in here."

Someone knocked on the door. One of the men was shielding his eyes to stare through the window, but the glare from the lamps and the darkness outside made it hard to tell exactly who we were dealing with.

"Who is it?"

A muffled voice, trying hard to do a flat Midwestern accent but stumbling miserably. "Is manager. We, I, need to talk with you about bill."

I was tempted to get a fisheye view from the peephole but figured they were waiting for something like that. Maybe a shotgun already flush against the door, ready to take me out of the game. Instead of falling for it, I trusted that the locks would hold and I shouted, "We'll deal with it tomorrow. Trying to sleep right now."

"No! Is very important you talk now. I have paper for you. Come, open the door and take."

"No can do. First thing in the morning, I swear."

Once Graham came out of the bathroom, I signaled, three fingers up, then I pointed towards the door.

He reached behind him for the gun he had left by the sink. He was just a little bit late.

Explosion, bright and sudden, the force dropping me to the floor. I fought to keep myself in the zone. The window cracked from the blast, and the men finished the job with sledgehammers. The bulbs in the lamps blew. Pebbles of glass flew across the room, bouncing off the bedspreads and our skin. I fired towards the curtains, heard a grunt and thought I'd hit one. Couldn't tell. Dark, dark, dark except for our guns and their guns.

I heard loud Arab voices and finally was able to focus on someone stepping through the hole in the window into our room. A glimpse of his profile—the greeter from the house in Ann Arbor, but much fatter. He had a gut. An oddly shaped gut.

I figured it out. Leapt from the floor over the far bed, pulled Drew from the mattress and covered her with my body, then turned to tell Graham, "*Get in the bathroom! The tub! Now!*"

The greeter screamed over my words. Graham planted his feet and fired at the greeter. Chest shot. Head shot.

Too goddamned late.

The greeter detonated himself.

It was one of those moments you never expected to see with your own eyes. On the nightly news, sure. The aftermath, dulled by editing and commentary, in a far away place overseas. A centuries old war that we had no part of.

So we thought.

The flash came first, blinding me. I turned my head on instinct, braced it against Drew's back. Then the *bang*, a real *bang*, not a movie extravaganza full of layers and reverb and resonance. It was a loud pop, fraction of a second, that I thought might have taken out my ears for good. Immediately heard two banshee wails. One in my head. It took me another long moment to realize the other was coming from Drew, pounding me with her fists from below. She must've thought I was unconscious or dead.

I pushed myself up, the dark disorienting me, colors flashing in my bad eye. Wiped it. Blood, glass, no pain but no sight either. Sprinklers raining down cold, steam coming off the floor and the walls. The charred flesh odor made me gag. I helped Drew up. She seemed okay, coughing and crying, clinging to me. We found Graham, felt him moving, and each took an arm, dragged him out of the room into the parking lot.

We were instantly surrounded, hotel guests and workers in their pajamas out in the near freezing air. I looked back at the room, some sight returning to my injured eye. The door was hanging open. Smoke poured out. It hadn't been as powerful as the suicide bombers overseas, but it devastated the room. No idea how I had survived, let alone Graham.

Then I looked down at him. Holy God.

He was alive, but his face was ground beef, unrecognizable. Blood was seeping through the skin. I didn't see a source. Everywhere. Drew knelt across from him, taking towels from other guests, trying to stop the bleeding. Graham was writhing but fading. I held his hands high. Three fingers on his left, gone. Two on the right burned to stubs. I ripped his shirt to ribbons—his chest was raw, pulpy—and tied off his wrists. Still couldn't hear anything, still seeing spots.

Frantic to save Graham. In the back of my mind, though, coming up fast, was the truth: he was gone. Too much trauma, too much blood. I wanted to pray. I shouted to him, "Hold on, help's coming. You be strong, you hear? Answer me!"

He stared at me, locked in. Nodded. I could barely hear the world around me so I knew goddamned well he couldn't. No way his wires were playing the scene straight for him. But he locked in and moved his mouth. Shards of teeth. He lifted his chin, motioned me closer.

He knew. Saw it in Drew's eyes that he was on his way out, saw in mine what I wanted to do about it.

I leaned closer, closer, ear touching his lips. I heard him breathing. The words came out wheezy: "Don't do it."

I turned my head, wanted him to read my lips. "I don't have a choice."

Head shake. More blood seeping. He winced, held his breath. Then again formed the words carefully. "Don't. Do. It."

I laid my hand on top of his head. "Okay. Okay. I hear you."

The next word was tougher to make out. It took me hours running through possibilities to understand. "Peace."

His breath stalled. Then he sucked in a lungful. Sirens. My hearing was coming back slowly, the banshee wail still louder than everything else. Drew called for a doctor, a nurse. A young black lady with glasses knelt beside her, said she worked in a pediatric clinic. A fit white guy stood above us, said he was a physical therapist. He recruited a couple of guests—"*Need ice! Water. I need lots of towels!*"

I backed away, sat on my ass in the parking lot. Counted my fingers and toes. All there. Legs and arms working, no broken bones. Sharp pains in my back. I imagined I was a mess. But alive, willing, and able. I crawled to Drew and pulled her away. She didn't want to let go. The nurse loosened Drew's fingers from Graham's shoulder. She slid towards me and dug her nails into me. Not crying anymore.

We were thinking the same thing. If we stayed here, we were useless. We were done for. We would have come all this way only to give up the rest of our lives to the Federal

Government, either as prisoners or "material witnesses", same sort of life—caged.

The sirens were closer. We needed to run before the cops showed up if we were going to do this.

"Let's go," I said.

It only took one glance. She stood, helped me up, and dug the keys out of her pocket. A few of the people on the crowd tried to stop us as we walked towards our car. I pushed them away. Drew dropped into the driver's seat. I climbed in the other side.

She cranked up, blew the horn to clear off the four people trying to keep us on the scene, then headed out for Ann Arbor.

TWENTY-FIVE

If there was an APB out on our vehicle—and how could there not be?—we must have slipped the net. We barreled down the dark highways and mourned quietly. I'd never thought of Graham as anything more than a well-meaning figurehead until this past week, and certainly not like a brother. Drew hardly knew him at all. What we'd seen together made us family, though. A family that didn't forgive all that easily.

The terrorists had broken their word so the deal was null and void. Ends justifying means, all that. I didn't even want to get into the ethics—how could they claim religious piety when their whole movement depended on lies? I just wanted cold vicious revenge. Graham deserved justice more than Asimov did. Regardless of the man's dying words, I couldn't let this one lie.

We had left in a hurry to avoid the cops and med techs and TV cameras, so we weren't prepared for our assault. Had to stop in a taco shack parking lot so I could grab a shotgun and revolver, pretty much all we had left. Two cops and a bass player do not an arsenal make. We had to make our shots count. I pulled out the guns, a few boxes of ammo, and noticed a couple inside the taco shack staring at us through the window. I grinned and waved. *This isn't for you. Enjoy your date.*

I spread myself and the guns across the backseat and we were off again, Drew like a bat out of hell. I watched her eyes in the rearview mirror. Hard on the road, no blinking. This might not have been what she was used to in her small-town, low-ambition lifestyle, but she hadn't wavered once. Like a rock. I had felt sorry for bringing her into this at first, but at that moment all I felt was pride.

Her eyes flicked up to me. "I don't hear shells being loaded."

Thumbed one in. *Schick.*

"That's better."

A few cruisers passed us going in the opposite direction. We were lucky. If they had lit us up,

I would have told Drew to floor it. We were above the law. Lucky was better.

We were in sync and didn't need words until we got to the outskirts. Drew pulled to the shoulder and I took the wheel.

"Don't pull up right in front," she said.

"I won't."

"I'm sure they know by now that we got out alive."

"Yeah."

Another quiet street. I slowed down at an intersection and turned left. Six more blocks.

Drew said, "I'm coming with you."

I expected her to say that. This wasn't a movie, no need for me to say, No, it's too dangerous. You wait right here. *She didn't need to say, "I'm just as big a part of this as you are. You need me in there."*

Movie guys never realize what they're pushing away until it's too late.

"Of course you are," I said. "That was always the plan."

At the final corner I slowed to a stop at the curb. "It's five down on the right."

"Counting the corner house?"

"Five driveways. Let's go."

Left the key in the ignition as we climbed

out, guns ready like they were extensions of our bodies. Let the neighbors see. That wasn't our concern anymore. What happened after was out of our hands. This was about something bigger than us. If we failed, then we'd probably be tortured like Heather and Ian before they took our heads off. I'd seen more horrible things done to the human body in the past few days than I had ever expected to see in my lifetime.

Two driveways. Dogs barked. Porch lights, a couple of Subarus, a basketball goal above them. Crickets.

Four driveways. Drew smoothed her palm across my back, slipped it off, wrapped it around her fingers already tight on the gun.

The fifth driveway. No cars. All dark. We stood on the sidewalk and stared, waiting for signs of life. A faint glow in one of the windows, maybe some lights on in the back room. We eased through the yard to the left side of the house. A motion sensor from the house next door caused a light in front of the garage to wake up and glow. We kept on. A tall wooden fence separated us from the backyard. Voices from nearby - the neighbor's backyard, a handful of friends sitting around having a few beers, laughing it up. I wondered if our terrorists had ever been invited over for dinner or had asked to borrow a cup of sugar, the whole time labeling everyone else in the neighborhood as the enemy.

I shook my head, sighed loudly.

Drew said, "Don't get sentimental on me. I need the corrupt side of you switched on right now."

I turned to her, whispered, "You really think of me like that?"

She worked the latch on the gate. "It's who you are. But it's not all you are, so deal with it."

No lock on the gate. They didn't want to look like they had anything to hide, right? Of course it also made it appear they had nothing to steal, and that wasn't normal either.

We slipped into the back yard, another motion sensor triggering near the back door. *Shit.* We flattened against the wall, couldn't do anything about the shadows.

"We've got to do it now," I said.

Drew nodded, lifted the .357, as long as her face.

She stayed on the wall as I heaved off. Slammed my foot into the back door. The lock held. Slammed again. Again. Again. The frame gave way and I followed the momentum inside.

Yes, the kitchen light was on. It had been left on for whoever happened to stumble across it once the mail piled up and the smell overwhelmed the neighbors.

Our clerk, slouched in a chair with a Glock in his hand, riddled with many more bullets than I'd plugged into him. They'd come from another pistol, the one in the hand of Aziz, dead on the floor barely six feet away. Just like the man had said—he'd taken care of the problem, then immediately cleared out.

"There's no one here," I said over my shoulder.

"Oh god." Drew had sneaked behind me, gripped my shirt into a tight snarl.

Then I thought, *Bomb, bomb, bomb—*

"Out! Go! Get out!" I turned and shoved her running into the backyard as far as I could without stumbling, then fell onto the ground beside her. Covered our heads. We waited.

Nothing exploded. We waited still. The chatter on the deck next door picking up in speed and volume—Should we call someone? Look, out in the yard! I don't have a gun. Yeah, just dial it, 911. I don't know. Maybe it is *the cops. Never trusted those guys.*

We sat up, looked back at the house.

Perfectly still and in one piece. Made sense—no need to blow up this house and bring more attention to themselves for a pointless act. They were saving the fireworks for the big metaphors. The bomb at the motel was a tiny sneak preview.

Drew said, "Long gone. Maybe they knew we'd come looking for them."

"They left as soon as we did. Graham was right. I don't know what else we can do."

More lights coming on in the yards around us.

Drew glanced from yard to yard, back and forth. "We need to get out of here. Someone's going to call the cops."

I shook my head. "I need to stay behind, try to explain."

"No, come on. You know what they'll do to you."

I tried not to think about it. If I ran, then I'd be putting both of us in more danger. Terrorists on one side, the government on the other. Running was the coward's way out. Now that Graham was dead, all the fight bled out of me.

I said, "You have your phone?"

"Yeah."

"Get to the car and go home. Call my

dispatcher, Layla, on the way. Tell her I sent you."

"I can't leave you."

"You need money?" I dug into my pockets, pulled out the wads of loose cash I'd accumulated at truck stop diners along the way. Enough to get her out of danger. "And my credit card for gas. In my wallet."

I reached for it as Drew grabbed my wrist. "I don't want to. Come on, let's get out of here."

She hopped to her feet and pulled me with all her strength. I couldn't do it, though. I didn't want it to look like I was trying to run away. Graham had died because of me. Drew was nearly killed because of me. I had to stop and take my lumps.

"Baby, you need to leave now. Don't let them get you. Go back to Minnesota, find Layla, and tell her what happened. I need you to do that, okay?"

She was still pulling. I worked my wallet from my jeans with my free hand, handed it to her. "You don't have much time."

Her breath was labored, frantic. She finally let go of my arm and took the wallet, clutched it to her chest and paced. More neighbors shouting, more dogs barking.

I yelled at her, "Would you fucking *run* already? Run!"

She did, sprinted through the open gate. I didn't move a muscle. Sat with my hands in my lap and waited. The sirens closed in. Drew only needed to run half a block. Then drive for two days without getting noticed. I hoped she could make it.

As for me, I would probably never see her again. They would hide me away, maybe one of those bunkers they had built to survive a nuclear war. No Drew, no Ginny, no Ham and Savannah, no Dodge Ram, no riverside cabin, no Mississippi, no Minnesota. Man without a country.

I hummed "America the Beautiful" to myself until the police showed up, pinpoint flashlights, garbled commands, and German Shepherds.

"On your face!"
"...from sea to shining sea."

TWENTY-SIX

Today

Rome was kind enough—or evil enough—to let me get a good four or five hours sleep before taking me back to Pale Falls. When the guard woke me, he handed over some water and a couple of Aleves. Good thing. The pain and jitters had ratcheted up while I slept.

They gave me back half my clothes. Didn't expect that. My black boots, my jeans and T-shirt, dirtied with ash and blood. Graham's blood. Another one of Rome's mindfucks. Outside, sans blindfold, I saw that it was early morning. So it hadn't been noon back in the interrogation room like Rome would have had me believe. Cold wind on a sunny day, Spring much farther along now. No snow on the concrete here, not even in the shadows. Still, I was goosebumped from head to toe without my leather jacket.

The guards helped me into the back of the FBI Suburban, black with midnight-tinted windows. Thick bulletproof glass separated me from the front. It was warm and cozy in the backseat. Rome finally showed up, his overcoat worth more than I used to make in a week, and bullshitted with the guards a minute or two before climbing in beside me with a McDonald's bag in one hand, a cup of coffee in the other.

"Black is all you get," he said. Great, a joke. More than I'd expected out of him.

"Perfect."

"And a breakfast burrito. Easier to eat with handcuffs."

"Gee, considering how *late* at night it is, I was hoping for pizza."

He smiled at me, then examined his watch, mock-confused. "Well, look at that. I didn't even notice. Battery must be slow." He spun the hands to what felt like the correct time for what I saw out my window: 7:13 AM.

"So, honestly, does that trick with the time ever really work on people?"

Rome stared straight ahead, tapped on the divider glass. "What trick?"

Two hours after we started down the two-lane highway that cut through cornfields, we closed in on Pale Falls. They wouldn't let me stop along the way at a Dairy Queen for lunch. I really wasn't hungry, but wanted some time to relax, maybe lose the knot that was tightening in my stomach as we edged closer to Yellow Medicine County.

The couple of times I had tried to raise a conversation, Rome responded with grunts, nothing else. So I spent most of the drive staring out the window, absorbing all the details of the Minnesota morning. Soon enough the tractors would be out there planting crops. The flattened yellow grass would rise, fill with green. The bare wicked-witch limbs on the trees would cover themselves with leaves again.

I thought back to the day after Katrina. Hurricanes swept out the clouds and the high pressure as they plowed through, and even in the face of apocalyptic devastation, I remembered sitting on the trunk of my police cruiser next to my gutted house, soaked to the bone, and thinking just how *clear* the air was, how deep the sky, and how I could close my eyes and imagine paradise, if only I didn't hear my wife's voice: "Oh God, there's another photo album. Ruined. Oh, not my hope chest."

I'd experienced that same feeling when the

world was overcome with ice, and the winds whipping so you couldn't stand up, and the snow piling higher, coating the ground and trees in such a way as you'd think you might never see either again. Same as watching it melt and fill the rivers and creeks, wondering if the level would overrun the banks, watching it come oh so close. I was learning to accept it all with wonder.

Familiar rhythms kicked in as we drew closer. Shit, why couldn't we just be there already? Maybe Rome was right to bring me here. I was already thinking of how much I'd like to get home, go sit by the river. How much I would like to unpack, really make a go at settling down here. My yard was already hallowed ground—Paul's last stand. Maybe staying there, tending to the house, the land, my own spirit, would help me discover just what the hell drove me to self-destruction, and how to stop it. So, yeah, I could open up to Rome a little more. I needed to trust someone at this point. I willed the Suburban to go faster as my patience wore thin.

"Can't they, you know, rev it up some?"

Rome eyed me with his chin on his chest, then tapped on the glass. The driver checked his rearview. Rome held up five fingers, closed his fist, then opened another five. The driver nodded and slowed down.

"Asshole," I said.

"Traitor," he said.

Not long now.

We arrived at the Sheriff's Department to a packed house. Every cruiser was accounted for, every deputy standing around outside, outnumbered by Federal vehicles and black suits. Not bad, my fellow deputies showing support. Home field advantage. Pulling into the lot, I watched the faces of the guys I had worked with. They were either blank or angry. Not that we'd ever been friendly, but a cop's a cop, right?

Rome opened his door, stepped out. Another agent opened mine and took my elbow, eased me into the cool air that smelled a bit like toasted peanut butter. Must be the soybean processors. On other days, the winds would shift and you'd be stung by the foul odor from the beet sugar plant off to the east. The first time I'd complained, the guy at the gas station replied, "Tell that to the farmers, they'll say it smells like money."

The deputies formed a gauntlet between the Suburban and the front door. That's when I got the picture. My colleagues, every last one, and a few folks from town were there to see the monster finally get what he deserved. I grinned at Clark, the bartender at the dive where Drew's band played their first gigs. No response. I tried to stop and speak to Spaceman's mom, who looked as if she'd aged ten more years since last I saw her a few weeks ago. I owed her an explanation, the least I could do. Soon as I was within a few feet of her, she spit at me. Yeah, this wasn't the homecoming I wanted, but it was precisely why Rome wanted me here—maybe I'd feel guilty enough to cry him a river of confession. Real officer thinking.

I passed Nate and Colleen, side by side. I grinned at him, happy to see he'd gotten somewhere with her. Before I could say anything, he shouted, "Nothing but a goddamned murderer."

I understood. They thought I was responsible for Graham's death.

Well, in a way so did I.

More taunts: "Hope you die like he did!"

"Traitor!"

"Motherfucking terrorist!"

"We don't want you here! Go back to Iran!"

I whispered to Rome, "Thanks for telling them what really happened."

He didn't turn to me. "I'm sorry? I didn't tell these people anything."

This was the guy I wanted to trust? "You're a professional liar."

"Coming from you, that's a compliment."

The mob's hand-clapping took on a pounding rhythm, along with the chant: "Trait-or! Trait-or! Trait-or!"

I tried to shuffle faster. The agent held me tight. I had to take my lumps. When a beer can whizzed over my head, the agents moved faster. Louder chanting. More flying cans. A rain of beer on my back. And then we were inside.

The muffled chanting sounded larger and angrier when the doors were closed. More cans and bottles ricocheted off the glass. Two agents led me to the middle of the room while others stood guard at the front. All the comforts of home - the smell of burnt coffee, old pastries from the corner gas station, Layla's favorite talk radio station. But now there were anonymous agents with utilitarian laptops sitting at the desks where the deputies used to field calls. We'd always been so casual. Seemed shortsighted in hindsight.

Rome stepped over to Layla's desk, where she stood staring at me, her arms crossed and her lips drawn tight. I had hoped she would be on my side. Didn't look it. My heart sank fast. If she thought I was the devil, then Drew hadn't succeeded in getting to her, telling her the truth.

The new sheriff, George Tordsen, stood beside her. That should have been me. Graham had taught me in those few days what it meant to really help people as a law enforcement office. I was his rightful heir. Maybe if I had listened to George in the first place when he told me to sit tight, I would be headed that way. Not anymore. He was dressed immaculately in a suit, maybe like a French mayor in World War Two welcoming the Germans, knowing he had no choice if he wanted to maintain his lifestyle.

Rome shook Tordsen's hand, then waved towards me. "I promise this will be temporary, hardly more than a few days. Then we'll move him on to a Federal institution, my promise to you."

"Fine, I understand. Anything to help."

"I take it from the reception that your staff isn't as reasonable?"

Tordsen sighed. "I have a handful I trust

with my life, and with his." A nod towards me. "Your team has arranged the cell as you asked. Round the clock electronic surveillance, blacked-out window, and makeshift sound insulation. Just egg cartons, but my son swears it works. He's in a band."

He turned to me when he said it, intentionally reminding me of Elvis Antichrist, all dead except little Drew, all of them local kids trying to forge their own identities out in farm country, struck down in a war they didn't know they were fighting. The sheriff's tone told me the people had found a way to pin that one on me, too.

I couldn't help myself. "You know damn well I would've died to save them."

The sheriff stepped closer. Breath like baked beans. The agents flanking me tensed. "Funny you should say that. We've got all these dead folks you claim to protect, but look who's still alive, Billy. A miracle. Can't seem to give your life for *any* cause, can you?"

"A dead cop's no good to anyone."

He was waiting for something like that. "I feel the same way about a living traitor."

The traitor tag was getting old. "All American, sir. One hundred percent."

He stepped back, blew out a long breath. "I can't do this anymore. We done with him?"

Rome nodded, a smug expression. I figured he thought each new spoonful of humiliation would weigh heavily, pile up, break me. Maybe he was right. All my colleagues really believed I had some part in killing Graham, my ex-wife's protector, confidant, and someone who'd been a good friend to me when I deserved even more shit than I was being fed now. The one time in my life I tried to put myself aside and serve the county…I was tired of thinking about it.

Tordsen cleared his throat and said, "Layla, show them to the interview room, please."

In the room, Rome and me. No two way mirrors, no videotapes. Just another legal pad, handful of cheap pens, and us.

"Here we are," he said.

Couldn't argue with him. "So what was all that talk about this being temporary? What do you have planned for me?"

"That depends. It's up to you now."

"Not even a hint?"

He picked up one of the pens and tapped it against the table, one two three. A pause. Four five six. "I'm going to listen to your story one more time. Like I already said, if we think you're finally opening up, it's a good future. We think you're holding back anything, I'll see if I've got any magic persuasion pills in my back pocket."

My mouth was dry, my stitches prickly. I didn't know what else to say. If I were to ask about Drew, he could twist me. I ask about my family, same deal. I couldn't win.

Still, in order to get out from under all this I would need to drop the tough guy pose and show Rome that I was cooperating. I gave him the stuff I'd kept to myself so far—not taking Ian into protective custody when I had the chance, not calling for help when I felt that Drew's band was in trouble, hiding Paul's body, holding back the news about Trigger and Spaceman's deaths. I let it spill. The bribe from the Malaysians, the plan Graham and I set up. Killing one of their cell members. Their retaliation. I'd given the Feds a cleaner version of the same story, but this time I let them have the details. I talked while I wrote. Rome stopped me every now and then, asked me to expand, clarify, asked what I'd been thinking. Asked how I could be so stupid.

"I guess that's who I am, and it's hard to change."

"But you *can* if you try."

I shrugged. "Didn't want to try. Too mad."

In fact, I was still holding out on him. Something in me couldn't give up Drew. If that's where my story fell apart, fine. I didn't care. No way was I going to turn on her, especially if it looked like they now had her. I didn't give a shit how many witnesses at the hotel saw her leave with me. Fuck it. I left her out of everything after that day in the dorms, and I dared Rome to call me on it.

He didn't. But I swore he knew more than he let on. That little smirk, the bored way he slumped in the chair. He had the straight flush to my full house, positive. I just couldn't tell which suit.

After about an hour, I was tired of breathing the same air, smelling my own stink. Fading out because of the long drive, the lack of real sleep. The jail cell would've been a welcome change. The cot was comfortable enough. I'd slept off hangovers on it a few times.

When I got to the part where the cops found me in the terrorist's backyard, I signed my name and pushed the pad away. I rested my head on my arms and waited for Rome to look it over, send me off to bed.

All he said was, "That's it?"

"Yep." It came out muffled through my sleeve.

"Well then we're not done. I warned you about this shit."

I lifted my head. "Excuse me?"

He slapped the back of his hand against my statement. "You had plenty of time to color in the details on the way over. It's still the same soup full of lies you've been feeding us from day one."

That woke me up. "That's the story! If you've got something else, you'd better lay it on the table so we can end this charade. *That's all there is.*"

Okay, so maybe it wasn't everything, but it was more than enough. I was catching on. They needed terrorists in custody to be happy. They needed to warp my brain enough so that I'd start believing that I was a terrorist-by-proxy and feel guilty enough to admit it. Fucking games. In order to be left alone, I had to believe they were telling me the truth about myself—I *was* a traitor.

When you're fucked, take a stand. I thought of Sean Connery in *The Rock*, a British spy squirreled away secretly for decades because he knew too much. The only way to fight the Feds is to keep living. That way they have to feed you, clothe you, talk to you, *humanize* you every day. You win by forcing your life in their faces. No longer a legend or a zealot. You're a real man.

I rested my head and eyes again, lifted my hand, flipped him off.

"You don't sleep until we've got the real picture."

"I'm done. I'm choosing to shut up."

He stood, lifted his chair, slammed it down again hard. Punctuating his words. "No! You don't get to choose!"

"Then you need to believe me."

He paced. Didn't have enough room to, but he tried. Two steps one way, two back. Fingers on his chin. How many chips did he have left?

Finally, the smirk returned to his face and he snapped his fingers. "All right. We'll see. Be right back."

He rapped his knuckles on the door. The agent outside let him out, and I was left alone. Hey, bring on the next round. I would never give him what he wanted.

I mumbled, "Do your worst." Then fell asleep.

TWENTY-SEVEN

Paul's head, forever exploding from a terrorist's bullet, spoke to me.

"I didn't mean for it to go this way."

"Why terrorists? We could handle street gangs. They needed us. But fucking terrorists?"

"Come on, they were wannabes. They weren't going to do anything. It was just another meth scheme, that's all."

The bullet entered in slo-mo, did its worst. A bloody piece of work, Paul's face sliding and tearing as he spoke. And when the bullet exited, spreading blood and brain into the air, the action froze and slowly reversed until I was seeing my friend's head whole again before the next cycle.

"These guys killed my friends, my connections, college kids. *You*, for God's sake. How was that supposed to make me sign up?"

"Intimidation?"

"I don't think they ever wanted me on board.

I was too much of a maverick. Soon as you told them about me, I bet they wanted me out of the way."

"Looks that way. I'm sorry, man."

I laughed. It was just like Paul to apologize when it was too late to matter.

The next thing out of his mouth was a drumbeat. Steady and hard.

Then I woke up. Rome was rapping his knuckles against the table. I lifted my head, blinked away the blurriness. The room felt colder than before. The door was open. Another agent held it open with his body, hands clasped together in front of him.

"Sweet dreams?"

"I…what do you want?"

"We're going for a little trip. Some sightseeing, for old time's sake. You up to it?"

I tensed, crossed my arms and hugged myself to stop shivering. It wasn't the cold, but the fear. I wondered how much of his anger at me was manufactured, all designed to bring us to this point.

The list in my mind:

- A face to face with Drew. Would it

make me crack to know she was under the gun? Maybe.

- A face to face with Spaceman's mom, the waitress with the enormous breast who trusted that I would take care of her son out there in the woods, the one time a corrupt cop was good for *something*, I suppose.
- Graham's grave.
- Ian's grave.
- Heather's grave. Guilt, guilt, guilt.

Then the SUV turned onto Highway 67, my river camp's road.

Maybe they had figured out that was where Paul died. DNA from the burn pile or something. If that was Rome's play, then I imagined he had me. I'd cop to manslaughter and say it was personal, an old beef from our Gulfport days. That felt okay to me, an easier road out than attempting to guess what sort of fairy tale these Feds wanted to hear in order to convince them I was a contrite enough turncoat. I never thought I'd see a day when the FBI actually preferred outrageous fiction to disappointing truth. Yeah, so I'd work up some tears and say, "I took Paul's life. I didn't mean to, but I was just so angry." It was a first class ticket to State & Local Land. Eventually I'd be a hero: I wasn't a terrorist. I *killed* terrorists!

We passed the riverside park where I'd fished and guzzled light beer with Nate, Tordsen, and Graham on weekends, and sometimes on a lazy afternoon shift. We passed the nine-hole golf course where I tried to muster up love for the game but instead lost a bunch of balls and bent a few clubs around trees. However, I did enjoy a few lusty evenings in the third hole sand trap with the course manager's niece, who worked the clubhouse between semesters at the university, once the last golfer had gone home. Her heavy Minnesotan accent intrigued me—I just had to find out what it would sound like while I fucked her. I'm sure the entire river valley heard her, too.

Had we kept going past the house, we would've found ourselves at the casino, and then another five miles to the bar where I'd first seen Elvis Antichrist play, a couple of months after Drew's prom night. She invited me, was so excited. They weren't *that* bad, but I was glad they eventually got better. I was there for every moment of the group's evolution. Right up until Drew came to me asking for help.

That chased away any chance for further good feelings the last mile. Rome stared at me, tight-lipped, until the agent driving us slowed and clicked the blinker to turn into my driveway. I nodded at Rome before I turned to the familiar sight of my little piece of heaven on earth.

Except that it wasn't there.

Some of it, pieces and rubble and ash. The garage was gone, too. Burned away. The evergreens, the rutabaga trees, the rusty abandoned farm equipment, the red canoe, my Weber grill, all gone.

When the agent finally pulled to a stop, Rome leaned towards me, unhooked the cuffs, and said, "Go ahead."

He knew I wouldn't run. I was trembling, barely able to pull the car handle and step out into the breeze, ashes swirling around my head. There was no warmth radiating from the remnants. An old fire. Pieces of the walls stood no more than waist high. Chunks of plastic—electronics, storage containers, kitchenware—poked out, strange and lumpy forms. Some furniture stood, singed but recognizable. The firefighters had soaked the place with water and foam. I couldn't get my bearings. Stumbling, spinning, trying to find something to save. Guns? Wine bottles? Photos of Ginny, my kids? My Mississippi license plates? My grandpa's duck callers?

I stepped into the ashes of what used to be the bedroom, found what used to be the closet, and went to my knees. I dug through ash, mud, charcoaled wood and half-burned papers. Nothing was saved. You wouldn't even know the thing in my hands had been a shoebox full of Polaroids. I wanted to scream, but I wouldn't give the Feds the pleasure of hearing it. So I bit my cheek and closed my eyes.

Rome's voice behind me. "You still want to protect these guys?"

"I've told you everything."

"What you told us doesn't explain *this*. Maybe there was something here they didn't want us to get our hands on. Or maybe someone sent you a warning. I don't know the details, but I've got this tingling, see."

I stood, turned to him. In my peripheral vision, one of the agents unbuttoned his coat. They really had a bad perception of me. "Ever heard of Joseph McCarthy?"

He wagged a finger at me, his face wrinkling.

"Don't you pull that. No, no. There's a big difference here. You got caught red-handed."

Nothing was going to shake him. I foresaw my ex-wife getting dragged into this next. He'd put her on a plane to see me. What could I do? The worst part was realizing that I'd missed something. He kept pushing because there really was a secret, a necessary key. Rome knew it was out there, but he didn't have enough intel. Problem was, I had *no* intel.

One more glance around the remains of my home. If ever there was a sign from God that I was about to pay full-price for all I'd gotten away with in the past, well…yeah.

"I'm tired."

"What are they hiding? What are they planning?"

The abandoned house next door was still standing. It looked as if only a few trees surrounding the house were taken down in the flames. A giant circle of scorched grass showed the extent. If I had the info he needed, you're goddamned right I'd tell him.

Instead, I walked through the remnants to the Suburban. "I don't know. I'm very tired."

I stood at the rear door of the vehicle, head down. I stopped listening to his maneuverings, waited quietly by the door. Didn't want to look back at the ashes.

Before long Rome said, "Let's go." An agent helped me into the Suburban, stopping to cuff me first. Rome climbed in beside me, obviously pissed. Fuming. Barking at the other agents. Bye bye Washington office. Bye bye big promotion.

A couple of miles down the road, I said, "You remember in the eighties, that movie about nuclear war came on TV? *The Day After*?"

Rome nodded. "Hm."

"It freaked everyone out, but when you think about it now, it really wasn't so bad. People survived, they moved on, even if it was hard."

"Surviving could be worse than dying, they said."

"Yeah, but so what? People would survive. It's not like every square inch of earth would be fried. They rebuilt Hiroshima. Listen, it's like all these movies though, they have these characters, just normal people, and we're supposed to identify with them so we'll feel bad if the bombs fall."

"Always some young couple," Rome said. "Always someone who doesn't believe it's going to happen. Bunch of stereotypes."

"But none of them were really special. Just normal people. And it was set in Kansas or somewhere like that. Nebraska."

"They had all the missile silos in the cornfields."

"But no one in Nebraska or Minnesota ever thinks they're going to be the bullseye. That's what's nice about living out here. The world leaves you alone, mostly."

"What are you saying?"

"I don't know. It's pretty innocent, that's all. People don't know what to do with nukes or terrorists or gangs or any of that shit. Why would anyone want to bother us?"

He turned his head to me. "You got an answer?"

"Well, if you want to really shake up the country, you don't hit New York or Los Angeles or Chicago, but still. I'm talking Sioux Falls, Kansas City. Fargo. You do some damage there, it's scary."

"I can't believe you're just now figuring that out. They're everywhere. They hate all of us."

I shrugged. "Just never thought of it before. Where can you be safe?"

After a long sigh, Rome said, "You can never be completely safe. But I'll take a little risk over boredom any day."

I grinned, said, "Me too." But then wished I hadn't. I thought of Ham and Savannah growing up in a world where *every* choice was like that—is it a risk worth taking? Driving to school. Shopping at the mall. Buying gas. What you eat, drink. Each day a little more dangerous than the one before.

Think about it: someone in another country was told that God wants him to dedicate his life to going undercover in America, pretending to like us, only to find a way to kill a bunch of us at once—and himself included—because I like Jesus and MTV better than Mohammad, and because I don't mind shoving it in their faces. Hell, I wouldn't kill nobody over something like that. That takes effort. You've really got to despise someone to go that far.

Then Umar spoke to me, his prayers running laps in my head. Eventually becoming words I could understand: *You hated me plenty enough.*

Maybe that's what they want. They want us to hate them as much as they do us. Seems that's the only way life makes sense for them. A constant state of war. But I can't do it. Neither can most of us. No matter what, we just can't seem to hate them as much as they do us. Like the bully on the playground who punches you until you react. He only wanted the reaction. Gives him an excuse to beat you even harder.

I was too numb to even feel the punches anymore.

TWENTY-EIGHT

Back at the station, one of the desks had been transformed into a buffet, every inch of surface covered with casserole dishes, aluminum trays, a slow cooker. Several different types of hot dish, the signature Minnesota meal, plus some cocktail sausages, sandwiches, and some spaghetti that sounded unappetizing as one of the men scooped out a spoonful and plopped it on his plate. Layla stood at a nearby desk filling glasses with iced tea, handing them to agents after they'd passed through the food line.

I passed by, starving, wondering if they would even offer. I took a long look at the hot dishes. I hadn't liked any I'd tried before, usually some combination of leftover meat, noodles, and cream of mushroom soup. The kind of stuff you hated eating as a kid. I missed muffalettas, gumbo, and fried catfish. I missed Mom. I'd give anything to start over again, try a different path in life. But here I was, stuck smelling Minnesota Hot Dish with shackled ankles and wrists.

Rome said to me, "You want some? Fix you a plate before we talk again?"

I must've made a face. Got him grinning. I thought of the stuff I'd really miss, so I said, "How about you run up to Hardee's, get me a roast beef sandwich?"

"Oh really? Like I'm your waiter or something? Seems to me you'd love this hot dish." He waved his hand across the desk like the food was a game show prize. "Smell that down home goodness. Mmm mm."

I turned my head, but that wasn't enough for him. A couple of agents laughed along, but most were stone silent. Rome got in my face. "Should I fix you a double helping? That's a good place to start, I think. How about it?"

Sheriff Tordsen raised his hand, got Rome's attention. "Why can't you just get the man a roast beef sandwich?"

Rome turned back into a suit, all business as he clasped his hands behind his back, stepped over to Tordsen.

"Sheriff, I'd ask you to not interfere with my suspect."

"You're still a guest in my department,

Mister Rome. I believe if Lafitte wants a roast beef sandwich, then what's the goddamned harm?"

Rome paced a circle around Tordsen. "And who'll fit the bill? You want the U.S. government buying fast food for traitors? Wouldn't our taxpayers find that pretty offensive?"

Tordsen dug in his pants pocket, pulled out a five and some ones. He motioned to one of his deputies, told him, "Do me a favor and run up to Hardee's, get him a roast beef. Make it a combo." To me, "You like curly fries?"

I nodded. "Yes sir. And a Dr. Pepper."

Tordsen handed the money to the deputy, watched him leave.

Rome crossed his arms, shook his head. "Your service to your country will be noted."

"Just a sandwich, is all. And he'll eat it out here, not in the cell. I expect you to treat Mister Lafitte with the same dignity you afford other men who haven't been proven guilty yet."

"Is that all?"

Tordsen began, "I wish you'd tell him. It's just not right." Trailed off.

"Sheriff, I told you—" Rome said.

"Tell me what?" Fear hit me cold, as cold as

I had been after climbing out of the river. "What is it? My kids? Drew?"

"That's enough!" Rome burned a hole in Tordsen before getting me out of there quickly, shouting for one of his agents. He shoved me into the interrogation room and slammed the door. If I'd known what it would lead to, I would've demanded a deep-dish pizza or fried walleye sandwich, something a little more difficult that would take a small effort to round-up. But I wondered what the new sheriff was talking about. Now I knew for sure Rome was hiding something. Fuck the roast beef. I'd just lost my appetite.

After a while of me listening to muffled arguments through the walls, not understanding the words but definitely catching on to who was saying what, Rome came in scratching the back of his neck. He stared at the floor. In his hand was a simple manila folder, very thin.

He slapped it on the table and took the seat across from me. Slouching some, knees out wide. He'd loosened his tie. Whatever he was about to tell me, he sure as hell didn't want to.

Rome spoke firmly, a very low timbre.

"Look, you've got to understand the pressure I'm under here. We need to make sure that you and I are truly communicating. Sometimes, that means I have to hold back some information, see if what you give me matches up—"

"It's just a sandwich. Isn't starving a guy something like torture?"

He flipped through his file folder. Two flips. Very little was in there. The fear crept in again, my arms sprouting goosebumps.

I said, "I've been thinking about all this, and I hope you realize I want to help you. Maybe I've done some shit I ain't proud of, but I never crossed the line into treason."

"Good, good. I need to tell you something."

Keep talking. Hold back the inevitable. "Believe me, if there's *anything* I can do, hell, I can change. I'll outline every dirty thing I've ever done as a deputy here. I'll even pay back the Katrina money. Come on, anything, I swear."

He'd tried to interrupt the entire time, until he finally raised his voice. "Shut up, okay? That's enough."

Quiet. Another flip through the file. He was sweating. Here I was scared to death, but it was *him* who was more afraid. I think I heard the words in my head before they came out of his mouth.

"Drew is dead. I'm sorry."

My fists shook, rattling the shackles. I swallowed hard. Dry. No saliva. Thoughts drifting: Car Wreck. Jail. Suicide. The terrorists forcing her to suck dick, then beheading her like poor Heather.

Rome kept on. "We intercepted the call she made to your dispatcher almost immediately, but we didn't catch up to her until two days later."

"She was okay? What happened?"

"We found her in a State Park. She'd slept in the car overnight. Guess no one noticed until morning, when we got word. She woke up surrounded. When she came out of the car, she had a shotgun. And she was ready to use it."

"Bullshit. She was just a kid. No fucking way you could consider her dangerous."

His eyes were telling me it was true, though. "Maybe you rubbed off on her. She wasn't willing to go quietly."

"No, she was innocent."

"Then why was she on the run?"

"I did it." Hearing myself say it was like a knife to the gut. "I didn't want her mixed up with you. I didn't want you to fuck with her mind, make her hate me."

"I see," he said. "Yeah, I can understand that. Because I told her you'd rolled on her. I thought if she was under the impression you had ratted her out, we would get past whatever charade you'd concocted with her."

I was confused. Was it an act, or was he as bad as I suspected? He was a damn fine liar. Then I thought about the file.

"Is that what I think it is?"

"I figured it was the only way you'd believe me."

Rome slid the file across the table. I didn't let the dread hold me back. I flipped it open.

Drew. On the slab. Head shot. Eyes wide open. The next showed more of her, laid out indecently, horribly, while the photographer clicked away. Another, just her hands. Another, her feet.

"Fake. Could be fakes." I didn't believe they were. I was grasping for straws. "It's a set-up."

"Wish I could agree with that. Like I said, I'm sorry, Billy."

"Sorry for what?"

Rome tilted his face towards the florescent tubes buzzing overhead, stared at them. "For being the one who took the shot."

It was almost like I didn't hear the words. Like that moment in time didn't even exist for me, even though I knew it to be true.

Rome brought his eyes level with mine and said, "It was me."

I swept the file off the table, let the photos hit the wall, fall to the floor. Rome was still as a dead man. I stood, planning to kill him—choke him with the shackles, kick his goddamn skull in. Paint the walls with his blood, Manson style. I started around the table.

But then he leapt up, gun already out. The real thing this time, not a stun gun. I stopped cold. I had hoped to get a couple of vicious shots regardless, adrenaline and rage keeping me alive just long enough to bite his throat out. If she was dead, I didn't want to be alive, but I wanted to take Rome out with me.

I don't think I really knew she was dead until I realized how scared he was.

"You think you'll *ever* get another word out of me now? You think I'm ever going to think about anything besides seeing you dead?"

He calmed his breathing, sidestepped to the door. I could've grabbed the gun. I was that fearless, done with the world. I thought I was saving her by sending her away. Goddamn it, thought I could keep her off the radar. Chalk up another failure. Not much further to the edge of the cliff.

Then Rome had to press his luck. He banged on the interview room door, waited until one of his agents opened it for him. Then he passed the threshold, turned to me and said, "I told you I was sorry. It was all down to her. All she had to do was drop the shotgun." A long pause as he stared down the hallway, at what I had no idea. "But before you get all righteous and turn to stone, don't forget—we've still got an eye on your kids and ex-wife. Maybe we should question them, see what we can find out."

I launched towards him. He barely got the door closed in time. I slammed into it with my shoulder. I swallowed the pain and kept slamming, pounding, screaming his name. Over and over, all the bloodlust seeping out word by word, blow by blow, until I slid down to the floor. Nose bled, blood vessel in my eye burst. I saw red. I sucked air through gritted teeth—*I will not cry. I won't let them see me cry*—until my thoughts went silent. It was another two hours before someone was brave enough to open the door and move me to my cell.

TWENTY-NINE

It's hard to kill yourself in a jail cell, especially if you don't want to attract attention. Several scenarios considered, discarded—beating my head against the floor until I cracked my skull (but they'd hear and see it, since I was being monitored by cameras, plus I'd probably pass out before I did any real damage); find a sharp edge to slice my wrists (I tried, believe me. Nothing worked); smother myself (again, passing out short-circuits it). Nothing to hang myself with except the sheets, but again they would see that before I got far enough along.

I sat in my cell, trying to imagine worse punishments than this. If the man who expected me to trust him could gun down Drew, then use my kids to threaten me, well, the ball game was over. I started wishing I *had* committed treason. Execution would take a few seconds and then be done. Seemed like a blessing compared to Rome.

Maybe Ginny's dad could call in a top notch lawyer to keep the Fed threats away. Otherwise, I'd just start making up shit, all sorts of crazy plots to keep the Feds running in circles for months. Once one story petered out, I'd give them another. No clue when they'd stop trusting me. Might be fun while it lasted, though.

I curled up on the thin mattress, trying to rest, but images of my house on fire kept breaking in. Drew and me on a beach watching my house burn while the Malaysians and Arabs marched towards us, knives drawn. We retreated into the water. They kept coming. We kept retreating, the surf splashing around our legs. Deeper. Our chests, our shoulders. Our feet couldn't touch the bottom anymore. We were too heavy to swim. The terrorists marched on as if the water wasn't an obstacle.

Dream Drew said to me, "I didn't believe they would shoot me."

"But why even try to draw down on Feds?"

"I figured that's what you would've done."

I was about to ask her more when something beneath the waves tugged at her feet, ripped her from my arms. Down down down into the dark. I shouted her name. I dove under. Dark and cold.

Then I woke up. Someone was at the cell door. I hugged my pillow, drew it across my forehead to wipe off the sweat. I was a mess, soaked to the bone and barely able to breathe. I couldn't take another late night interrogation, no indeed. Not one more question. My stomach was churning like the tide during Katrina.

It was George Tordsen. He smiled, painfully, like an angel of mercy. I had crawled as close to the wall as I could. He eased over to my bunk, sat down. "He told you, right?"

I nodded. "Tell me it was another lie."

He hung his head, frowned. "Afraid not. I found out shortly after you got here that he hadn't told you. I don't like that kind of thing." A long sigh. "I guess. So…I hope you'll forgive me for what's happened, and how I let it go on too long."

"Please, George. Don't."

Then the sad smile returned. "Okay. But the good news is that for you, everything's going to be just fine."

I blinked when I heard it. "Why are you here?"

"Come on," Tordsen took my arm and eased me up. "Let's get you out of here. I'm setting you free."

Layla handed me some clean clothes. "My son's old stuff."

Jeans, a flannel shirt, a windbreaker. I changed in the men's room. Washed my face, got my bearings. Looked at my face in the mirror, saw a ghost. A patchy beard. Not like me at all.

Out in the squad room, I sat at one of the empty desks, stared at a blank Fed computer screen, and waited to wake up from the dream.

"Someone going to explain this to me?"

Tordsen nodded. "You can thank Layla here. I was ready to believe you were the Devil, but she convinced me you'd never do the things they were accusing you of. But try telling that to Rome, he threatens your job, your family, goes a little crazy. So we made a few calls to his higher-ups and discovered that there had been witnesses to what happened at the hotel. About how you and Drew tried to save the sheriff after the bomber blew himself up. Until then, we'd thought you led him into a trap."

"That's what Rome was saying about me?"

Layla said, "He'd gone rogue. They didn't know what he was doing, except that he'd apparently fabricated some documents, said it proved you had a hand in Graham's death. George here got him shut down, so you're almost free and clear for now."

"For now?"

"Well," the sheriff sat on the edge of my desk. "You went vigilante on us, were present when Sheriff Swoboda died, and have been blundering through with these people from the start. We can't allow that to slide, but if you cooperate I'm guessing they'll only give you a slap on the wrist. You'll have to admit to a few things, maybe not illegal but certainly not smart. That'll get you out from under the Feds. Then if you want to stick around, we'll help you find a job. Maybe a security guard, something like that."

I was way out of it and unable to process what they were saying. "You need to slow down."

He put his hand on my shoulder. "You're going to be all right. Don't worry about it. I've got a guest room for you at my house until you get everything settled. I'm sorry about what happened to yours."

I stood, turned to Layla. The look on her face reminded me of Ginny's mom, how she'd always been so calm and collected with me when I called in a drunken fit. I understood now that there was more sympathy in her than I first believed. "Tell me about when Drew called you."

Layla said, "We'd made a plan with her mom to get her out of here, down to her aunt's house in Kansas City. So all she had to do was show up, I was ready. But she was so tired, stopped to sleep at Whitewater State Park." She choked on those last words. Then, "I should've gone to pick her up. I had no idea…"

"No, no, please. It's all my fault. Don't."

She made a noise like a horse, but it soon turned to tears. I reached out to her and she fell into me, crying for Graham, the dead college kids, and for no longer feeling safe at home. If not for me coming here, and then for Paul knowing I was here and what sort of person I'd once been, well…wherever else I might've gone, it would've been the same story.

Yeah, terrorists in the heartland, and it was all on me.

Soon Layla dried up, sniffled, and eased away.

Tordsen stepped over to us and said, "You can get some sleep. I waited until now to wake you so Rome wouldn't try to interfere. His agents know what's going on, though. That's why they're gone. Tomorrow I'll drive you over to The Cities so we can start clearing this mess up. Need to get you a lawyer, too. If you want to think about pressing charges against Rome, well, there's that, too."

I shook my head. Fuck justice. I wanted to see Rome wrapped in tin foil and left in the middle of the desert. Then again, if I were in his shoes, I'd probably follow his methods exactly, even perpetrating worse things to get a confession out of a pig like myself. "I'm not pressing charges."

"Sleep on it. It'll look different tomorrow." Then he noticed my expression, something I was doing unconsciously, I guessed. "Don't let that idea in your head take root. Like I said, sleep on it and you'll have a new perspective in the morning."

I nodded. "I've had enough trouble for a while."

Tordsen grunted. "I don't think you know what 'enough' means."

He was right. I was stunned by his

generosity, but it wasn't enough to settle my boiling blood. The trick was to look weak, defeated, relieved. And I think I pulled it off.

"Oh, by the way…" He looked at Layla. She dug a set of keys out of her purse. My keys.

I took them. "Really?"

She started for the door. "See for yourself."

There it was, good as new in the front parking lot. Layla had gotten her husband to rescue it from my house, fix the damage and put on new tires. My big red truck.

I leaned against the truck's grill, finally feeling relieved, but also anxious.

Layla said, "Don't worry. Graham called me from the road, said maybe I should come pick it up, get my husband to knock it back into shape. No one searched it."

"Much appreciated." I grinned. "You think anyone's going to miss me if I take a hunting trip instead of helping out?"

Layla raised her eyebrows. "Hunting for what?"

"They're still out there, and all this time Rome's had me locked up, God knows what they're up to. I can bring them in, I know it."

She laughed, patted my arm. "Oh, really? Suddenly you're some kind of action hero? Honey, they've already caught up with your terrorists and are just waiting for the right moment to move in for the kill."

"Wait. Rome said –"

"Shit, Billy, he'd made it personal, all messed up in the head. He'd convinced his boss that you were some type of leader for those guys. Hey, we're all out of this now. Not our problem anymore."

I pounded my fist against the hood. "The fuckers burned my house down! You think I can just let that go? Goddamn it, it's not fair."

She said, "Is that what he told you? He told you it was the terrorists?"

"Well, *yeah*, it was the fucking terrorists, right? Killed my friends and then came back and torched my house."

"Oh, honey, no. No no no. That wasn't those guys. Dear God, no."

"What was it, then? Lightning strike? Dry brush?"

"It was Doctor Hulka. Raving drunk. They caught him dancing around in your front yard while it was burning. Says you ruined his life the night you took him home from the casino."

What the hell was going on? "Are you sure?"

"They caught him. He admitted it. Right there in your yard. I'm so sorry, hon. I had no idea. I need to tell George to add that to the list of Rome's fuck-ups."

Just when I thought the bastard couldn't sink any lower. Unbelievable.

It got worse. Layla said, "I'll bet he didn't tell you that Drew's shotgun wasn't loaded either."

That was all I needed. A couple of tears warmed my cheek. Layla's eyes grew wide. It took every ounce of will I had to keep myself from jumping in the truck right then and there. But I had to play the nice guy, right? Had to fool them just a few minutes more.

Until, "Well, no. He didn't."

A long silence, the wind picking up, whistling between the cars in the lot. She reached over, rubbed my arm. "So sorry."

I shrugged. "I think maybe filing charges would be a good idea after all."

"Maybe so."

I opened the door to my big red truck, got inside, slammed it shut, and eased down the window. "See you tomorrow, Ms. Layla."

She hugged herself and stepped back. "Don't you want to wait for the sheriff?"

"Just tell him I felt like sleeping under the stars tonight."

I was gone.

THIRTY

Free. Unarmed. Angry. And I was pretty sure that Tordsen would realize his mistake soon enough and come after me. So I had to move fast.

I had a good idea where Rome was staying. When he moved here to work at the casino, a couple of other deputies and myself kept tabs for a week or so, just to see if he was involved with any dirty dealings we could profit from. He came up clean as a whistle. Still, that meant I'd spent a night or two a block down from the small ranch house he'd rented in Pale Falls, on a quiet street near the hardware store and post office. I was hoping he hadn't abandoned it for the town's only hotel now that his cover had been blown. He surely wanted a better bed than his agents.

This time I parked two blocks away, thinking

he might have a couple of agents keeping an eye out, just in case. That was a long shot, though—as far as he knew, I was in jail and the wannabe Al Qaedas were under the gun a long way from here. The strange thing was that I knew what I needed to do in order to get into Rome's house, but I had no idea what I would do once inside. I would have to improvise, make it look like an accident or suicide, make people believe that's what it was, even if they knew good and Goddamn well it was really all thanks to me.

I took my time easing through backyards on my way to his rear door, the grass still slick with melting ice. I was lucky that Rome lived on a relatively dog-free street. No fences bordering yards here, everyone a big happy community. My former citizens, snug in their beds, no idea the Bastard Traitor Deputy was on his way to commit a *real* crime for a change.

Rome's porch light was on, but otherwise the house was dark. It was a tiny thing, gray vinyl siding stripping away any charm. Just what you'd expect a Fed to fall in love with. It was indistinct in every way. His yard was bare except for an uncovered gas grill which, from the looks of the rust, he probably left out all winter. The porch was a concrete slab with a couple of cheap patio chairs on it, a stained Igloo cooler between them.

I slipped over to the door, my fingers on the knob, when it occurred to me—the guy had to have a security system, right? Especially him, always on the hunt for evildoers everywhere.

"Shit." Through my teeth. Seething.

But I'd come so far. I mean, trying to imagine what tomorrow would be like, or the next day, or the next week, it just wouldn't come. I had already started over once after Katrina, already lost too much, and wasn't looking to do it again. Without Drew, without Graham, without a chance to reconcile with Ginny, might as well go out fighting.

I tried the knob. Locked, but simple to break. I wished I had rescued the picks from my cruiser when I had the chance, but no biggie. All I had to do was keep turning left, hard as I could, squeeze it until it felt like all the bones in my hand were about to break, then pop the door with my shoulder. I'd done it a thousand times before. And it worked this time just as easily.

I was standing in Rome's kitchen. The porch light showed me old yellow linoleum, slightly curled up at the edges. A cheap card table, a half-opened pizza box on top. The whole room smelled like stale cheese.

I eased the door closed, stood still as the air while listening for movement, letting my eyes adjust to the dark. I was planning on the fly—*look for a knife. Maybe he keeps a spare gun on top of the fridge. I used to do that.* Whatever part of me didn't think this was a good idea kept quiet.

My eyes adjusted and focused past the porch light slicing through the blinds on the window over the sink to the archway into the rest of the house. And something was standing there.

Someone. Rome flicked the lights. I flinched, blinked, squinted to see him there, waiting, in sweatpants and a white T-shirt. Cell phone in one hand pulling away from the light switch, pistol in the other, lazily aimed at me.

Rome waited a long time before saying anything, neither of us moving. Must've been a few minutes. His expression never changed, a complete blank except for a tiny hint of dread. None of the fear I'd seen in the interrogation room. He must've been working hard to hold it in.

He said, "I was just doing my job."

I nodded. "I get it."

"The sheriff called me almost as soon as you

left the parking lot."

"I figured."

"Hoped you wouldn't come here." Stopped himself, shook his head, and said, "No, I guess not. I've been looking forward to this."

"You could've let me help find these fuckers. Could've trusted me. How in the hell did you decide I was one of theirs?"

He readjusted his grip on the pistol. "Don't run your game on me. It's too late. You going to pull an O.J. now? Tell me the real terrorists are out there still?"

"I know you've already got them in sight. I can't wait until they're questioned. You're going to look like a total fool, man. Bring up my name, these guys will be all, 'What? Who?'" I smiled, started laughing. "It's going to be sweet."

Rome stabbed the gun at me as he said, "*You're* the fool here. You can't come here looking to avenge your little girlfriend, thinking how right you are. I know *damn* well you're part of that cell, and she was helping you. And if you want to deny that, then what in the hell was she doing waving a shotgun at us?"

I was getting angry, raised my voice. "An unloaded shotgun. She was harmless."

He matched the volume. "*I* didn't know that! How was I supposed to know?"

"I don't care. It doesn't matter any more." That's right. Son of a bitch could think he had me where he wanted me at gunpoint. But I didn't care if I croaked. I was waiting for the right time to launch. Scanned the kitchen—drainboard by the sink, some forks. I could aim for that. "I'm taking you down."

He sighed. "Man, you just did all my work for me. Here I was thinking I'd be throwing your new sheriff in jail tomorrow for obstruction, get some court orders and shit before I got cut off for good. It's much easier now, you breaking into my kitchen like this. I'm going to call my agents and we'll get you out of dodge, back to Minneapolis. Another nice cozy cell in solitary, that sound all right?"

When he dropped his gaze just enough to punch the call button on his phone, that was the cue. I stretched for the fork, couldn't reach, bent over sideways until I had one in hand, and I charged.

Rome was stunned, dropped the phone and tried to get his other hand on the gun. "Get on the fucking floor! I will shoot you if you don't—"

The charge only took a few seconds, but halfway into it, when the bullets didn't tear into me like I expected, when I grabbed Rome's wrist and the gun didn't go off because he didn't have his finger on the trigger, I got it: he couldn't kill me. He *needed* me. Without me, the free rein license he had from his bosses at Homeland Security disappeared. He'd told them I was the key. He was so Goddamned sure. My death was the end of his power.

We collided and I sent him sprawling on his back in the living room, barely missing his coffee table. I banged his wrist against the table until the gun clattered across and fell onto the carpet. I stabbed the fork into his shoulder and he let out a grunt. He got a hand on my face and tried to gouge my eyes. I pulled back. He shoved me off, yanked out the fork, and got to his knees. He went after the gun.

I kicked him over before he got it, slamming his head into a CD rack on the wall. Jewel cases rained down on him. I stood, found the gun and gripped it. But then he was up and behind me, grabbed my collar and slammed my head into a small TV on a stand in the corner. Pain pulsed across my scalp. Jesus, it stung. He banged me again. The glass cracked. A smear of blood on the screen.

He reached for the gun. I tucked it between my legs, doubled over. He scrambled and grabbed. I stomped on his toes and sent him reeling.

I thought I'd end it for us both right there—one in the head for him, one for me. But I turned right into his fist. Popped me in the face, my cheek, almost got my nose. He kept coming, a football tackle into the far wall that knocked the wind out of me. His fingers circled my wrist, squeezing the circulation out of my hand. I was blacking out.

Breathe in. Come on. He gets that gun, you're his bitch for life. Locked away without parole, without a trial, without anything.

He punched me again, pulled back for another. When he tried again, I opened my mouth, caught his knuckle and bit down *hard*. Caught a nice big vein over his index finger. My teeth went numb from the shock of the punch, probably loosened the ones up front.

He stumbled off me, holding up his closed fist while blood flowed heavy out of the wound, dripping on his T-shirt. He sat on the floor, his back against the couch, wrapping the shirt around his hand.

I pushed myself up, gulped down air, then got my bearings. I aimed the gun at his face. Thought maybe I'd torture him first, get a few laughs out of it. But after all that I just wanted it over. We both stared at each other, exhausted of hate, of smart-assed remarks, of anything besides heavy breathing and the smell of sweat.

I said, "Okay. That's enough."

Rome held up his good hand. "Wait, first. Look."

"No more talk."

He shook his head. "Not that. There's something else. I was waiting before I gave it to you."

I stepped right up to him, gun on his forehead. "Don't fuck with me."

He closed his eyes. "Drew wrote you a letter. We found it in the car. I was going to give it to you tomorrow."

Half of me didn't want to believe him, and the other half didn't want the letter. But he'd put the bug in my head now, the nagging voice. I couldn't let it go.

"Where is it?"

I helped him to his feet, got him to the bedroom. The letter was in his briefcase on the dresser, folded tight, in an evidence bag. It was sitting underneath my hunting knife, also in a bag, blood all over the inside.

"How'd you get this?" I asked.

"We caught one of those Malaysian bastards on his way back to Detroit. Had this in the trunk. That was the next thing I was going to use against you."

"I told you it was stolen from me."

He shrugged, eased down onto his bed. "I can't believe a word you say, man."

I put the knife aside and looked at the note. Nothing on the outside. Could be that Rome was full of shit. Maybe he'd written it himself.

I said, "You know what it says?"

"Of course I know what it says. It's my job to know what it says. How about you? Want to read it?"

I stared at him a long moment. Flipped the note in my hands. Did I really want to know?

Finally opened the bag, pulled out the note.

THIRTY-ONE

Dear Billy,

I hope you get this, because if you do it means you're safe and that you've made it back home. I'm hoping I will too, but I wanted to write this now while it's on my mind. Layla has promised to help, and I hope she gives this you. Know that I'm so grateful for everything you've done to help me, even though so many terrible things have happened because of it. I'm sorry I ever asked you to get involved. I hope I can leave this behind and sort this mess out in my head. I've never had to face so much death before, so many people I cared about.

And you. I want you to know that I do truly care about you. Maybe in another life, another time, I could've loved you. But I hope you'll please understand that that's impossible now. I could

never trust you the way I need to, and I don't want to be reminded of what happened for the rest of my life.
Please know that you have been so good to me. I'll never forget your kindness, your sacrifice, or your love. All I ask is that we leave it behind, and that you do not try to contact me. I'm sorry if this hurts you, but understand how much I'm hurting inside, too. All I ask is that you leave me alone.

Always your friend in memory, with love,

Drew

I read the letter silently three times, hoping I'd missed a word or sentence or was imagining it. Tried in vain to believe it wasn't her handwriting. Each time it was exactly the same, Drew's words written in Drew's hand, just like in her notebooks back when she was trying to think of a name for the band. I remember that list, six pages long. The favorite before Elvis Antichrist was "Gore Bunny".

She had washed her hands of me before the FBI ever found her car. If she'd only dropped the goddamned shotgun.

Rome said, "Look, I know you wanted to

protect her, but come on. I know it hurts."

I stared at the paper, my hands trembling. "You really think she was looking for a showdown after reading this? Because that's what you told me."

"Shit, I just used what I had, a little exaggerated. Like I said, it's my job."

"Yeah."

The whole time I'd been lost in Drew's note, Rome had been scooting toward his nightstand, finally close enough to reach for the drawer. I caught his fingers twitch in my peripheral vision, and I was back to reality. Dropped the letter and brought up the gun.

Rome reached for the drawer but I kicked his hand away. Grabbed his briefcase and swung hard, papers and a cell phone and a couple of clips flying around as the corner smashed into his temple. I swung again for good measure, connected with his chin. He collapsed on the bed, hands covering his face, whole body writhing.

I lifted his gun. Almost forgot I'd been holding it. Or had I? No, I knew. The whole time, all it would've taken was a quick squeeze of the trigger. Revenge, my only reason for coming here in the first place.

But I couldn't do it. I had killed two men in my life, that gangbanger on the Coast and the terrorist lackey Umar. Guess I was done with it. Not someone I knew. Not another law man just doing his job, regardless of how wrong he was.

I wanted to tell him something, anything, to justify breaking into his house. I wanted him to feel the pain that was gripping my heart worse than having my head pounded into a TV screen. But when I opened my mouth to really let him have it, I had nothing.

On my way out of the bedroom, I heard him groaning, then my name. I waited, didn't look back.

"You won't get very far. I'll be seeing you real soon, motherfucker."

He might as well have said: *Have a Nice Day.*

I kept the gun, picked up Drew's now crumpled letter, and left Rome seething on the bed. I took the front door out, walked back to the truck, and drove away.

THIRTY-TWO

Two hours north of Pale Falls I found a cheap hotel in a town called Alexandria. The walls were mint green. The bed had seen better days. They had cable, but the TV's color was messed up, a big streak of yellow down the left side. Everything smelled like cigarettes and industrial glue. A small round table and two torn vinyl chairs shoved tight against the AC unit that ran along the front window, the rising sun spreading gray light across the floor. I sat in one of those chairs with a bottle of cheap Syrah I'd picked up at the off-sale liquor store a few blocks away. Drew's letter was smoothed out on the table.

I didn't know how much time I had left before the Feds found me. Really didn't even know if they would bother looking. If it was up to Rome, probably. You don't do what I had done to a man like that and expect him to let it slide. If Tordsen was right and Rome would be off the case as of this morning, then at least we'd eventually settle our beef on a personal level, no more weight of the law to keep either of us from bearing our fangs. Not that he'd been a fragile flower last night—far from it. I could only imagine how much nastier it would get from here until one of us was dead

If I even wanted it to go that way. I didn't know. Maybe another game of Russian Roulette, but this time with Rome's automatic, the odds definitely in my favor. Yeah, it was an idea.

On the other hand, maybe I could catch Ham before he left for school, catch Savannah before her busy day of playing with toy ponies began. Reconnect with my kids, see if Ginny and the in-laws might be open to me paying them a visit once they learned the truth about what happened to Graham. They needed to understand that he gave his life trying to save my ass. I would've died for him. For Drew. They took a stand for me. Maybe the only way to make it up to the universe was to take a stand for my own flesh and blood.

Those were my choices. On the nightstand

beside the bed were the phone and Rome's pistol. Halfway through that bottle of wine, I decided which one to pick up.

THE END

By the same author.

- *Slow Bear*
- *Slower Bear*
- *Slowest Bear*
- *The Butcher's Prayer*

About the author

Anthony Neil Smith is the author of numerous crime novels, short stories, and essays. He is an English Professor at Southwest Minnesota State University.

He likes British beer, Mexican food, and Italian crime flicks from the 70s. His newly adopted dog is named Edmund, and he is the devil.

You can find out more about his work on his website

www.anthonyneilsmith.com

Books in the Fahrenheit Pocket Noir series.

- *If You're Not One Percent by Todd Morr*
- *A Briefcase Full Of The End Of The World by Todd Morr*
- *Instant Karma by Todd Morr*
- *Yellow Medicine by Anthony Neil Smith*

Other books from Fahrenheit Press

Pure by Jo Perry

Caught in a pincer movement between the sudden death of Evelyn (her favourite aunt) and the Corona virus, Ascher Lieb finds herself unexpectedly locked down in her aunt's retirement community with only Evelyn's grief-stricken dog Freddie for company.

As the world tumbles down into a pandemic shaped rabbit-hole Ascher is wracked with guilt that her aunt was buried without the Jewish burial rights of purification. In order to atone for this dereliction of familial duty, Ascher – in her own words 'a profane, unobservant, atheist Jew, frequent liar and grieving loser' – volunteers to become the newest member of Valley Haverim Chevra Kadisha, a Jewish burial society on-call twenty-four-seven during lockdown and performing Mitzvot at no cost to the bereaved.

What follows is a journey through the insanity of lockdown in Los Angeles as Ascher attempts to bring peace to a troubled soul, and perhaps in the end redemption for herself.

"The mystery will get under your skin, for sure, but the humanity of this novel will resonate far beyond the page."

The Perception Of Dolls by Anthony Croix

The triple murder and failed suicide that took place at 37 Fantoccini Street in 2001, raised little media interest at the time. In a week heavy with global news, a 'domestic tragedy' warranted few column inches. The case was open and shut, the inquest was brief and the 'Doll Murders' - little more than a footnote in the ledgers of Britain's true crime enthusiasts - were largely forgotten.

Nevertheless, investigations were made, police files generated, testimonies recorded, and conclusions reached. The reports are there, a matter of public record, for those with a mind to look.

The details of what took place in Fantoccini Street in the years that followed are less accessible. The people involved in the field trips to number 37 are often unwilling, or unable, to talk about what they witnessed. The hours of audio recordings, video tapes, written accounts, photographs, drawings, and even online postings are elusive, almost furtive.

In fact, were it not for a chance encounter between the late Anthony Croix and an obsessive collector of Gothic dolls, the Fantoccini Street Reports might well have been lost forever.

"It's almost as if history is trying to erase the whole affair." - Anthony Croix

Red Honey by Saira Viola

Red Honey is the much anticipated new book from the hugely critically acclaimed Saira Viola. With an introduction from Todd Robins, editor of Vautrin Magazine, Red Honey is a collection of never before published short stories & flash fiction from a recognised giant of the genre.

"Saira's prose seeps from the page, through the senses and into the soul without appearing to trouble the brain. In a way, that wide-screen, surround-sound experience of reading her work is a double edge sword. It's like watching a firework display; the pretty sparks falling all around can make you forget it was born of gunpowder." - Russell Day, Author of King Of The Crows

Printed in Dunstable, United Kingdom

66908348R00224